BRAVING FATE

LINSEY HALL

For my love, Ben. With you, anything is possible.

PROLOGUE

Central England, AD 60, eve of the Roman conquest of Britain

THE WOMAN he loved lay dying in his arms. Blood spilled over her breast, trickling from the dagger she'd sunk into her chest. Drops of blood hitting the dirt floor of the stone roundhouse echoed hollowly in his ears, amplified by the dawning knowledge of what he'd done. What she'd done. What they'd done.

"Why, Boudica?" His heart and voice were breaking. "Why do this?"

She shuddered in his arms, her broken body cold and fragile with looming death, but no less fierce than when she'd fought on the field of battle the previous dawn. She was their warrior queen, the force that had drawn thousands of British Celts together to revolt against Roman occupation, and he her top general.

She was his love. The one bright spot in the miserable spectacle of blood and death his life had become.

Boudica drew a harsh breath that rattled in her wounded chest and glared at him, her eyes alight with hatred.

"Why?" It was clear she would have screamed it if she could. Another faltering breath. "After your betrayal, you ask me why?"

"Betrayal? I did it for you."

Her bitter laugh died on a cough. "I thought you knew me. I was wrong. You only know what you think me to be. I'm a warrior, the leader and symbol of our beaten land. I led my people in battle for our lives, our homes, our freedom." She paused to catch her breath. "But we've lost. Irreparably."

His jaw clenched, his chest aching with the weight of their past and his future. For she would die this night, her future forever erased. *Because of him.* Because he hadn't been able to protect her. As he hadn't protected his village and family before he'd joined her.

"The Roman dogs are at our door." She coughed. "My daughters dead at their hands. Our lands stolen. Why would I live when capture is inevitable and my very life will be used as leverage? My head will be on a pike in Rome before summer's end. More likely, they'll use me against our people." She raked him with a scathing glance and coughed again. Blood marred her colorless lips. "What would you do, O great warrior?"

"The same." His throat burned. Capture *was* inevitable. And unbearable. Now, with the final battle lost and thousands of their families and allies dying in the fields around them, the fate that awaited her at the hands of the Romans would be worse than death, not only for her, but very likely for her people as well.

He'd tried to save her from this, but she hadn't let him. He would have committed any deed, no matter how terrible, to save the woman who'd changed his life when he'd met her a year ago. But Boudica was a warrior first, his woman second. And she would die believing he had betrayed her.

She coughed, her pallor more pronounced. "And yet you would deny me my honorable death?"

"I love you. I'd do *anything* to save you."

"And I thought I loved you," she whispered. And as her eyes closed, the enormous life force that had propelled Boudica, Celtic Queen of the Iceni, evaporated.

The crushing weight of grief squeezed the breath out of his lungs. Collapsing over her, the black night swallowed his roar of pain. *He would have vengeance.*

1

C adan Trinovante jerked awake, the sheets tangled in his fists. He ignored the vibrating phone that had awakened him from the nightmare and stared at the wide wooden rafters supporting the ceiling above him, struggling to catch his breath. Of all the memories that had faded in his two thousand years of life, the memory of Boudica's death was the one that never had.

Guilt tugged at him and he reached for the phone.

"Cadan," he said as he glanced at the clock on the bedside table. The gleam of Edinburgh's streetlights shone on hands pointing toward one a.m. The yells of revelers stumbling from pub to pub filtered in through the open window.

"Cadan, it's Warren."

Cadan merely grunted in response and walked to the window. He listened with half an ear as he stared out at the gothic spires of Edinburgh's churches and the soot-blackened stone of the surrounding buildings. They rose tall and narrow, pressed cheek by jowl on either side of the sloping cobblestones of the city's oldest street. Cadan shut out the cool night air and the sound of fading revelry.

"You've a new assignment," Warren said. "Can you be here in an hour?"

Finally. He needed something to keep his mind off the past. The damn dreams had been hounding him more often lately and he was ready to forget, to slip back into work.

"Aye, I'll see you by two," he said.

Damn it. He could still hear the revelers below. Living for so long was wearying, but listening to others take such joy in life was just salt in the wound.

In less than an hour, he strode through the great iron-sheathed wooden doors of a building on the campus of the Immortal University. The eyes of the eerie stone gargoyles who guarded the entrance followed him as he entered the cool halls of the Praesidium, named over a thousand years ago when Latin was still the language of education.

Fucking Latin. Fucking Romans.

He dragged a hand through his hair. The short drive to the outskirts of Edinburgh where the university was located hadn't fully banished his dreams.

His footsteps were soundless on the marble floor of the wide, familiar hallway. It was a habit he'd never broken, though there was no need for stealth here. Terrible, unforgivable things happened when you let your guard down. But this was the safest place for a Mythean in Edinburgh since it was hidden from the prying eyes of mortals, who shouldn't know of the existence of the supernatural beings who walked among them.

He pushed open the old oak door at the end of the hall and entered his friend's office, a book-filled room lit by a small fire that smelled of autumn. Warren looked up from his cluttered desk and leaned back in his chair.

"Cadan, thanks for coming in so early."

"No' a problem," Cadan said. He sank into an old leather chair across from Warren's desk. "Who's it this time?"

As one of the few Mythean Guardians in the world, it had been Cadan's responsibility for nearly two millennia to protect those mortal or supernatural beings deemed important to the fate of humanity.

Warren glanced down at a rumpled piece of paper. "Looks like a Celtic warrior."

Interesting—a man who'd been alive for as long as he. "Why's the bloke need protecting if he's made it this long? Destiny just revealed to him?"

And why haven't I met him before? Though he didn't get out much, Cadan knew, or knew of, nearly all the Mytheans in Great Britain. The ones who hadn't gone rogue, at least.

"Well, that's where it gets a little strange. The warrior hasn't been alive. The soul has just been reborn."

"A reincarnate? They're damn rare. Doona think I've ever actually met one."

"It doesn't happen very often," Warren said, picking up the Slinky on his desk and fiddling with it.

Why wouldn't Warren meet his eyes? The claws of nerves crawled up Cadan's back, little pinpricks sinking into his skin that wouldn't shake loose. It took him off guard; he hadn't felt that in centuries.

"I've spoken briefly to Aerten about it." Warren finally glanced at him, but looked away almost immediately.

Shite.

"What does the goddess of fate have to say about it?" He hadn't seen her in ages. Hell, he'd only seen her a few times since she'd offered him a spot in the Praesidium. Whether he should thank her or curse her was something he hadn't figured out yet.

"That only select souls are reborn. Those who were so strong in life that their souls never left this plane." Warren set the Slinky down. "Their souls wait in stasis until humanity needs them. At that point, they're brought back to perform a task that only they can accomplish."

"So, I'm going to be protecting a child who will save the world?" A cold sweat broke out on his skin. Killing and guarding adults—no' a problem. But dealing with children was something he was entirely unqualified for after being alone for two thousand years. Fuck, what a mess.

"No' exactly," Warren hedged. "Apparently with Druidic reincarnation, the soul is reborn in another person, but the person doesn't become conscious of their previous life until they reach the approximate age at which they died originally."

"Shite, they develop split personalities?"

"Ah, no' exactly." He paused, seemingly unaware that he'd grabbed the Slinky again and was juggling it faster and faster. "They doona survive that long. Once they remember who they are and complete their fated task, they die."

"Die? That's some shite luck."

"Aye. The tragedy that took the soul too early the first time follows it. History is destined to repeat itself, after all. You need to protect the reincarnate until the fated task is complete, longer if you can."

That would be a challenge, but then, he liked a challenge. "Do we know what this guy's task will be, once he regains his memory? And where is he, anyway?"

"Doona know the task, but Aerten has prophesied that a catalyzing event will spur the memory of the reincarnate and lead them to Arthur's Seat, likely today or tomorrow. That's where you'll meet." Warren hesitated before continuing, finally meeting Cadan's eyes. "And the warrior isn't a man."

Cadan's breath stuck in his throat and a chill broke out on his skin. Nay, it couldn't be. "Who is it, Warren?"

"It's Boudica."

2

Clayton, Maine

A DEEP, hollow grief filled her, so strong that it nearly overpowered the lightning bolt of pain that streaked through her chest. Cold crept insidiously through her veins, a sickening contrast to the burning pain. Every breath that she struggled to drag into her lungs felt like she'd plunged in the dagger all over again.

The moans of the dying filtered weakly through the walls of the house in which she lay, creeping through the thatch of the roof and wrapping around her brain, her soul, and sucking the life from her all the faster. Her warriors lay dying outside in the mud and blood of war.

The sounds of her failure to protect her people, her daughters, reverberated through her mind and soul like thunder.

She gasped as a streak of pain tore through her chest. Why did it take so long to die? Perhaps because she didn't really want to die, and hadn't plunged the blade to its greatest effect. But it was only right.

Her death would ensure the end of the war, and she'd rather it be at her own hands than those of her enemy.

"Why?" the man holding her rasped. "Why do this?" His pain was palpable, but the only thing she felt was rage at his betrayal.

DIANA LAUGHTON'S fingers stopped on her computer's keyboard and she stared at the words she'd just written. What the hell? She was a historian, damn it. She wrote historical analysis, not historical fiction.

But *it* was happening again.

Only...different. Worse. She rubbed a sore spot on the back of her wrist and inhaled deeply of the brisk October air that blew through the open window. It smelled of leaves and carried the heavy, wet scent of impending rain.

She scrubbed at her eyes, which were gritty with exhaustion. The dreams that had haunted her on and off since childhood were coming more often, taking over her mind whether she was asleep or not. She felt what the dying woman felt, smelled what she smelled, and saw what she saw.

And wondered if she was finally going crazy.

A knock sounded on the door. Diana jumped. A statuesque woman, her striking face topped with wild dark hair, popped her head into Diana's small office.

"Hey, Diana," Vivienne said. "I've a break between classes. Do you want to go grab a coff— Oh, hey, are you all right? You don't look so good."

Diana looked up at her friend. The Egyptology textbooks in her fellow professor's hands, combined with her flowing, colorful scarves, presented an image of worldly and adventurous scholarship that Diana never failed to appreciate. For what felt like the thousandth time, Diana admired the casual bohemian elegance of her closest friend.

Whereas Vivienne spent much of her time traveling through Egypt's deserts in search of ancient sites, Diana had spent the last few years preparing her latest manuscript. That meant research and libraries, not world travel and exotic sites. She'd been content, mostly, to stay back and work on the research that had obsessed her for years. But sometimes...

"Ugh, it has been *a day*," Diana said. "I could definitely use a break. I was about to head out anyway to meet the postman."

She mashed her finger against the delete button and almost sighed as the muscles in her shoulders began to relax.

"Is it that dream again?" Vivienne asked.

"Yeah. It's been getting worse."

"Did the dream still feel familiar?"

It sounded crazy when Vi said it like that. Hell, it was crazy. Vi was her closest friend, and the only person she'd ever told about the dreams besides her dad, who had reacted...badly.

"Yeah, but I'm a freaking history professor. I should be familiar with battles and the theoretical consequences of war. What I shouldn't be able to do is feel the dying woman's last emotions." Such miserable emotions.

Diana stood to put on her coat and barely resisted straightening the mussed pile of papers at the corner of her desk. They were fine the way they were. She no longer had to make sure everything was neat as a pin. That necessity had died with her father. Her hand squeezed into a fist. It might have been a dozen years since she'd experienced the repercussions of not following his rules, but such things were hard for the subconscious to forget.

"Let's go." Diana turned quickly from the pile of papers.

They walked down the barren hall, Vivienne's stilettos clacking at a higher pitch than Diana's comfortable beige kitten heels.

Fortunately, the coffee shop was close to their department.

With her erratic sleeping patterns, coffee was the only thing that had kept her going during the last month.

Outside, they crossed the historic street that ran down the center of the university town of Clayton, barely dodging a child racing down the sidewalk on a bicycle. A gust of wind blew russet leaves off nearby trees. Halloween was coming and jack-o-lanterns grinned eerily from shop stoops. Normally, this was her favorite season. But this year, with the dreams coming more frequently and the unsettled feeling haunting her waking hours, she hadn't been able to appreciate it at all.

"Was there anything new in the dream?" Vi asked.

"No, basically the same, but this time the man spoke. I couldn't make out his face, but I think I loved him." Diana shook her head. "I mean, the dying woman loved him. At least she *had* loved him. But she felt betrayed."

"By what?"

"Don't know."

Honestly, it was creepy and she didn't want to think about it anymore. She rubbed the back of her wrist, which had begun to tingle again as the cuff of her jacket rubbed against the sensitive skin. Yet another mystery to be filed away for later.

"Very cool." Vivienne paused when Diana shot her a look. "But sad. I wonder who she was?"

They slipped inside the coffee shop and out of the brisk air. The wind slammed the door at their backs, but the warmth and inviting décor, punctuated with local art and plush furniture, welcomed them.

"How about a figment of my crazy imagination? Maybe all my research is getting to me."

"Or, your memories are getting to your research."

"No, the dreams have nothing to do with my book." *Liar.*

Hadn't she always been drawn to the more gruesome parts of ancient history? The warriors, battles, death? Ever since she was little, she'd been the girl who wanted to play with wooden swords and watch *Xena, Warrior Princess.* Combined with her love of books, it had led her to a career as a history professor with a specialty in the warrior women of the Bronze and Iron Ages. She had almost finished converting her dissertation into a book for the university press.

"The manuscript is almost done, by the way," Diana said. "And with it, my application for assistant professor will be all but in the bag."

She hoped. She really needed that promotion. Currently, as a lecturer, she had no control over what she taught, how or when she taught it, and no certainty that she'd even have a job next semester. She wanted that certainty and that control, desperately. The tenure-track job as assistant professor would get her one blissful step closer.

The line went quickly as they chatted. Their turn to order came and Diana thrust her card at the barista, nudging Vivienne's out of the way. "Both, please."

"Diana, you don't have to." Vivienne nudged her own card at the barista.

The girl glanced at Diana, then shook her head at Vivienne, no doubt deciding that Diana was the scarier one.

"I know. But you've spent so much time listening to me complain about my nightmares that the least I can do is get you a coffee."

"Thanks. And it's not a problem. I think they're interesting, though I'm sorry they cause so much trouble."

Black coffee in Diana's hand, a frothy latte in Vivienne's, they headed toward the door.

"All right, Vi, I've got to run. FedEx is delivering an old treatise to my house today. They usually show up around three and I don't want them to leave it out on the stoop, what with this weather." She nodded up at the gray clouds. "I'll see you later."

~

LATER THAT EVENING, Diana jiggled the key in the lock of the front door of her townhouse. Rain pounded on her head, and the groceries she'd run out for after receiving her package made opening the door a pain in the butt. *Damn.* She needed to get the stupid lock fixed, but there just never seemed to be time between writing and classes.

Snick. Finally. The door swung open and she stepped out of rain that wasn't nearly as charming as it was when she was snuggled up cozily at her desk.

Letting the door swing shut, she kicked off her shoes and hauled her grocery bags down the hall to the kitchen. Fresh veggies, tofu, and red wine—it wasn't exciting, but they were the healthiest things she could find at the small shop down the street. That had to count for something when it felt like any control she had over her life was disappearing with every terrifying new dream or hallucination. Not to mention her manuscript deadline and her upcoming—*please, God* —promotion.

A sudden clap of thunder rocked the house, making her jump. She fumbled to find the kitchen light, but her hand stilled when she heard the front door creak open.

Damned wind. She must have forgotten to lock the door. She never used to forget things.

Footsteps thudded down the hall and her stomach dropped to the floor. *Who is that?*

The footsteps thudded slowly but inexorably closer. She heard the intruder turn into the small library at the front of the house, but he'd be in the kitchen next. No time to call the police.

She clamped a hand over her mouth and her eyes darted around the kitchen in search of a weapon. Dim light from the porch lamp streamed through the window, its faint yellow glow illuminating the neatly modern space.

Damn, nothing on the counter, not even a stray knife. Why did she have to be so organized?

The back door. Maybe it was unlocked.

She tripped in her haste to reach the door to the porch, a crash of thunder seeming to propel her forward. The handle was slick beneath her sweaty palms. The door wouldn't budge. Swollen from the rain, damn it.

Turning around, she pressed herself against the panes, her skin cold and the hair on the back of her neck standing upright. There had to be a weapon in here. A knife, a meat hammer—anything was better than nothing.

She spied her enormous skillet sitting by the sink and snatched it, wincing as the heavy cast iron dragged her arms down. *God, this thing is heavy.*

She cursed herself for not taking self-defense classes. With research and teaching, it was another thing she had no time for. And now, she really wished she'd made time. Thank God for skillet corn bread, she thought, as her fear bubbled into panicked hysteria.

An enormous figure stepped into the kitchen and she bit her lip to stifle a gasp. Over six feet tall, its freakishly slender form was draped in a long coat that looked to be made of raw leather. Long black hair streamed from its head. When she finally caught sight of the face, a scream was strangled in her throat. It couldn't be human. The dim light glinted off dark, burnished crimson skin and eerily feminine features. Beady eyes, a nose that was almost beaklike, and thin lips all gave the appearance of a bird.

She was not a she, she was an *it.*

Monsters aren't real. They aren't real!

But this was no Halloween costume. It was far too realistic.

Diana cringed back against the wall. *No, no, no.* This couldn't be happening to her. She shook her head, but it didn't disappear. Her heart thudded in her chest, beating in a painfully frantic rhythm against her ribs while her breath was strangled in her lungs.

"You're Diana," it said, as if expecting her to confirm.

She heard a squeak of fear and realized it had come from her own throat.

It nodded, clearly taking her squeak as confirmation. "We've been waiting for you."

Two heavy steps and it was almost upon her. Her feet were glued to the floor. She couldn't even move, not even to curl up into a ball like her brain screamed at her to do. She tasted something metallic in her mouth. She'd bitten straight through her lip.

A claw-tipped hand reached for her. Fear clogged her lungs and she jerked the skillet out from behind her back and swung haphazardly at its head. Luck alone landed the wild blow.

Its roar of rage drowned out the sickening sound of the iron connecting with its skull. The impact made her arms vibrate and she nearly dropped the pan.

Eyes on fire and mouth gaping, the beast shook itself, then backhanded her across the cheek. Pain exploded in her head as she whirled from the force of the blow. As agony seared her skull, a rage like she'd never known engulfed her, so strong it felt like a living thing. Gasping, and as terrified of the unfamiliar anger as she was of her attacker, she felt it wash over her.

The rational part of her mind faded to the background as instinct and something otherworldly took over her body. The pain in her head forgotten, Diana lithely jumped to her feet.

Hurt it. Kill it. She turned on her attacker and leapt on it, throwing its spindly form to the ground with her weight. She raised the skillet. Its weight felt natural in her palm, as though she was meant to do some damage with it. Somehow she knew exactly how to kill this creature, but she wanted to hurt it first. How *dare* it try to beat her? *No one* did that to her. *Never again.*

Through her rage, she barely recognized the thoughts. She'd never been beaten before, and she rarely got angry, but now she was inflamed. She swung the frying pan hard at its head, beating it as if to drive her own demons away. The thud of the metal against its skull was a joy to hear and fueled the raging beast within her.

Though an otherworldly power sang through her veins, the creature was stronger. With a great heave, it threw her off and the pan flew from her hand. She was on her feet in seconds.

"Come on," she said, beckoning it to her. She barely recognized her voice. She should be running, but some part of her *wanted* it to try something. So she could kill it.

The creature obliged, coming toward her with murder in its eyes. Snarling, she ran at it, ducking beneath its outstretched arms with a grace that felt entirely unfamiliar. She spotted a knife strapped to its calf and nimbly plucked it from its sheath. With deadly precision, she sank it into its back, punching through the skin and then sinking into the muscle. She twisted right where its heart should be and was rewarded with its howl. The creature clawed at its back, attempting to reach the knife, but within seconds its strength had leached away and it tumbled to the floor. It shuddered, then lay still.

With the threat gone, the fog of rage that had overtaken Diana's mind evaporated. She stumbled away from the woman —the creature—the *thing*—sprawled on her kitchen floor. Tripping over her own feet, she collapsed in the corner, a sob rising in her throat. The floor was hard beneath her as she started to rock back and forth, weak with exhaustion and fear.

What did I just do?

She hadn't recognized herself, not even a little bit. Where

had those instincts come from? She was losing her mind. She was losing *herself*. The self that she didn't even know.

Panicked, remembering the body in her house, she looked up. It was still lying there, with the knife protruding grotesquely from its back. Diana tried to take deep, calming breaths, but the air had gone thick and worthless, heavy with the coppery and sinister scent of blood.

The back of her wrist began to burn again, as if fire ants were crawling over her skin in a pattern. She rubbed it and looked down, temporarily distracted from the corpse in her kitchen.

Her mouth fell open when her wrist began to turn red in a thinly lined pattern. Fine black lines replaced the red, as if she were being tattooed from the inside.

This could not be happening.

She squinted at it, scrubbing panicked tears from her face as she tried to make out the design. It looked like...*a mountain range?* No, not a mountain range, but close. Scrawled across her wrist where it met the back of her hand was a beautifully embellished depiction of a craggy hill.

She rubbed it more fiercely, desperate to make the image disappear. To make all of this just go away. All she wanted was to go back to her normal life and continue on her nice, safe, sane path.

A sizzling sound distracted her from her assault on her wrist and she looked up at the creature lying on her floor, its black blood creeping across her lovely limestone tiles. Strike that—it *had* been lying on her floor.

Its skin had begun to steam with heat and its extremities were disappearing. She shook her head. No way. There was no way that creature was sublimating in the middle of her kitchen.

But before she could blink the rest of the tears out of her eyes, the last of the arms and legs vanished. The torso began to steam and shimmer out of existence as well. Within moments, the creature's knife clattered to the floor when the torso it had been buried in disappeared. A black substance—it must have been blood, though it looked more like tar—coated the wickedly serrated blade.

She scrambled to her feet, shock and terror thick in her throat. This couldn't be happening. Now she couldn't even tell herself that the awful beast had been some kind of criminal with weird red tattoos. And how could she explain her own tattoo? She'd think she was going crazy if she didn't have proof on her wrist. Scratch that. Just because she had proof that something really weird and really wrong was happening didn't mean that she wasn't *also* going crazy. Diana laughed, sounding insane even to herself. She had to get this thing off her.

She leapt to her feet and ran to the foyer to wedge a chair beneath the handle of the front door to make up for the broken lock. Within moments she was scrubbing her hands beneath scalding water in the downstairs bathroom, but the heat didn't stop the pervasive cold streaking through her veins. She frantically rubbed the lavender soap against the back of her wrist, feeling the thin raised lines underneath the black ink. She had to get it off.

Look at it, a dark part of her whispered.

No. She wouldn't look at it until she couldn't feel the raised lines anymore. She scrubbed harder.

Look at it.

Willpower, Diana. But her gaze was drawn down to the tattoo. Still there. Terrifying and beautiful.

Wait a second—she had seen that before. Arthur's Seat in Edinburgh? The famous landmass, an extinct volcano jutting from the center of the Scottish capital, had a well-known profile. One that she was familiar with from the treatise that FedEx had delivered earlier. She'd looked at the first couple of pages before running out to the grocery store. There had been a frontispiece.

She'd been drawn to the small illustration, captivated by the delicate curves and jagged lines that told the story of the mountain's past.

Get it together, Diana. There was no way the tattoo was going to wash off. And she'd actually just killed a monster with some new strength and bravery she couldn't define. Bravery that was long gone now and she was all alone. Though she normally didn't mind being alone, her small townhouse now seemed cavernous and dark outside of the bathroom.

She had to get out of here. Diana turned off the water with a trembling hand and grabbed a towel. After scrubbing her hands dry, she ran to the library to grab the book and went out the back door. It took her a few minutes of yanking on the stuck door, but she managed to get it open. It was worth the effort. Anyone could see her if she went out the front. But the back led to a miniscule fenced-in plot protected from prying eyes.

Rain pounded her as she ran across the tiny yard to the little gate she'd added at the side. It swung open easily into an identical tiny and private yard and she ran across and up the back steps of the neighboring townhouse. She cradled the book to her chest, protecting it from the rain, and pounded on Vivienne's door until it swung open.

"Di, what's wrong?" Vivienne beckoned her inside.

Diana bolted out of the rain. A small rush of warmth flooded her when she entered her friend's cheery kitchen, but not enough to banish the cold that had gripped her heart with icicle claws.

Vivienne was the only person she knew who wouldn't immediately call for a straitjacket, and she was so damned grateful they were neighbors.

Vivienne rubbed Diana's shaking arms and said, "Come on, let's go to the living room. You look like you've seen a ghost."

Vi dragged her into the brightly colored room. Such a

contrast to her own, and so welcoming that Diana almost wept. They sat on the couch.

"Tell me what's up." Her friend's face was creased with worry.

"Oh my God. I don't even know. Um, a monster broke into my house." With a trembling voice that bubbled just under hysteria, she described the attack.

"What?" Vivienne's voice was incredulous.

"Look." Diana thrust out her arm. "This appeared."

"Holy crap." Vi ran tentative fingers over the black lines.

"Yeah. And it looks like the frontispiece illustration in this treatise. The one that I ordered." Diana flipped open the book and showed Vivienne. Diana watched her inspect the two, waiting for Vi to speak, her breath caught uncomfortably in her throat.

"Well...huh..." the normally eloquent Vivienne said. Silence.

"I know."

"This is crazy. I mean, I believe you. But it's insane."

"The worst part was...it knew my name, Vi. The monster said that *they* were waiting."

"Who are they? More monster things? Are you sure it wasn't some kind of freaky gang?"

"Lord, I don't know. I don't know anything anymore. But it really wasn't human. That body *disappeared*. I need answers." Her wrist burned again, screaming at her. Was it a sign? She laughed bitterly. Of course it was. But of what?

"They know where you live. You have to get out of there. Stay with me."

"No. I snuck through the backyards, so no one saw me come here. But I can't be seen staying here. What if they send more after me? What if they find me here? Then you're dead, too."

"We'll figure something out." Vivienne frowned, no doubt trying to figure a way to smuggle Diana in and out of her townhouse. Their little backyards were great for privacy because of the fences. But there was no way to get out of them. The only other option was the front door. "You can't just wait around there for the next monster to come through your door."

"Or worse," Diana said. "They could appear at the university and threaten everything I've worked for." She'd sacrificed too much for her position to lose it like this. It was all she had.

"You need to get your priorities in order," Vivienne said. "Come stay with me. It'll be okay."

"No, Vi, I can't. Everything has just been getting worse. My dreams have been winding me up until I'm about to break. Before, they just happened at night. Now it's night and day. All this shit is happening to me. I can't just sit around and wait for it all to explode. I've got to do something, because no one else is going to do it for me."

"Di, you never talk like this."

"Nothing's ever been this bad before."

"What are you going to do?"

"I'm going to Edinburgh." The idea came to her in an instant. "I have to get out of town, and the only thing I know about this whole miserable business is that my tattoo is of a landmark in Edinburgh."

Edinburgh could have monsters, but there might also be answers. There were definitely monsters here, and likely no answers. So, leaving: one point. Staying: zero. And maybe she'd figure out what the damn dreams meant and find some peace.

"That's a good idea," Vi said. "You can't exactly go to the police with mystery tattoos and stories about your dreams and say that you killed a monster. And if you stay on the move, then they can't find you."

Diana's stomach clenched at the idea of staying on the move, not to mention flying so far from home. That's what people did in thriller movies and adventure novels.

No, no, no.

There was no time to freak out. She had far bigger issues to deal with than a little transcontinental flight to Scotland. Like the disappearing dead monster. Or the mystery tattoo. Or the split personality. Something terrible was happening to her, and she had to figure out what it was.

"God, you're right, Vi." She felt sick even as she said it, knowing that she was about to make a decision that could possibly kill her. But staying here would definitely kill her. "Will you watch my classes for me? If I'm only gone a week, it shouldn't be a problem with the department."

"Of course. Just call me when you get there. Do you even know where you'll stay?"

"No, I'll figure it out on the way. The sooner I leave, the better."

E *dinburgh, Scotland*

NEARLY TWENTY-FOUR HOURS LATER, Diana passed through Immigration at the Edinburgh airport, grateful to finally be off the airplane. Two flights and an obnoxiously long wait in New York had left her rubber-legged and exhausted. She mumbled something about vacation to the Customs and Immigration officer, and within minutes she had her passport stamped and her bag slung over her shoulder as she headed toward the taxi queue at the exit.

No line. Thank God for small favors. She slid into one of the classic-looking black cabs that always appeared in movies about the UK.

"The MacDonald Hotel, please." Her throat was rough from exhaustion and the rest of her didn't feel much better.

"Aye, lassie. The one at the base of the Royal Mile, near Arthur's Seat?" His Scots brogue was thick.

"Yes." She'd used her phone in New York to book a hotel at the foot of the small mountain. She had no idea what she was going to do when she got there. Stand at her window and stare at it? Wait for it to talk to her? Fear had driven her away from home, but now that she was here she was at a bit of a loss.

The streets were dark and silent as the cabbie navigated through the city. In less than thirty minutes, the cab rolled to a stop next to a wide expanse of grass that surrounded the small mountain she'd come to see. Buildings crouched at the edges of the park, though they were set back a ways across the grassy expanse at the mountain's base.

She squinted up at it, nearly blinded by the streetlight right outside her car window. The dead volcano looked bigger from the base. It positively loomed. One side was a sharp vertical cliff that rose up from the grassy park. It sloped down on the other side, undulating to form small hills and valleys.

It looked just as it did on her wrist. Bigger and not as stylized as the tattoo, but there was no mistaking it. It wouldn't take long to climb to the top, she estimated. Maybe she'd do it in the morning.

"Ach, lassie, I'm sorry." The cab driver's voice made her jump. "The construction for the new tram has made it all the way down here. I took some back roads to see if I could get around it, but no good."

She glanced out the window to her left. A maze of wire fence construction barriers crisscrossed with walkways.

"Your hotel is just ahead, not a hundred yards down the street. Only work lorries allowed through, no' cars. There's a walkway there, through the barriers. Think you can walk it? It's a fine neighborhood—the Palace and Parliament are right here —so no need to worry."

"Sure, no problem." She handed him twenty-five pounds and slid out of the car, dragging her small bag behind her.

She stood for a moment in the pale yellow light as a fine fog began to creep along the ground, ushered in by the cooling air. But as she stared up at Arthur's Seat, the revelation wouldn't come. No epiphanies, angels on high, carrier pigeons, nothing. Nothing at all to tell her what was going on in her life and why an outline of this mountain had appeared on her wrist at the same time an evil creature had burst into her kitchen.

Her nails cut into her palm as she squeezed the strap of her shoulder bag. She had to fix whatever this was and get back to work, to finishing her book and getting her promotion. The longer she was gone, the more the kindling under her career smoldered. It would eventually go up in smoke, and then she would have nothing. Nothing to show for her years of work and nothing to show for the sacrifice.

As the cab sped away, she turned on her heel to head to her hotel, determined not to dawdle no matter how curious she was. Out of the corner of her eye, Diana caught sight of three familiar spindly figures with long black hair creeping out from behind the construction barrier. *No.* The cabbie had said she was near the top government building in the city—it should be safe.

The creatures crept closer along the only walkway connecting the city and the park. They blocked the only way to the safety of the hotel. Her heart jumped into her throat and she managed to let out one strangled scream before her body kicked into action.

The bag slipped off her shoulder as she spun to run across the lawn at the base of the mountain, hoping that someone had heard her and would come running. Running as she was now, with her feet pounding the ground and the wind tearing through her hair.

CADAN FELT her presence like a wrecking ball to the chest just moments before a scream cut through the silence. He sped toward the noise, racing down the sloping hill from his perch on an outcropping of Arthur's Seat, his lungs and muscles burning in tandem. He'd waited here all day for Aerten's vision to manifest.

Finally, it had. But she'd said nothing of attackers.

Terror lanced through him like acid in his veins. The wind tore at his clothes with icy claws as he hurtled down the eastern slope, with only faint moonlight to illuminate the scene below him.

A small figure fled from three taller ones at the base of the mountain, hair flying like a flag behind her. She stumbled and fell, and he swore he could hear a sob burst from her throat. *Protect.* He embraced the instinct and pushed himself harder, adrenaline singing in his veins.

Almost there. Only fifty yards. The beasts were upon her now, and her terror made a growl rise in his throat. Hurtling over a pile of rocks, he tackled the closest assailant, crashing to the ground in a tumble. The creature, a spindly red demon with eerie feminine features, bucked beneath him, attempting to throw him off. Cadan didn't hurt women, but this demon was more evil than woman.

Cadan thrust his elbow at its face, the satisfying crunch of cartilage and bone like music to his ears. He plowed a fist into the demon's mouth. Regretful that he couldn't hurt it more without leaving Boudica at the mercy of the other two, he slit its throat with a knife plucked from his boot.

Pain tore through his shoulder. He reached back, yanked on the knife sunk deep into the muscle. With predatory grace, he swung around and grasped the demon's arm and twisted it up behind its back. The crack of snapping bones sang in his ears.

Vengeful pleasure seethed through him as he reached up and broke the demon's neck with his other arm. *For her.*

A scream caught his attention. Just ahead of him, the woman struggled beneath the last demon. She brought her knees up and kicked the beast off her, then scrambled to her feet. Her gaze locked with his and she gasped, eyes flashing with fear and confusion. Fear dominated, and she turned and fled into the night.

Gods damn it, he was here to save her.

The demon she'd kicked off glanced at her fleeing form, then charged him. Cadan stabbed the beast in the heart, twisted the knife out, and took off after her. The demons' bodies would sublimate once they drew their last cursed breath, returning them to the hell from which they came.

Must find her. Fear turned the blood in his veins to ice until he felt they would burst. With Boudica's return to consciousness, someone who wanted her dead knew that she was back. Even now there could be more creatures chasing her.

He headed in the direction that she had run and soon caught sight of her slim form racing across the field in front of him. Damn, she was nicely shaped. Better than nice.

Focus on the task.

When he was only steps behind her, she glanced back, eyes flashing in fear behind scholarly glasses. He leapt, wrapping an arm around her waist, and tackled her to the ground, careful to twist and take the brunt of the fall. She struggled in his arms like a hellcat, all claws and writhing woman.

"Settle down," he said as she nearly ended any hope of future children. He rolled her beneath him to still her struggles.

"Get off me!" Her voice broke.

"I'm here to help you." Her struggles caused her soft thighs to part, allowing him to settle between them. He stifled a groan.

Her hair tangled around their arms as he wrestled her wrists above her head, trying to keep her neat but sharp claws away from his eyes.

Finally, he caught sight of her. Little black glasses over angry brown eyes. Sexy librarian glasses. Christ. And lush, pink lips that formed curses far more inventive than he'd expected to come from such an innocent looking face. Close up, her hair appeared to be a pale red.

At first glance, she was nothing like the woman he'd known, who'd possessed a strong, raw type of beauty. Boudica was a blur in his memory now. Had been for centuries.

But this woman was *very* different. Delicate and soft where Boudica had been strong and fierce. Not a beautiful face, but a compelling one. One from which he couldn't look away.

Her struggles did nothing but make him more intimately aware of her form. Made his cock more aware of her closeness. He stifled a groan. She was curvier than he'd noticed when she'd run across the field. Too soft to be a warrior. Her panting breaths pressed her small breasts in a tantalizing rhythm against his chest. The feel of her made his heart punch against his ribs, so loudly it echoed in his eardrums.

He recognized her. Not her form, or her voice, but something in her called to him, caused long-dead desires to flood him. After Boudica's death, women had come in a seemingly endless stream of nothing. Looking at her now drove the wisps of their memories from his mind.

Something in Boudica had connected to his soul. It had been severed when she'd died, and a part of him had died with her.

Nay, this woman was far different from the one he'd known, but it didn't seem to matter. He'd felt dead for two millennia, but here, lying in the grass atop this woman, his woman, made him feel alive again. He would do anything to protect her. Even if he couldn't keep her.

She heaved up and head-butted him in the forehead.

Ow! That had hurt. *Right, no more head-butting.*

It hadn't even fazed the giant of a man who loomed over her, his strong jaw set. His face was cast in shadows, giving him a sinister air despite the evenness of his features. He was hand-some in a rough way, with dark hair and eyes, and for some reason, it scared her even more. Evil should be visible on the surface. Diana's heart beat so fast that it felt like it might vibrate right out of her chest.

"Let me go!" She thrashed beneath him, pushing against the broad wall of his chest. Futile. He was huge, his muscular form pinning her to the grass, trapping her like a bird in the paws of a greedy feline.

He stared down at her, searching her face as if he thought he should recognize her. Her breath caught when the confusion in his gaze morphed into desire. *Don't look at me like that.* But she shivered. Visions of him kissing her flashed through her mind even as it chanted *get off, get off, get off!*

Did she have some type of fetish for men who scared her? It was sick. She should fight him.

But even as her heart pounded, the chill that thrilled along her nerves began to falter. She should be scared, and she was, but she could swear there was something familiar about him.

He removed his left hand from her wrist, but she wasn't fast enough. He trapped both hands above her head with his right hand and ran his other hand down her waist to her hip. He squeezed and her stomach dipped. The smell of crushed grass wafted around her, mingling with his heady, masculine scent.

He was looking at her like he'd been waiting to see her for ages, but when he slid his hand back up her waist, she tensed.

"What's your name?" His voice rasped over her nerve endings.

He was attacking her. She should be afraid of him. But her body wasn't, almost as though it recognized him. *No.* She was stronger than her body, and this was madness.

"Get off me!" She thrust her knee upward, nailing him between the legs.

He cursed, and a grimace twisted his handsome features.

She used his shock to her advantage and funneled her anger and fear into a great shove against his chest. He'd dropped his guard, and she was able to wriggle out from under him. She scrambled on the wet grass, then heaved to her feet and sprinted down the field.

Desperate to reach the dim yellow streetlights ahead, she pumped her arms faster, breath sawing in and out of her lungs as she ran. The lights ahead glowed, beckoning. If she could just reach the lights...

Footsteps pounded behind her, sending her heart into her throat. They were coming fast. Way too fast. No escape. She was swept up into his arms before the thought left her mind.

"Stop running," he said. "I'm here to help you."

She whimpered and began to struggle. He glowered at her, beautiful in a terrifying way. A dangerous way. She twisted in the iron cage of his arms.

Trapped. She didn't stand a chance against his power. With her rage gone and fear overwhelming her, the strength seeped out of her muscles. Though she pressed weakly against the hard planes of his chest, she knew she wasn't going anywhere.

Out of tricks.

He strode toward an inconspicuous black car in the small parking lot next to the park. He yanked the passenger side door open, almost growling as he did so, but placed her gently on the seat.

"Where are you taking me?" She cowered in the seat next to him. She was beyond caring that she was acting like a terrified mouse, cringing from a broom. He hadn't blindfolded her, which meant he wasn't planning to let her live. She had no control over what he could do to her, and it terrified her.

He started the car without answering. The quiet streets of one of Edinburgh's outlying neighborhoods flew by, a black and white blur illuminated by the moon. She desperately tried to remember the turns they were taking and the street names, but the lefts and rights had long since begun to collide in her mind. He drove so quickly, with a cold control that made her nervous and even less likely to remember where they were going.

"To the university."

She flinched at the dark timbre of his voice, and he scowled. Apparently he didn't like that she was afraid of him. Too bad.

"What do you mean? The University of Edinburgh? Why would you take me there?" This had to be some kind of joke. They had left the city and the University of Edinburgh miles behind, and were now in the rolling countryside surrounding the city. A dark copse of trees, looking like something out of a Halloween tale, passed on their left.

"No' that university." He jerked the steering wheel left, and she sucked in a breath as the car turned smoothly off the road and headed straight for an enormous oak only a few feet ahead of them, its twisted branches reaching for the dark sky. She opened her mouth to scream, but before she could utter a sound, the car passed smoothly through the tree.

"What?" she squeaked. The trees around her began to disappear.

"This university." A towering wrought iron gate appeared. Two large gargoyles clutched gas lanterns at the entrance, and he slowed the car to a crawl as the gate parted to admit them.

She expected to hear it creak ominously and spiders to drop down from the pinnacles at the top, but it swung open noiselessly. Wait, had one of the stone statues grinned evilly at her?

There was nothing ahead of her but a manicured lawn dotted with large oaks. After a moment, a collection of enormous buildings came into view. The elaborate stonework that decorated most of the buildings suggested that they were old, and that this was no normal university.

She laughed bitterly. As if elaborate stonework was all that indicated this wasn't a normal university. Disappearing trees and a gate that could keep out an army suggested something wasn't quite right.

They approached a stone courtyard surrounded on all sides by ivy-covered buildings. The sculptures and stonework that decorated the eaves and windows stood out in stark relief. Creatures of myth crouched, frozen in stone. Twisted and curving decorations filled the spaces in between. Were they Pictish? Viking? Celtic? They looked like a bit of each.

Though it was dark, several beings rushed around the courtyard—all of whom looked very human, thank God, intent upon reaching their destinations. If only she could get their attention, but if they were part of this crazy place, would they even care that she was being abducted?

Her captor parked beneath the single huge tree in the middle of the courtyard. Its twisted roots pushed up through the cobbled ground and looked as if they had been doing so for centuries.

"Doona even think of calling to them for help." Her abductor glanced at her, knowledge of her plans in his dark eyes.

"I—I wasn't going to."

"Sure you weren't." He reached over and unbuckled her seatbelt. She scrambled away from him and out of the car, hanging onto the door for support. He strode around the back of the car.

"Come on," he said gruffly when he reached her. He grasped her arm, as if he knew somehow that her brain had shut down from too much foreign and impossible information, and led her toward a building at the back of the courtyard. Its mullioned windows gleamed in the light of Oliver Twistian lamps while elaborate gray stone carvings of scenes from history covered the facade.

If she squinted, she thought she could make out Caesar, Vercingetorix, William Wallace, and dozens more. At the very top of the building, directly above the large double doors that marked the entrance, a female warrior stood, draped in ancient garb. She looked familiar, but Diana couldn't place her. Something wasn't quite right about her, though. She was whisked inside before she could figure it out, and she tried not to let her mouth drop at the sight before her.

"Where are we?" The foyer was enormous, with a strange false sunlight streaming through the glass dome above and gleaming softly on the parquet floor. There was no way this room could be so big given the size of the building she'd just walked into, but after being attacked by actual monsters earlier, she had bigger problems to worry about than a trick of the light.

He didn't answer, but led her through a doorway and down a wide corridor. She caught a glimpse of a cavernous library on her right and almost craned her head to see more of it. Bookshelves rose two stories high and books were piled upon tables and chairs.

"Where are you taking me? Who are you?" To her relief, her voice didn't shake nearly as much, as if the books had imparted some of their strength to her.

"You'll see soon enough." He opened a door at the end of the corridor and nudged her inside, shutting it behind her.

4

Tonight, Esha Connor hunted evil.

Wet gravel crunched beneath her boots as she crept through the deserted underground streets of Edinburgh. Shivering, she pulled up the zipper of her snug leather jacket. She felt a bit like the Tomb Raider, if Lara Croft had worn jeans instead of shorts, brandished magic instead of thigh-holstered guns, and been accompanied by an irritable black cat. She rarely wore anything else, favoring the practical, and forgettable, ensemble. It allowed her to go about her business without drawing attention. Or so she told herself.

The truth—that other Mytheans could usually feel her coming and would run for it—just sucked. Their loss if they did, but why give them a heads-up? Especially the one she didn't want to run away.

Her black cat, the familiar who was ever present at her side, nearly blended into the surrounding darkness as he strolled quietly along, slinking from one strange scent to another, ever watchful. Though she could smell only rain, dirt, and the light scent of decay, her companion would pick up on the subtler aromas. They were usually the interesting ones.

The unrelenting dark of the tunnel-like street was softened only by the small ball of cold fire she held in her palm. Its dim light glinted off the soot-black fur of Chairman Meow.

She could barely hear the bustle of the city above, though the steady drip of water through the dirt overhead echoed as it hit the ground. Drip, drip, drip. She spent so much time down here hunting rogue Mytheans that she barely noticed the annoyance anymore. The Chairman stopped abruptly near the crumbling stone wall that formed the side of the subterranean street.

"What do you smell, Chairman?" Her voice was soft; it would be inaudible to anyone but the cat, who listened for it constantly. He turned to look at her, citrine eyes glinting in the light of her carefully cradled flame. He had the strong, masculine visage of a large tomcat, his fur shiny, medium length, and constantly disheveled.

One low, deep meow reverberated in the stillness, and though reading his thoughts was beyond her powers, she understood his intention. The Chairman smelled evil, greasy and dark, a smear on the night that had been left behind by someone, or something, passing in the shadows.

Shit. It was exactly what she'd been afraid of when she'd entered the underground for a routine rogue hunt and realized that something felt very off. She'd immediately set out with the Chairman to find the source of it.

She smirked. Curiosity wouldn't kill her cat, and it wouldn't kill her, either. She'd made it alone this far through brains and brawn—magical brawn, at least—and she looked forward to the rest of her immortality.

Esha was a soulceress, a Mythean whose power was linked to souls. Not only did she draw her power from the immortal souls of other Mytheans, she had the ability to see the evil in a being's soul manifested as black shadows that hovered around them.

From the feeling of the underground tonight, there were

shadows here that were growing freakishly large. And from the Chairman's meows, she'd almost found them.

Good. Once she located them, she'd dispatch them, as she had with the rest of the truly evil ones.

"It's just too easy, Chairman," she said to the cat. Her ability made her a natural justice dealer and even paid the bills. Every kill meant a deposit in her account by the university, who paid her to off the most evil Mytheans who might reveal their existence to mortals.

She continued down the corridor after the Chairman, sidestepping the bones of some creature she couldn't identify.

Access to this underground world, and the large Mythean community from which she could draw her power, were the primary reasons she'd settled in Edinburgh. The city had long been a haven for the supernatural community of the British Isles. The eclectic inhabitants of London's northern sibling had at times been composed of everyone from kings and the literary elite to the unsavory beings of the thriving underground world.

Chambers, streets, and alleys had been dug out beneath the teeming streets of Edinburgh over the centuries. In the past, the chambers and corridors had been workshops, the sites of legal commerce, dens of iniquity, and the tragic underground slums housing the poorest members of society.

Modern mortals had turned some of the old workshops and slums into pubs, dance clubs, and tourist traps. But they were the exceptions. Far more Mytheans had taken over other underground spaces for various purposes, both legitimate—at least, as legitimate as possible—and nefarious.

Underground, mortals and Mytheans managed to exist side by side relatively peacefully, primarily because mortals thought they were alone. They occupied separate sections, with a dead zone of abandoned tunnels in between. Any weak areas were blocked by magic, but all the same, it was a careful balance.

Esha skirted around a shadow hovering in a cubbyhole. The remnants of old evil attached to the ghost might have made Esha shudder, if she did that sort of thing. But it was weak, and so she continued on. It was because of such beings that Edinburgh was the most haunted city in Europe, and who was she to mess with that reputation?

"Haunt on, ghostie," she said to the spirit, because that little one wasn't the shadow that had been growing, pulling at her from the abandoned spaces in the dead zone. She couldn't be sure that the evil she sensed was from past souls, but it was *something*, and she was determined to find out what.

The Chairman looked at her again, meowing deeply once more, but not with portents of evil.

"No, we can't eat yet." She glanced at him wryly. He looked and sounded like such a badass until he complained about his stomach. Then he ruined both their reputations. Thank goddess only she could understand him. "Let's go a little farther, then we'll get food."

He glared at her before stalking off into the dark. She followed him down the sloping corridor, constantly scanning the dimly lit tunnel. Eventually, the Chairman began to slow, not in fear, but in caution. He was never afraid, but she recognized his stance as one of wariness in the face of danger. She slowed as well, creeping along in the gloom. The smell of decay assaulted her nostrils here, and as the space widened into a larger chamber, the air became staler instead of fresher as one might expect.

She squinted into the chamber, but unable to see, focused on the fire in her palm until it glowed brighter. She looked up from the light and gasped, stumbled back, pressed herself into the stone wall. The Chairman hissed, arching his back.

A great, writhing mass of shadows pulsed in the corner of the large chamber. It was enormous, far bigger than any she'd ever seen, and the blackness at the center appeared endless.

She reached for the cat. "Chairman."

His corporeal form vanished, and turning into shadow, he appeared at her side instantly. He twined about her legs, and when she felt nothing but the energy of his being, they disappeared.

5

Cadan strode down the wide hallway, the figures in the paintings on the wall glaring at him as he stalked past.

Space. He just needed some space. The lassie was going to be a problem. Her presence was a force he hadn't felt in nearly two thousand years and seeing her had been like a punch to the gut. This new version of Boudica could really fuck with his equilibrium.

He tore off his shirt and threw it against the wall as he stalked into the empty workout room that the Praesidium kept for guardians. Various pieces of workout equipment were scattered around the space, but it was the tear-shaped punching bag hanging from the ceiling that caught his eye.

Frustration was best exorcised in physical activity. And if it couldn't be exorcised between the sheets, which it *could not*, it'd have to be here, beating the hell out of something to help repress the memory of her struggling beneath him. The thought made sweat break out on his skin and his palms itch to touch her again.

He laid into the punching bag. She was not an option. Two

thousand years ago, his love for Boudica had distracted him and he hadn't been able to protect her. She'd died. In the cold and the dirt. When she recovered her memory of that, she'd blame him for his failure. She'd be right to. Worse, he'd be that much closer to losing her.

No, damn it, he'd lost her long ago. Best to accept it.

He hit the punching bag harder, causing the last of the screws to come loose and the bag to bounce off the nearby wall. *Shite.*

"What'd that bag ever do to you?" The voice came from behind him at the open door. Warren. "Want to spar? You've killed the damn thing."

Perfect. Just what he needed—someone to hit him back. He swung around to face his friend, who stood in the open door of the big room. "Aye, all right then." He hopped lightly up and down, rolling his head to loosen up.

Warren stepped onto the floor mat that roughly marked the sparring area of the gym. They started off circling each other, looking for the best opening. They'd been doing this for centuries, and though he knew Warren's few weaknesses and many strengths, he could never tell when something might be off one day that would give him an edge.

"How'd it go, bringing Diana in?"

"Diana's her name? Figures. Classic, like she looks."

"Just heard it from Lea. So, she fancy you?" Warren threw a low punch at his ribs, his fist fast and almost accurate.

Cadan dodged it and barked out a bitter laugh. "Nay. She was too busy screaming and running or whimpering and cowering."

He grimaced at the memory of her looking at him as though he were the same as the demons who had chased her across Edinburgh. What the hell had made Boudica's soul choose the small redhead? Boudica had been an excellent strategist, but you wouldn't know it by her choice of Diana for her next life. Hell, did Boudica even get to choose? Or was it just fate that had made Diana a reincarnate? He had no idea, but whatever she'd been reborn to accomplish, Diana wasn't nearly strong enough to do it.

"Huh. Well, I guess you canna expect her to be exactly like Boudica," Warren said as he landed a punch to Cadan's cheek that made lights burst behind his eyelids.

Aye, she was nothing like what he'd expected. From her lithe form and rounded curves to her fine features, she was nothing like the woman that he had known. Boudica had been magnificent—strong and tall, beautiful in a harsh way. Her passion and dogged commitment had shone like a beacon, drawing those around her to her cause.

The woman he'd just rescued was a mouse. A delicate, intriguing mouse, but a cowering mouse nonetheless. Despite the difference, something deep within him had recognized her. It had clutched at his insides and been impossible to ignore. It made him want, but his world would eat her alive unless he could keep his cock in his pants and his mind on protecting her.

"Have you heard anything new? This is worse than it seems, isn't it?" he asked Warren.

When Warren had said that the tragedy that haunted Boudica's first life could follow her to this one, he hadn't wanted to believe it. Hell, he still didn't want to believe it.

But after seeing three demons stalking her, he didn't have a choice. Tragedy, that spectral wraith with the crimson claws, had most certainly stalked Boudica in life. And now Boudica had returned, destined to perish. Yet again.

What the hell was his withered heart supposed to do with that? Fate was a bastard. It gave him back the love of his life, twisted into a totally different person, and then threatened to take her away almost immediately.

"Aye, Cadan, someone like Boudica isn't reborn for a picnic. That's why she has to remember who she was as soon as possible."

"Gods damn it." That's what he was afraid of. He didn't want her to remember the horror of that night. To have to suffer that pain again.

To suffer with her. Her suicide had broken him. She'd left him. With one quick plunge of the knife, she'd just left. It had taken centuries to get over her. He'd vowed to himself that he'd never fall for a woman like that again, and he hadn't. Whenever the loneliness became too much, or he'd just wanted to lose himself in someone else, it was easy to find someone for the night. But it ended there.

And now she was back. He couldn't let the past repeat itself. He was supposed to be able to protect his woman, and his failure two thousand years ago had been eating at him like a poison.

"You still care for her, do you no'?"

"Nay." Losing his heart to her again was not an option. He wouldn't survive losing her again. Oh, his body would, but the rest of him wouldn't. His soul and mind would be done.

Warren's brow scrunched, and seeing his opportunity, Cadan delivered a punch to his jaw that made Warren stumble backward.

Warren shook the pain away. "Good, so I suppose you doona mind if I have a go? Even terrified out of her mind, she was a looker."

A red fog of rage rolled across Cadan's vision and he charged. The force of his blow took Warren to the floor in a tangle of limbs. The feel of flesh and bone beneath his fists was as satisfying as whiskey down his throat.

"Stay the fuck away from her." He punctuated the words with blows that made his fists ache.

Warren hit back and they rolled in a tangle of flailing fists and limbs across the black mat. As Warren whaled on his midsection, the red haze of rage dissipated behind Cadan's eyes. With a great shove, he heaved Warren off him and they lay panting, side by side, on the mat.

"Sorry, mate, dinna realize you were no' over her."

"I am over her, damn it."

"Okay, sure thing. I hear you, she needs some time to adjust." Warren pushed his hair off his forehead, then paused, as if he was unsure how to phrase what he had to say next, but barreled on regardless. "It's a good thing you're over her. Apparently, since you and Boudica were fucking in your past life, doing so again could be a trigger. Something about intimacy and trust—you could be a catalyst for her memory. In fact, we're countin' on it, since no one believes you can keep your hands off her."

What the hell? Sleeping with her could help her recall her past? Diana was fated to die as a result of her task, and they thought he'd sleep with her when it meant she'd remember her identity and set out on the path to her early death? Like hell he would. He took a deep breath and tried to speak nonchalantly. "You'll lose that bet, mate. But I doona want you or anyone else near her."

It was now clear that if she was to survive, she couldn't be allowed to discover her past identity, at least not until her fated task was accomplished. And there was no need for her to face her task, not when he'd take care of it for her. She finally had a second chance at life. The least he could do was make sure she got to live it.

～

DIANA'S HEART pounded in her ears as she looked around the room into which she'd just been pushed. A bit of the panic bubbling up within her dissipated as she absorbed her surroundings.

In...heaven. Books lined the six walls of the hexagonal room all the way to the ceiling, which was easily twenty-five feet above her head. Paintings and trinkets were propped against some of the shelves, obscuring titles that she was desperate to see. Light, trilling music drifted from the far corner where a petite figure was fiddling with an old Berliner Gramophone. Dumbledore would walk around the corner any second now.

Or maybe it wasn't the room that was calming her. Perhaps she'd gone as crazy as a bag of cats and this was all seeming pretty normal.

She looked more closely at the small woman in the corner. A woman that she hadn't seen properly because she was partially transparent. Most of the calm that she'd gained disappeared.

"Where am I?" Diana asked.

"I'll be with you in a moment." The woman waved a hand at her, but didn't turn. Her voice was as musical as wind chimes, but not so sweet as to be silly. "Have a look about. Entertain yourself."

Diana glanced around. Entertain herself? Where should she start? She settled on examining the bookshelf full of old marble busts. Books were stacked behind them and she peered through a gap between one of an old man and another of a young woman. *The History of the Immortal University: From Warriors to Scholars*, a large, leather-bound tome sat next to *Great Mytheans of Our Time*.

Though her fingers itched to pull one out and learn more about this place, she was too polite a scholar to touch such an old-looking book without asking. Bad form and all that.

Diana shifted her gaze to the bust of the young woman. She wasn't beautiful, precisely. Nothing so bland as that. She was striking, with a noble profile that spoke of wisdom. Diana read the small inscription below the bust.

EMILY THE WISE, *founder of the Immortal University, created a haven for those who were persecuted by mortals for their supernatural powers and abilities. Her dedication and bravery have created a home for us all. May her soul rest in her afterworld, for she died too young.*

VERY IMPRESSIVE AND VERY WEIRD. Impressive for such a young woman to create something so grand, presumably far in the past, yet downright freaky that this place was supposedly filled with supernatural beings like the transparent Gramophone fan who was puttering around on the other side of the room.

Her gaze shifted to the bust of the older man, but rather than focus on his face, her gaze was dragged down to the plaque beneath.

BENJAMIN TUCKAWAY, *inventor of the spell that would cloak the Immortal University from the eyes of mortals and remove it from their consciousness. Mytheans everywhere owe him a debt of gratitude for the freedom that concealment from mortals brings us all.*

HUH, that must be why the car had been able to drive through a tree onto a road she hadn't seen until they were actually on it. It was all an illusion created by the clever Mr. Tuckaway.

But Mytheans were *what*, exactly? Probably the same supernatural beings that Emily's bust referenced, but what did that mean beyond the monsters she'd seen? Witches, warlocks? Ghosts?

"All right, sorry for the delay."

Diana whirled at the sound of the other woman's voice. She'd come to stand behind the large, cluttered desk that stood between them. Despite the woman's near translucence, or perhaps because of it, she had an ethereal beauty, with her silver blond hair and flowing moss-green robes. The sharp green eyes peering out from behind gilt-framed glasses were the only truly bright color to her.

"Are you a ghost?" Diana asked. She couldn't believe she could be so rude as to blurt it out, but she couldn't help but ask.

"No." The woman smiled.

Had she become slightly less transparent? Diana squinted. Yes, she was definitely more opaque now. "But why are you..." Diana gestured to her.

"Don't you know it's not polite to comment on someone's opacity?"

"Oh, sorry."

"Just kidding. Well, not really. But I'm *not* a ghost—they're creepy. All that *oooohhh* and chain rattling." The woman shuddered. "I'm just...fading."

"Why?"

"That's a story for another time. I'm Lea, by the way. Resident historian. Reincarnates often have a hard time accepting what they are, so Aerten thought it would be best if I talked with you as soon as you arrived, since my profession makes me at least a little bit familiar to you."

A fellow historian. Someone who spoke her language, except that she couldn't understand most of what was coming out of her mouth.

"Reincarnates? And who's Aerten?" Diana asked.

"A friend of mine—the Celtic goddess of fate. She's the one who prophesied the return of your soul to Earth. But she's not allowed to leave Otherworld often, so she comes to earth only if she's had a particularly interesting vision. I'm filling in just for this bit of convincing."

The ground felt like it had dropped out from beneath Diana's feet. Panic began to claw at her frayed, and hard-won, control. It pushed aside the fear that had been lingering at the corner of her mind and demanded answers to the ten things in Lea's statement that she didn't understand.

"Convincing? What, that I'm a reincarnate? As in, I've lived before?" That was ridiculous, but even so, her legs began to tremble.

The woman drifted to a plush chair behind the broad dining table that served as her desk, indicating that Diana should sit in the chair opposite. "Exactly. You were born Diana Laughton, twenty-nine years ago this past August. But long before that, your soul was born for the first time into another body."

Diana was glad she'd taken the seat. "You're joking."

"Of course I'm not. You, Diana Laughton, are a reborn soul. A reincarnate. There are very few people like you. I've only met one other in my three thousand years of life."

She had to be exaggerating. This was madness. She didn't look a day over thirty. "Three thousand years?"

"Well, yes, but that's enough about me. You're the person of interest here. How could it be impossible that you are a reincarnate? Look at the tattoo on your wrist. You can feel it and see it with your own eyes, and it led you to this place, in a roundabout way." Lea's brow furrowed; her tone suggested she was thinking of the attacks on Diana, which were still a sore subject due to the fact that the bruises were beginning to appear on her arms.

"You sent those monsters?"

"Of course not. We sent your rescuer. Tea? You look a bit worn out, and a bit of tea helps everything." A silver tea service appeared to her left. No poof of magic, noise, or light had accompanied its arrival, making Diana wonder if she'd just missed it sitting there all along.

Lea didn't wait for a response, but poured the tea, adding a drop of milk and one of the smaller, broken sugar cubes, exactly as Diana liked it. She didn't have the strength to dwell on how the odd fading figure sitting across from her knew about that little tidbit, and instead sipped her tea.

"My rescuer?" The caveman who had all but thrown her over his shoulder and kidnapped her? "That madman is the good guy?"

In which case this ghostlike figure was the good gal, which seemed a bit of a leap at the moment. She didn't look like a monster, but she did look crafty.

"Of course. Cadan is your guardian, assigned to watch over you."

"Watch over me? Why? And why am I even here?" Frustration was quickly being replaced by exhaustion. She just wanted a nap. *No. Buck up, buttercup. This is* not *the time to be napping.*

"To remember who you were and to accomplish what you must."

"What I must?"

"Precisely. Whatever you were reborn for. You've already experienced catalyzing events back in America. Soon, something will jog your memory and you'll remember your past and the task that you were reborn to accomplish. But enough of that. Go on now—Cadan will meet you in the morning so that he can keep you safe while you do so."

"Cadan? The bodyguard?" The thought exhausted her even more. She didn't want to see him again.

"Guardian. Cadan is a Mythean Guardian. He works for the Praesidium, the department that protects us. Now off to bed with you—that tea is beginning to make you drowsy and it is best if you're in bed before it takes full effect."

It was the last thing Diana heard before she collapsed back into her chair.

6

Esha opened her eyes in her flat at the university, shaking so hard that her knees felt like they'd give out. Thank the gods for her ability to aetherwalk with the Chairman. Traveling through the aether that filled the space between earth and the afterworlds normally didn't take so much out of her, but after what she'd witnessed down there, it was no surprise.

"Oh, Chairman, what the fuck was that?" Her voice was unnaturally high, frightened even. She hated hearing it. How was she supposed to be tough if she sounded like a scared little girl? Shameful.

The Chairman didn't respond. What could he say, after all? Meow? The familiar earthy scent of the plants she kept throughout the room didn't soothe her as it usually did, and though the moonlight that shone through the windows on every wall banished some of the gloom, her terror lingered, crawling over her skin with sharp little claws.

Hell. Oh, hell. She'd never seen shadows that big. Shadows always accompanied a soul or a body or a ghost. But there had been nothing but the writhing, snaking, endless black of evil.

She stalked to the southeast window and yanked it open so that she could lean out and squint toward Edinburgh. The city was barely visible from her tower, perched high above the university to the northwest of the bustling metropolis. Sparkling lights in the distance revealed nothing out of the ordinary.

She imagined the many people going about their business, blissfully unaware of what lay under their feet. Stupid, happy, smiling people opened their doors to friends invited over for dinner parties, welcoming them into the light and brightness of their homes. Children sprinted through the streets, desperate to make it in before curfew, while others loitered with friends around parks and shops without a care. Stupid, happy people with no idea what was going on beneath them.

But nothing looked out of the ordinary, at least from what she could see. It wasn't like there was a great cloud of evil shadows billowing up from the sewers, power flickering out and the screams of the damned echoing as hell reached its greedy talons up to drag them down. She huffed out a breath, then whirled away from the window. *Damn it.*

She glared at the cat, who lounged in the center of the room, deeply unconcerned as always. "Couldn't you be a little worried?"

Not that it would make a difference. She didn't know what was going on in the underground and the Chairman didn't know *or* care, which left only one option.

She'd have to tell somebody, and she knew just the person. Somebody she didn't particularly want to talk to because she always put her foot in her mouth around him, but whom she'd be quite happy to stare at for a while.

Decided, she headed out the door in pursuit of her prey. It took her less than five minutes to run down the narrow, spiral staircase that led from her tower and across the rolling, oak-studded lawn that surrounded the university buildings to reach the main section of the campus.

Esha drew her jacket closer; the night had grown colder and the heavy rainclouds that had hovered over Edinburgh threatening to unleash their burden had finally started to spit minuscule drops of rain. She passed a lone figure in the distance, hunched and draped in flowing robes and digging a large hole beneath an oak. *Weirdos.*

Soon, she arrived at Warren's office door. She gripped the knob, took a deep breath, and silently called the Chairman to her. He appeared as shadow, and since he seemed inclined to stay that way, she swung open the door without knocking.

And there, jerked out of a nap on the couch, was the man she'd wanted since the first time she'd set foot on the university's campus ten years ago. She saw him around campus rarely and spoke to him less. He avoided her like everyone else did, but she wondered if it was for a different reason.

From what she could tell, he kept to himself and focused almost all of his energy on work. Whereas her isolation was forced on her by others—their loss—his was self-imposed. He was the only person she knew who was more isolated than herself, and it intrigued her.

"What the hell?" Warren's voice was rough from sleep, his shirt only partially buttoned and disheveled. He rose to his feet and his startled gaze met hers. "Do you no' know how to knock?"

His sandy hair was mussed, there were dark circles under his eyes, and the hand that he dragged through his hair only made the problem worse.

"Hello, vampire." She knew she poked at him, but he made her feel awkward, and feeling awkward always led to her mouth running away from her.

"I'm no' a damn vampire, and you know it." He eyed the cat circling her ankles; the Chairman ignored him.

"I figure if I keep guessing, I'll hit the nail on the head eventually." Actually, she was almost sure even he didn't know what species he was. Mythean, for sure. But exactly which kind...

"What do you want, witch?" His tone was acid on her skin and she ignored the jab. She didn't flinch, but it was close. Practice made perfect.

Anyway, she'd started flinging barbs first, even if she did regret it now. The instinct to push people away before they could do it to her—which they inevitably did because of her species—was deeply ingrained. Sometimes she even observed herself doing it, as if she were standing outside of her body and watching herself do the porcupine routine, all while screaming *No, stop! Act normal!*

Warren crossed the room to his desk, its vast surface covered with books, papers, small weapons, and various odds and ends that she couldn't identify. He quickly buttoned the rest of his shirt as he walked and she mourned the lost view of the muscles that played subtly beneath his skin.

Only his strong throat and the delta-shaped hollow beneath remained uncovered. She dragged her eyes from it, meeting his slate-blue ones—eyes the color of the stones she'd collected as a girl on long, solo beach walks. The look in them was about as soft as the stones had been.

"There's a problem. In the underground." Her voice was harsh, like that of an angry outcast high school girl who had a crush on a jock but didn't know how to talk to him. *Gods*, who was she kidding? She was that girl. She felt a scowl scrunch her face.

The black mist that snaked around his ankles drew her eye. They were the shadows of evil deeds, visible only to a soulceress. Normally, she'd only see them on rogues or other evil beings. On them, the shadows hovered like a black mist. But on Warren, they hovered around his ankles, like they couldn't stick to him.

Why? Was it because she couldn't see his soul? She'd heard of some Mytheans who used magic to hide theirs. Because a Mythean's power originated from his soul, it was closely guarded, even hidden at times. The whys of his shadows intrigued her.

"What kind?" He rested a hip on the side of his desk, crossing his arms. His eyes had grown alert at the mention of a threat.

"Well..." She tried to think of a way to describe what she'd seen, what it had made her feel, but came up short. "Honestly, I don't know what it was. Neither did the Chairman."

"Your cat dinna know what it was?" He arched a brow.

"I'd suggest that you not underestimate him." She left it at that, knowing that the Chairman would handle the slight to his honor if he were so inclined. It was doubtful that he cared anyway, what with being a cat. "I was in the underground beneath New Town. Around Princess Park, specifically."

He cocked an eyebrow. "The dead zone? You shouldn't be there. Why did you go?"

Mytheans rarely went to the dead zone unless they had an inclination to break the laws of both the mortal and the supernatural realms. She went there to hunt rogues or to steal the soul power of those she didn't have to feel guilty taking it from, generally demons and other unsavory elements of their society. But Warren didn't have to know that.

WARREN WATCHED ESHA, unable to look away. What was it about this American soulceress that got to him? She was all contrasts. Light and dark, soft and hard. An enigma as always, with her damn cat constantly at her heels.

Her abilities intrigued him. *She* intrigued him, with her

couldn't-give-a-shite attitude, and the heaviness that occasionally crept into her amber eyes. He'd made a point to look for it
on the rare occasions he saw her. What put the shadows in those
haunting eyes?

She was hell on his celibacy and peace of mind. Most things
in life he could pack into neat boxes in his head so he could get a
moment of peace. But Esha defied boxes. He did his damnedest
to avoid her because of it. He'd been pretty successful, until now.

It was one thing to change his route when he saw her from
afar or to avoid places he knew she'd be. But standing right
across from her, so close that he could breathe her soap-clean
scent, made keeping his eyes off her an impossible task.

She dragged a hand through her midnight hair, mussing the
utilitarian ponytail she forced it into. "I went to the underground
because I was hunting rogues. That's what the university hired
me to do, remember? But I felt something off. So we went to
check it out."

Alone? With a house cat for company?

The irritable animal hissed at him as if it sensed his
thoughts. Esha had never been afraid of anything in the decade
he'd known her. She wouldn't have hesitated before heading
into the underground. The woman had a shell as hard as granite
and balked at nothing.

"We looked around for a while, went through most of the
tunnels on the north side, until we reached a huge chamber, the
one located under the statue of Sir Walter Scott in the park.
There was an enormous group of shadows. Fucking huge *evil*
shadows. But there was no one, alive or dead, in the area. I've
never seen anything like it."

Was that fear in her voice? Not possible. Not from what he
knew of Esha. "What do you mean, evil shadows?"

"Come on. Don't give me that. You know what I can do."

He did. She could see the evil in people's souls as shadows.

What did she see in the blank space where his soul should be? He knew she could see the shadows of the evil that he'd committed. It made him wary as hell and was another of the reasons he avoided her. Although she didn't care what anyone thought of her, he did. He'd worked hard to regain his honor. To do right in the world. He hadn't yet succeeded and probably never would, but he didn't know how to deal with the fact that she saw the truth of him. It made him itchy.

"If there were no people—or ghosts—in the area, where did the shadows come from?" he asked.

"I don't know. That's what is so freaky about this. It was huge and looked like you could walk into it and never walk out again." She actually seemed shaken—there was fear in her wide, amber eyes.

"Until we know what this threat is, I doona want you going back there," he said.

Esha sighed as she began to pace near the door. "Why not? You can't see the shadows and neither can your guards."

"It's too dangerous."

She laughed. "Seriously? Too dangerous for me?" She stretched out her arms.

He scowled. But she had a point. For Mytheans, creatures of myth and legend, Esha was the thing that went bump in the night. She sucked the power out of other Mytheans and used it against them. She would be fine. He shouldn't worry about her. And given that her kind had stolen his soul, he definitely shouldn't be worrying about her. But he did. He just didn't want to examine the whys of it.

"Just stay away. I'll do something about it, I promise," he said. "But in the meantime, doona go back there."

The cat glared at him again. It had been slinking around the room, alternately turning from smoke to corporeal form, sniffing anything that came into its path.

"Do something? What do you mean *something*? We have to address this immediately. I'm not joking when I say it's really bad. The worst shadows I've ever seen." Her eyes were bright, her face hard, her posture stiff. Her chest rose and fell with her heavy breaths and he struggled to keep his eyes on hers.

"I'll look into it. As soon as we have some information, I'll tell you. But doona, under any circumstances, go back there alone. I will handle it."

He turned his back on her in dismissal, skirting the side of the desk and walking to the window. It was a dick move, but he had to get her out of here. He heard her huff, stalk across the floor, and slam the door behind her.

Warren leaned over the desk, gripping the edge until it cut into his palms, and tried to drag calming breaths into his lungs. Damn it. He focused on his breathing, trying to forget the sight of her, the scent of her. How she made him feel.

One of her kind had stolen his soul and made him a monster, had made him kill those he loved. He shouldn't want her. He shouldn't like her. He shouldn't feel this way about her. He shouldn't feel at all, not if he wanted to keep the demons of his past from howling until his mind cracked.

He leaned back on his heels and slowly counted backward from one hundred. One by one, he carefully packed the demons back into their coffins and locked the lids. They'd break free eventually, but for now he had a measure of rigidly self-enforced control that in its own way led to peace. As long as he wasn't around Esha, he could maintain this.

When his breathing had steadied and his mind had calmed, he picked up the phone. "Lea, it's Warren. I need a favor, if you could."

He explained what Esha had seen and asked if Lea could check the records for anything similar occurring in the past.

When they hung up, he called four guardians and assigned

them to guard duty on the chamber Esha had mentioned. They likely wouldn't be able to see what she had seen since they lacked her power, but they could at least be there to protect her if she went back.

Because if she got hurt, there'd be hell to pay.

7

The warrior beneath him arched her back, highlighting the curves and hollows that he was so desperate to touch, to taste. Firelight glinted off her pale skin.

He groaned as he pressed the head of his cock to her sex. She was soft. Hot.

"Now, Cadan." Her voice hitched on his name, her eyes vacant with pleasure.

"A moment, Boudica." Though he ached to thrust into her trembling body, he wanted to savor this moment, to make it important. Tomorrow's battle would seal their fates. This was the last time he'd make love to her.

He bit off a groan as he felt her nails sink into his ass. Yes. He loved her aggression, but not now. Now was a time to be savored. A time for tenderness.

She thrust her hips, desperately trying to take him inside her. As the heat of her entrance closed around the head of his cock, a groan was torn from his throat.

His fingers dug into her supple hips as he attempted to hold her still, but her panting cries tore at his control. He swooped down and plunged his tongue between her lips, savoring the sweetness that was

Boudica. She returned his kiss in a frenzy, writhing against him in a desperate attempt to coax him inside her.

He leaned up and looked into her eyes. "Savor this, Boudica, for tomorrow we ride at dawn."

"Just fuck me, warrior." Her voice was hard, the lust in her eyes replaced with determination. She jerked his head down to hers, delivering a punishing kiss meant to show him his place. He was used to such kisses, but he wouldn't tolerate them tonight.

He tore his head away and looked down at her. "Slow down."

She might be his commander in war, but not here. This wouldn't be a race to the finish. He dragged his mouth down her neck, kissing her as she rolled her body beneath his.

He met her eyes again. "I love you."

He'd never told her. In the year they'd trekked across Britain, engaging the Roman army at every opportunity, they'd grown closer with every battle won. His family was gone, as was hers. They'd make a new family.

"Just fuck me."

Had she even heard him? He gazed down at the strongest, bravest woman he'd ever known. He'd followed her across the country, fighting for their homeland. She loved him back. She had to. After all they'd been through, she had to love him.

"I love you." He repeated it again.

She stared up at him unblinkingly, undulating against him. "No, you don't. It's the horror of war that makes you think that. Put it from your mind and fuck me. I have no love to give. This—" She pulled him hard against her. "—is all that I have for you."

This is all? "Fine."

His lust was now fueled by rage and despair. He pulled back from her and flipped her over onto her hands and knees. She cried out as he drove into her, his cock plunging deep into her pussy.

"Take me," he rasped, knowing that he was almost too big for her, but that she liked it. She had never minded pain, on the battle-

field or in bed. He wondered if she used it to drown out everything else.

She moaned, arching her back to take him deeper. "Harder."

He obeyed, pounding into her as the sound of their flesh slapping together drove him to boiling. She always wanted it harder, faster. Always avoided the intimacy that he sought. He'd give her harder. He turned her over onto her back, pinning her hands above her head. She cried out as he thrust into her, her eyes rolling back at the force of his thrust.

"You're mine," he growled. "Say it."

She shook her head.

"Mine."

"I am no one's. I am my own." She cried out as her orgasm took her, causing her sheath to clench around him in spasms that rocked him to his core.

He bellowed his despair as his orgasm shook him, spilling all his pleasure and pain into her.

CADAN JERKED awake in a cold sweat, ill with the sense of loss that always followed dreams of the past. But now the past had merged with the present and Boudica's reincarnate waited for him.

DIANA'S EYES popped open in alarm. Who the hell was banging on the door at this hour? It was a Sunday, the only day she didn't go into the office, preferring to work from home. So why was someone pounding on her door with a battering ram?

Wait, where am I?

Smooth sheets rustled under her palms. She glanced down

at the red satin coverlet. She plucked at the shiny fabric. *Oh right, I'm in Narnia.*

How had she ended up in this bed? Had that strange woman put something in her drink last night? She never should have drunk the tea. *Stupid.* But her head felt suspiciously clear and she'd had no dreams last night—she must have been drugged.

The pounding on the door thudded even harder. "Diana." The deep, commanding voice caused a shiver to run down her spine. Not the caveman. "Come on, lassie. I know you're awake. I'm coming in."

She gasped, sitting up and pulling the covers up to her chest. Someone, hopefully her loopy and drugged self, had stripped her naked before bed. She *never* slept naked.

"Um, a—a moment, please." But she was so quiet that she almost couldn't hear herself. *Toughen up, Diana. You deal with beautiful, untrustworthy men all the time. Especially when you're naked.* Right.

"Give me a minute," she yelled.

"You've got five minutes. It's already ten in the morning. We've got to get started."

Get started with what? She could almost feel his impatience radiating through the door. She raised a hand to the mess of hair on her head. The rats had clearly started building a nest sometime last night and had been at it ever since. She hadn't showered since the horrifying night of the first attack nearly two days ago.

"You're going to have to wait fifteen minutes," she shouted, trying to keep the note of hysteria from her voice. She was a professor, for God's sake. She should sound dignified. "I need to shower."

"You've got ten, then I'll be in there with you."

There was no way she was winning this argument. She leapt out of bed.

Her overnight bag sat on the chair near the door. She thought she'd lost it during the fight last night. Had someone gone back to get it? She shook her head. There was no time to figure that out now. She grabbed the bag and headed into the small bathroom located off the corner of the room.

She speed-showered, then hopped out and rifled through her bag. Jeans and a loose, thin sweater were a few of the semi-appropriate things she'd brought, so she yanked them on. She should have taken more time to pack. *Really, Di? While the monsters were hunting you?*

It hit her then, that actual monsters were chasing her, and she had to brace her hands on the sink and breathe deeply to keep her vision from going black at the edges. God, she was terrified out of her mind and losing control of her life. She'd spent her entire life trying to avoid conflict, first as a child when her father had made it an impossible task, and now because more often than not, it made her freeze up.

She'd always been content to stay at home, reading instead of doing. Doing made her palms sweat. *Doing* was dangerous and it often involved breaking rules. She hated breaking rules. Her childhood had seen to that, and no matter how hard she tried to forget it all, she still instinctively trod the straight and narrow.

But she was well off the straight and narrow now. The only way back was through that bathroom door.

I can do this. Pull it together! She nodded at herself in the mirror, unable to help sneaking in a nervous and appraising glance at her clothes, and swept out of the bathroom just as Cadan walked in.

The sight of him stopped her in her tracks. He stood near the doorway, his stance casual, but still as tall and broad as she remembered from the previous night. The man was huge.

"Time's up, lassie, we need to go." His voice was deep, almost rough, and the Scottish brogue that shaped his words made a shiver run down her spine.

He felt vaguely familiar, as he had last night. Her gaze roamed over him, searching for anything recognizable and coming up short. She didn't know anyone with such tightly leashed discipline. From his board-straight posture and impeccable T-shirt and jeans to his dark, military-neat hair, everything about him spoke of self-control.

She wrinkled her nose in suspicion; he looked too big and perfectly shaped to be from the real world. He should be on a billboard somewhere.

The light of day didn't make him look any safer than he had last night, though; her original assessment of *dangerous* held true even in these civilized surroundings. Perhaps *because* of these civilized surroundings. Actually, a billboard wasn't the right place for him; he should be out on some battlefield in the Highlands, wearing a kilt and beheading an Englishman.

She was probably giving him the third degree with her eyes and felt heat creep into her cheeks. "You're here to help me figure out who I was?" she asked.

"I'm here to keep the demons off your back while you figure out who you were."

"Do you know who I was, then?" Tension gripped her heart in an iron fist, squeezing until it felt like it couldn't deliver blood to her starved extremities. This was even worse than nightmares. *Her soul wasn't her own.*

"Yes." His voice gave away nothing.

"Assuming that I believe you, can't you just tell me? This would all go a lot faster." And she could finally figure out what these damn dreams meant.

"Of course you believe us, lassie. You're intelligent, what with the university job. Recent events—the tattoo, the appearance of demons—indicate that the world isn't all you thought it to be.

And nay, I canna tell you who you were." End of story, the undercurrent of his voice said.

"And why not? Precisely?"

"Rules."

"If you are half as intelligent as you say I am, you'll agree that *rules* is just another deflection of my question. Why can't you tell me who I was?" The professor voice was the only one that would do in this circumstance.

"Fine. I'll explain. But the rules *are* important. They're the only way we keep our society secret from the mortals. They need to be followed." He gave her a hard look to make sure she understood.

Diana was all too familiar with the consequences of not following rules, so she nodded.

He nodded back and said, "Reincarnates usually experience a catalyzing event that returns their memories. The appearance of your tattoo was a small event that sent you to us, but you still haven't experienced one that will allow you to understand who you were. I could tell you that you were Queen Victoria, but it wouldn't do you a damn bit of good because you wouldn't have her memories. You'd have no idea what your task is. It could even divert you from the proper path if you went chasing off after loose ends. You were reborn for a purpose, and for you to misinterpret that purpose would lead to dire consequences."

Dire consequences? As in, more dire than being attacked by monsters and kidnapped by a previously unheard-of magical organization?

"Gather your things. I'll meet you in the hall outside in two minutes." He spun on his heel and walked out.

8

Cadan paced in the hall, clenching and unclenching his fists while he waited for Diana. They needed to get the hell out of here so that they could leave Edinburgh and her pursuers, yet the idea of being in close proximity to her had his heart sinking and his cock stirring.

What had that been in there? Seeing Diana, being near her, had felt like drowning. She'd made him *feel*, and he wanted to despise her for that. He'd worked so hard over the years to cut off emotion that he didn't know how to fucking deal with it anymore. Who the hell could live as long as he had, alone, and keep feeling and expect to stay sane?

The door creaked behind him and he turned, heart thudding just a little bit harder. The small, black overnight bag was slung over her shoulder.

"Where are we going?" She sounded calmer, more collected. With her glasses perched above a straight nose and the intelligence shining behind her eyes, she looked like a 1940s librarian. The kind from a pin-up calendar posted above a bunk on a WWII battleship. He hadn't known he had a fetish for sexy librarians.

Shite. His self-control was going to be a problem. Staying away from her, keeping himself focused, was the only way to ensure her safety...and he was already failing.

"We're leaving Edinburgh. It's no' safe for you here." There were too many Mytheans in this city, and he was afraid that some of the more dangerous ones already knew she was here. She'd been a soldier for good in her first life, and the underbelly of Mythean society wouldn't want her fulfilling her destiny.

"Come on, I'll take your bag." He reached for it.

"I can carry it." She clutched it closer and glared at him.

"Sure you can, lassie. But I'll be taking it all the same." He grabbed her bag, ignored her protest, and turned to head down the hall. Her light footsteps quickly caught up.

"Is that your idea of chivalry? I can carry my own damn bag." She scowled at him.

He supposed it was, though normally he was smoother. He never had any trouble with other women. But this one...

"And quit calling me *lassie*. I'm not your lassie."

"Never said you were. Lassie." He didn't know why he baited her. To see her reaction, probably. Was she as volatile as Boudica had been?

"Whatever. Why are we leaving?" she asked. "Shouldn't I stay here to discover who I was in my past life?"

He glanced at her. She moved gracefully even as she hurried to match his longer strides. The sight of her, fresh from her shower with a thin sweater clinging to still-damp skin, confirmed that she was shaped like a woman from his fantasies. She was smaller than he liked, true, but she made his hands itch to touch her again. Returning to Arthur's Seat for her bag had been worth it just to see her in that sweater. He'd wanted her to have her own things, something to comfort her, but the sight of her now reminded him of last night. There, in the shadow of the mountain with the moon hidden by clouds, she'd felt like a goddess beneath him.

"Well?" Diana's voice pulled him out of the memory. "Shouldn't I be here if I want to learn about my past?"

Gods, he needed to get his mind back on the here and now. "So, you agree that this isn't all a giant hoax?"

"Like you said, I have to accept this. I'm not an idiot, and I don't have many other options, do I? I want to know why monsters are stalking me, why this tattoo has appeared, and why I've been having the same dreams my entire life." There was frustration in her voice, but also something more he couldn't identify.

"Dreams?" He hoped his dread wasn't evident in his voice. How much was she remembering?

"Yes. It all makes a terrible kind of sense. I've had these dreams forever, and they've always made me a step shy of crazy, especially during my childhood. It's like I know myself, but something is missing. Like I'm living a second, horrible life when I'm asleep." She shook her head. "God, it's hard to explain." She hesitated before speaking further, as if unsure she wanted to tell him. "I'm dying. It's cold and dark." She shuddered. "Damp."

His arms ached to wrap around her, to protect her. The way he hadn't so many centuries ago.

"I'm in the arms of the man I love, but he's betrayed me. I don't know why or how, but I think that's the key."

Betrayed her? His jaw tightened. Her soul was still angry after two thousand years? But the love she'd spoken of hadn't been past tense. "In the dream, do you still love him?"

"I don't know. It was complicated. But if I did, he's long dead, isn't he? My dreams take place more than a thousand years ago, at least. If we're leaving Edinburgh, how am I supposed figure all this out? Are we going to another university, one with a library? Other scholars?"

They passed through the grand front doors of the building and stepped out into the muted sunlight filtering through heavy gray rainclouds. The cobblestones of the courtyard gleamed dully, a sheen of rainwater darkening them. It was unnaturally silent, with only rustling oak leaves breaking the silence. The smell of wet leaves and grass gave the morning an earthy scent that always reminded him of the calm before a battle.

"Nay, we're going to my home. It's known only by a few. Anyone tracking you won't be able to find you." And he could keep her from figuring out what her task was so that he could accomplish it for her. The sight of her this morning had only confirmed that she didn't have a chance of surviving it.

He opened the passenger door of his car for her and she slipped gracefully inside. His gaze followed her. He needed a bigger car. She'd be sitting far too close.

He skirted around the front of the car and slid in under her watchful gaze, then turned the key in the ignition. The engine purred to life. It was far more powerful than the body of the subtle sedan suggested it would be. After centuries of living without modern conveniences, he appreciated them all the more. Particularly cars. Traveling by horseback was too slow. He might have saved Boudica had he been able to move more quickly than his horse allowed. But then they would both be dust by now.

They passed through the elaborate gates of the Immortal University and headed north.

"Are you hungry?" he asked. "We can stop at a café on the outskirts of town if you want breakfast."

"No. Food is the last thing on my mind right now."

"Aye, all right."

They rode in silence for a few minutes until she asked, "If we go to your house, how am I going to figure this out? I need to start researching. Do you have the resources that I'll need?"

"Like what?"

"Books, of course."

Books, right. Those must be the resources she'd mentioned, but he was having a hard time paying attention to her words when she was so close to him. From the exasperation in her voice, she was noticing.

"How am I supposed to learn about history without books?"

"Ah. Such a scholarly lassie."

She arched a brow. "Well, I am a professor."

"Aren't you a bit young to be a professor?" He looked sideways at her, skepticism plain on his face.

"No. I'm not tenure track yet, but I will be soon, if my promotion goes through. It's possible to attain a professorship before you're thirty in certain fields. If you work hard enough, that is.

Impressive. "Well, I've a library at my house. You'll have access to the books you need." He had a large collection—two thousand years of solitude resulted in an impressive collection of reading material—but he'd be hiding most of the books about Boudica before Diana could look at them. He didn't know what kind of information she might find about her upcoming task, but he wanted to find it first. "Do you really expect to find the answers in books?"

"I don't know. But I'm not just going to sit around and wait for another *catalyzing event.*"

"Nay, I suppose that doesn't sound very appealing."

She let out a little laugh. He felt a burst of pride at the sound, then crushed it. *Idiot.* She wasn't his, couldn't be his, and it didn't matter if he could make her laugh.

Though the interior of the car wasn't warm, he turned up the air to cool his overheated skin, but it made her scent drift toward him. Clean and bright. He clenched his fists on the wheel and shifted in his seat. The familiar roads passed in silence until they were well out of sight of the university. He could barely restrain himself from peppering her with questions about her life.

"Where is your home?" she asked.

He glanced at her, but she was staring out the window. *Look at me.*

Instead, she stared out at the damn mountains. They would be in the Highlands soon, where the hills would turn to mountains and the roads would wind ever higher, twisting and turning amongst the rock-falls and the sheep.

"On the cliffs of the Isle of Mull, overlooking the sea. It's in the northwest, but we'll be taking the more remote northern roads before turning west. We'll avoid Glasgow, though it's faster. Sitting in traffic with your pursuers on the loose is no' a grand idea."

"You think?"

He felt a grin tug at his lips.

"So, when we get there, you'll be protecting me from the monsters while I research in your library?" This all sounded like bad business to her.

"I'll no' let you out of my sight."

"But you said they can't find the house, right?"

"Aye. It will be harder to find than any other, at least."

"Unlike mine."

His head whipped toward her. "What do you mean, unlike yours?"

"The same kind of monster that attacked me at Arthur's Seat broke into my house. I killed it, but I came to Edinburgh because I was afraid there were more looking for me back in Clayton."

"You really killed a demon? When did you learn to fight?" He sounded impressed.

"I haven't," she answered. "I'd never been in a fight before."

"Then how'd you do it?"

"I don't know. I didn't really feel like myself. At first I was afraid, but then it hit me in the face. And I realized it could kill me. I had to protect myself. I started hitting it with a cast iron skillet. They're very heavy, you know, well suited to fending off an attacker."

He chuckled. The sound reached into her and tightened something in the best way possible.

"I eventually grabbed its knife and stabbed it." *Then collapsed on the floor in a shaking mess. Won't add that part.*

"Well done, lassie."

She flushed at the compliment.

"That's one thing we'll be doing when we reach Mull," he said. "I'll be teaching you to defend yourself. You've entered a violent world, and you're going to need to learn how to get along in it."

Her stomach turned over at the thought of learning to fight, of being in situations that required it of her. But being able to harness her latent skill to protect herself was necessary. Sure, the massive warrior next to her could probably fight off demons with one arm tied behind his back, but he might not always be around. And there were monsters out there.

She swiveled to look at him. "Wait, you keep saying *demon*. Do you mean an actual demon? From *hell?*"

She had to get out of this new life. Monsters were scary, but a demon from hell was so much worse. Probably because demons proved the existence of both monsters and hell, two things she'd happily believed didn't exist until now.

"Aye, lassie. From hell."

"But how are they getting out?"

"Depends on which hell they're from."

"Which hell? As in, more than one?" She swallowed hard, not sure if she wanted to hear this.

"Aye. There's a lot of them. As many as there are religions that created them. Though mortals have warred for centuries over the one true religion, they've got it wrong. Most religions are real. Belief is the key, and if enough people believe in something, it becomes truth. The heavens and hells of different religions are separate, but equally true, realities called *afterworlds*. But they normally doona come into contact."

"Come into contact? Like people can go back and forth from earth to hell or from one hell to another?"

"Nay, mortals can only get into a heaven or hell through death and they canna get back out once they are there. Some Mytheans can go back and forth."

"What about the demons that are chasing me? Where are they from?"

"Doona know. I doona recognize their type. They could be escaping somehow from a dead religion's afterworld that has long since been closed off."

Oh crap. A vision of murderers and thieves attempting to escape hell and overrunning earth made her stomach pitch. "How often does this happen? Shouldn't somebody be keeping control of this?"

"That's what the university tries to do."

"Shouldn't it be the FBI or something? Scotland Yard?" Wasn't that what they used over here?

He laughed. "Mortals canna know about this. Anyway, it's no' a brute force operation—usually. It's more of a diplomatic or intellectual one. The university doesn't teach many classes—it's more of a research institution that tries to keep a handle on what heavens and hells exist. When necessary, we keep the peace, either through diplomacy with the gods, magic, or the Praesidium."

"So, if it's all about belief, are you an immortal in the Praesidium because of your religion?"

"Nay, those of us called *immortals* are simply those whose bodies won't deteriorate with age. And we're damned hard to kill. The title *Mythean* suits us better than *immortal*, since we're all immortal, in one way or another."

"Everyone at the university?"

"Everyone on earth. It's no' easy to snuff out the energy of a soul. Those people who die on earth lose only their physical bodies. Their soul and their consciousness pass on to the next place they believe they'll go—Christian Heaven or Hell, Valhalla, Elysium, Hades, reincarnation, take your pick. Mytheans are aware of the existence of the heavens and hells, though we spend most of our time on earth."

"Belief is all it takes?"

"Belief is like a window. It allows people to see the road they need to take to get to the next place. For mortals, earth is just one stop on a very long journey."

"Then why would someone ever choose hell?"

"Ah, lassie, that's the beauty of the universe. Just because you believe in heaven and think you'll end up there doesn't necessarily mean you will. You're still subject to the general rules of your religion, though the university still doesn't know all the details of how that works."

"That's a good argument for ascribing to a religion that has no hell, then, isn't it?"

He grinned and the sight made her catch her breath. "Truer words were never spoken."

"Were you born a Mythean?" she asked.

He shook his head. "I was made one when I was invited to the Praesidium. When the last of my family died, I..."

"You?" she prodded gently.

He shifted in his seat, clearly debating whether or not to tell her. She wanted to prod him again, but resisted.

"My family was killed before I was made immortal. My mother and sisters—gone to our enemy's blade in an afternoon. A year later, so was the woman I loved. I...failed them." His jaw clenched. "When I attacked the army responsible, I dinna intend to come back."

"You were going to kill yourself?"

"Nay. I expected one of them to handle that job. But none of them were up to the task. Apparently killing that many soldiers in one go impressed Aerten, the Celtic goddess of fate. She granted me a post as an Mythean Guardian."

"But why would you want to live forever?"

"I dinna. Still doona. But I failed my family. This is a way—" He swallowed hard before continuing. "—to make amends."

"You must have loved them very much."

"Aye."

"It's been a long time since then, hasn't it?"

He hesitated, a frown pulling at his mouth. "Over three hundred years."

"Wow, that's an incredibly long time."

He nodded, shifted in his seat. "You have family back in America?"

"No."

"At all?"

"No. My parents died." Her hands tightened into fists.

"I'm sorry."

I'm not. She almost clapped a hand to her mouth. What a terrible thought. She was an awful person. "Thanks."

"Do you miss them?"

"My mother died in a car accident when I was an infant, so I never knew her. I'd have like to, though. And my father was—" She racked her brain for a nice way to describe her father. "—very controlling. *Very.* He cared. I'm sure he did. But he was a difficult man to live with."

That was the nicest way she could possibly put it. He'd suffocated her with a million tiny little rules that dictated every aspect of her life, from her clothes to her friends to what she ate for dinner. The yelling and throwing things that resulted from not following his rules had made teenage rebellion not an option. The rules *would* be followed. But he had cared for her, in his way. She had to think so.

"He died of a heart attack right before I went to college." And his death had allowed her to study whatever she'd wanted. The sudden freedom had been exhilarating, the adjustment difficult. Over time, she'd managed.

"I'm sorry to hear that."

She could do nothing but nod, caught up in memories of the past.

THEY NEARED their destination for the night an hour later. It would take two days to reach his home on Mull. The ferry only ran occasionally at this time of year, on the edge of the wilderness of Glencoe. Because this part of Glencoe was closer to the coast, the mountains had become more rolling and less peaked. The valleys had supported flocks of sheep for hundreds of years, shepherds tending them as the sun rose and set countless times on the faces of mountains that never changed. Now, the sun shone through the low, wispy gray clouds, spreading dim beams of light across the valley.

He turned right off the main road. After about ten miles on

one of the tiny lanes, he pulled up to the old inn he'd been staying at for centuries. Ownership hadn't changed, nor had the interior, and he appreciated the familiarity. Watching the world change could be as wearying as it was exciting.

"Is this where we're spending the night?" She scanned the stone front that had been carefully built so many years ago. Flowerboxes were fixed to the windowsills, but frost had killed the plants that awaited the first winter snow. What had originally been a four-room mountain inn had been expanded over the years until there were nearly a dozen rooms from various periods fitted together in a hodge-podge beneath the slate roof.

"Aye. There aren't many visitors to this part of Scotland so close to winter. There shouldn't be many other people here, which is good."

"In case there's another attack?"

"Aye. It'd be better to be away from people so there's less to explain."

"I see." She adjusted her sweater nervously.

They checked into their room at the pub bar, which also acted as an informal reception desk, and with her overnight bag slung over his shoulder, they walked through the winding corridor to the back of the inn. He slipped the skeleton key into the lock, jiggled it, and the old door popped open. He ducked under the lintel as they walked inside and slung the bag onto the small double bed.

"Are you staying next door?" she asked.

"Nay."

"Down the hall?"

"Nay again."

"You can't stay here." She glanced pointedly at the bed, but as she did so, she wondered how much she meant it.

"Aye, lassie, I am. I'm no' leaving your side 'til I know that you're safe."

Diana frowned. "How long could that possibly be?"

"A while. Though when we're at my home you'll be more secure, so we won't have to share a chamber. Doona worry. I'll take the chair." He nodded at the big chair near the window.

"Um, okay. Thanks." Was she happy about that? Strangely, she didn't feel the relief she'd expected. In fact, she didn't know what else to say, and suddenly the room felt very tiny. "I guess I'm going to go shower."

9

What the hell have I gotten into? Diana's mind tumbled over itself as she tried to relax beneath the gentle fall of water, the thin stream leaving a lot to be desired in the pressure department.

One day she had a nice stable life and the next she had a destiny that involved fleeing from demons while she tried to figure out the mystery of her past.

It sounded crazy. She shivered despite the heat of the shower. This mess felt like a carrot being dangled in front of her starving rabbit self. Finally, a chance to figure out the nightmares that had stalked her to this day. All she had to do was get past some demons. No big deal.

Just like the wildly attractive man now pacing in the room beyond the door. What was she supposed to do about him? She didn't date much because of her workload, and she'd certainly never been around a man quite like him.

His past was tragic, though how he dealt with it was admirable. She felt strangely comfortable in his presence, despite their short acquaintance—as though he could actually protect her from this nightmare.

Diana sighed, shut off the water, and grabbed a towel from the rack. She swept the curtain back from the old clawfooted tub that had been converted into a shower. She shivered as she stepped out of the tub onto the tile floor, then immediately slipped in a puddle.

A curse broke free of her lips as she tried to catch the shower curtain and scrabbled for purchase. The curtain rod snapped, clanged like falling steel pipes, and her curse bounced off the walls of the small bathroom.

Damn. She'd probably alerted the cavalry.

She swore again as Cadan burst through the door and caught sight of her sprawled on the ground. She clutched the towel to her chest; it barely covered the essentials.

He strode toward her, concern in his dark eyes, and swept her up.

She gasped as he pressed her against the wall, his strong hands gripping her upper arms gently. The heat and roughness of his palms burned into her skin, and she thought inanely of the towel that threatened to slip off. Her sanity wavered under the intensity of his gaze. She barely knew him, but her body didn't agree with that sentiment.

"Are you all right, lassie?" His voice was rough with worry, his dark brows drawn over eyes that burned with some intense, unrecognizable emotion. Anger, lust, something else? Whatever it was made it almost impossible to drag air into her failing lungs.

Kiss me. Rational Diana slipped to the back of her brain. She raised her hand to his chest, biting her lip when the muscles tightened beneath her palm.

"Diana," Cadan whispered roughly, emotion in his voice that she couldn't recognize. Maybe he couldn't either.

He cupped the back of her head with a callused palm, lifting her face to his. She pushed futilely against his chest. *No, I shouldn't want this.*

But she couldn't make herself speak the words. Didn't want to speak the words.

He drew her to him, her token resistance a fly that he swatted away. His eyes darkened, a storm within them, and he glared at her before crushing his mouth to hers.

A moan escaped her as she felt his mouth close warm and firm over hers. She struggled to resist, but when his tongue pressed against the seam of her lips, she parted them, eager for the heat of his invasion.

His tongue stroked hers, sending a lightning bolt of pleasure through her body straight to her pussy.

"Ah, lassie, you taste sweet," he murmured against her lips.

She stood on her toes and wrapped her arms around his neck, sinking her hands into his hair. Her movement caused him to groan, a dark sound of delight that made her shiver. Encouraged, she bit his lower lip, laving it with her tongue as she held it fast.

He gripped her hair with his fist, tilting her head for better access, and wrapped one strong arm around her waist to yank her against him. The move pulled her up against his chest until she could feel the ridges of muscle in sharp definition. He took control again with his mouth and his hands. The things he could do with his tongue made her shiver and the strength left her legs.

Finally. She was darkly thrilled to have her hands on such a magnificent male. She'd wanted this for so long, but had never found anyone who made her feel anything more than vague apathy. But he, stranger though he might be, felt like what she'd been waiting for.

Running her hands down his strong neck, she tentatively began to explore the muscular contours of his shoulders and chest. How could he possibly be built like this? It wasn't natural.

Normal humans didn't have such a perfect combination of muscle and lean strength. Her hand inched toward the hem of his shirt, intent upon feeling the heat of his skin against her flesh.

Cadan shuddered. "That's it, love."

He trailed his lips lightly across her cheek to her throat. She gasped as she felt his warm mouth close over the sensitive spot at the curve between her shoulder and neck. Heat shot through her veins, and she felt a throbbing deep in her center.

She cried out softly as his teeth sank lightly into her flesh, careful not to break the skin. It felt like a lightning bolt joined the spot with her clitoris, and she arched into him.

"You like that, do you?" His voice rumbled in her ear, and she shuddered. How had he found that spot so quickly? She didn't even know she had it. But now that she did, she didn't want him to ever stop kissing and biting.

He didn't seem to want to stop either. She could feel his strong arm supporting her back and the erection bulging against her stomach and wondered what it would be like to reach between them to cradle him in her palm. She licked her lips and ran her hands over the muscles beneath his shirt at his lower back instead, too shy to touch what she was really interested in.

The hand that fisted her hair shifted and moved south, squeezing her hip briefly before running down her thigh. He gripped her leg and hoisted it up next to his hip. The movement almost put her core level with his shaft and she wriggled, not caring that she was whimpering in his ear.

She felt aching and empty and she wanted to ride the bulge of his cock.

Please, she almost whispered, but the words wouldn't come. She was losing her mind, every second that she was trapped between him and the wall turning her into a mass of feelings and need with no coherent thought. She felt helpless, a bird trapped in a cage of pleasure.

Fight it, something in her whispered, *you barely know him*.

"No," she said, almost too softly to hear. Or was she telling herself no? Because part of her didn't believe her own protests.

He began to slide his hand along her thigh toward the hem of the towel. *A little farther. Grip my ass and sink your fingertips into me. Touch me.* The thought was insane, she barely knew him, and he was breaking her resistance the way cannon fire destroyed a sail.

She was losing control—and she hated losing control.

"Stop it," she said, this time more firmly. She fought for the strength to stop, desperately, but it was like walking through quicksand. With more regret than she'd ever felt for anything, she reached down and stilled his hand. "I mean it."

He shook his head as if to clear it, his breathing heavy and his chest heaving, then set her down gently and pushed himself away from her. She sagged against the wall.

He shoved a hand through his hair, frustration radiating from his tense muscles. "Damn, I'm sorry. I'm your guardian. That was bloody inappropriate. Against the rules. It canna happen again."

Bloody inappropriate? Diana flinched.

With the harsh tone lingering on the air, he spun on his heel and left the bathroom. The door slammed behind him.

S *hite.* Cadan leaned back against the wall next to the bathroom door and squeezed his eyes shut. What had he just done? When he'd heard the crash, he'd rushed in, thinking that someone had gotten in through the window. Instead, Diana had been clinging to the side of the bathtub, damp hair slicked back from her delicate features. Her full bottom lip had trembled, and her vulnerability had roused a fierce, protective instinct.

Helping her to her feet had been the right thing to do. But from there.... The feel of her under his hands had been like a drug.

At the first of her welcoming responses, his control had begun to slip. He'd ignored the voice that told him to let her go. Becoming lost in her again would only compromise his ability to defend her. Even worse, sex could lead to the return of her memory. He'd told her it was inappropriate and against the rules. It was a lie, but he'd needed to say *something.*

Any voice of reason had been silenced as soon as he'd heard her desperate cries. The feel of her trembling, and then arching into him, had clouded his brain. Her surprised gasp when he'd bit her shoulder had made his cock throb, desperate to be free of its confines.

Had it ever been like that with Boudica? He'd wanted her, aye. It had been good between them, but fraught with a struggle for dominance and a desire to bury the darkness of their lives.

It had been nothing like it had been with Diana in the bathroom. That had been nothing but passion. Brain-clouding passion. He had to stay away from her, but the idea of never touching her supple skin again, never feeling her move beneath his hands, made him ache with loss.

He forced himself to walk away. He'd already spent too much time standing outside of doors thinking about her. He had to keep his mind off her and focus on the threats circling in the shadows.

Cadan crossed the room to the wing chair in the corner and scrubbed a hand across his face as he tried to ignore the sound of her moving about the bathroom. Instead he forced his mind to turn to more productive thoughts.

Why was she here? When he'd lost her the first time, he'd thought she was gone forever. Before they'd left the university, Warren had told him about a vision Aerten had seen—an ancient scourge returned. But whom? And to what end?

The door to the bathroom creaked open. He tensed.

Diana stepped through, shrouded head to toe in gray silk pajamas. His jaw clenched. He had a feeling that she considered the sleeping attire conservative.

His body said differently. The soft fabric clung to her curves and drifted over her hollows in a way that hid nothing and emphasized everything. The feel of her under his hands rushed to the front of his mind. What wouldn't he give to run his hands over her silk-clad form, molding them to every inch of her body. He'd slowly push the silk up her stomach, exposing the soft skin beneath to his lips and tongue.

He realized that she was staring at him expectantly, so he cleared his throat as he stood up. She looked away as soon as he met her eyes. How long had he been distracted, staring at her like she was a piece of steak and he a starving man?

"The bed is yours," he said. "I'm going to shower."

As much as he ached to feel her soft form against him again, he wouldn't rest until she was safely at his home.

"What about sleeping?"

"Damn it, Diana." Just her presence was stringing him tighter than a wire. "Doona worry about me. Until you're safe, I won't be sleeping."

She huffed, then stalked toward the bed. He didn't look at her as he walked into the bathroom.

He flipped the water on. Lying in the same bed or not, he didn't know how the hell he was supposed to keep his hands off her. He prayed she wasn't one of those active sleepers. The sound of sheets on her soft skin....

Cadan stepped under the spray, intending to turn it down to cold. It wouldn't work. A shower in the Arctic wouldn't get rid of his raging hard-on. He sighed, and tilting his face up into the spray, letting the water pound down over him.

The soap was slick in his hands as he lathered up and attempted to remain detached as he ran his hands over his body, washing away the sweat of the day. The sweat caused by rubbing against Diana.

Unbidden, images began to flash across his mind. Diana, sprawled naked in a bed, her honey-red hair tousled and her white flesh gleaming. He tried to resist, but eventually gave in to the fantasy, and his hand drifted to his cock as he imagined her turning her head and looking at him expectantly.

Please, she said. *I need you. Fuck me, Cadan.* Her lips parted as she breathed heavily, slipping a small hand down her stomach to the glistening pink between her thighs.

He knew what she wanted, what she was desperate for. He could almost feel her need on the air. The scent of it made his mouth water. She bit her lip and looked at him with eyes full of need, desire, and...love.

He tore his mind from that thought and turned it toward the baser elements of the fantasy.

Dream Diana said, *Please, Cadan, I need to feel you inside me.*

He fisted his cock, the flesh warm and hard beneath his hand, and wished it were Diana stroking him. Diana on her knees before him, his cock disappearing between her plump lips.

Dream Diana licked her lips and undulated her hips as she languorously stroked her pussy. He strode over to her and she looked up at him expectantly, her eyes full of need.

In the fantasy, he dropped to his knees on the floor beside her, his only thought that he wanted to taste her. The idea of her sweetness on his tongue made him bite back a groan. She cried out in thwarted desire, but he reached over and yanked her toward the edge of the bed.

Spreading her thighs, he draped them over his shoulders. His hands gripped the supple flesh of her ass, and she cried out as he lifted her to his mouth. He thrust his tongue between the glistening folds. Her sweetness drenched him. *Delicious.* He began to lave her clitoris.

Diana cried out and sank her hands into his hair. A groan tore from his throat as she squeezed, pressing his face tighter to her and clenching her thighs around his head. The taste of her was exquisite, and when she began to writhe against his mouth, he gently eased a finger inside her. Her wet heat gripped him, muscles clenching down as her orgasm began to wash over her.

Cadan savored the feeling of her legs quivering on his shoulders, her hands fisted in his hair as she pressed herself to him. He thrust another finger inside, curling them up to stroke the sensitive spot that would ensure she soaked his tongue with her release, and he felt her muscles contract harder. She screamed, a sound of passion that made him grip his shaft hard.

As his dream Diana drenched his tongue with her orgasm, he felt the pressure in his balls and shaft increase unbearably. He couldn't suppress a groan, and stroked his cock faster.

His knees weakened and he had to prop an arm on the wall next to the tub. He bit his lip as the orgasm crashed over him, stifling a shout. The pleasure made him blind, the image of Diana arching her body while his tongue was inside her the only thing he could see in his mind.

He shuddered as the sensation and the image drifted away, leaving him out of breath.

Lonely.

Breathing heavily, he turned into the spray and rinsed himself clean. *Damn it.* He punched the wall in frustration, then cursed at the pain. That was the best orgasm he'd had in centuries, and he'd only been dreaming about her.

Gods damn it. He didn't have the will to last an entire night in the same room with her.

11

Diana would never fall asleep as long as Cadan was naked only a few yards away. She couldn't get that kiss out of her mind. It had been amazing, mind-blowing, out of this world. All the way up to the point where he'd pulled a one-eighty and stormed out. He'd mentioned the importance of rules to Mytheans, and it made sense that following a strict code was the only way to ensure their survival. And technically, he was on the job. And that job was to protect her from demons. She really didn't want him to fail at that. But still, it sucked.

The sound of a low groan carried through the door and she twitched. Had he slipped? She started to get out of bed to see if he needed help, but paused when another groan sounded. This one did not sound like an exclamation of pain. Heat crept into her cheeks.

She slipped back under the covers as silently as she could and closed her eyes. It would be best to look like she was asleep when he came out. She couldn't hear any more noises, but the silence only egged on her imagination.

Was he really masturbating in the shower? She remembered

the hard bulge of his erection pressing against her. Yep, he was definitely relieving some pressure. The idea of him naked under the spray of water made her clench the sheets in her hands. What did he look like? Was he tan or pale? Which hand was he using? Both? Did he stroke quickly or slowly? Roughly or gently?

Was he thinking about her? She felt a coil of heat between her legs, reminding her of being pressed against the wall by Cadan's hard body.

She began to glide her hand down her stomach to the sensitive flesh between her thighs. Her skin was soft under her fingertips, and in just a few short minutes the dreadful pressure and want would be gone. She'd become quite proficient over the years.

The sound of the shower turning off had her cursing softly and withdrawing her hand. He would be out any minute, and there was no time for her to take the edge off like he had. Maybe it had been a bad idea to stop him earlier.

She'd only lain there a moment when the bathroom door creaked open. Too curious to resist, she lifted one eyelash infinitesimally. Cadan walked out of the darkened bathroom, rubbing a towel against his hair.

She swallowed hard. He was dressed only in tight, black boxer briefs. The snug cotton concealed nothing, and his semierect shaft still pushed against the fabric. She dragged her gaze away from the enticing sight, taking in the rigid muscles of his abdomen and the broad planes of his pectoral muscles. He had those muscles along the sides of his stomach, the ones that led down his pelvis like an arrow. *This way,* they said.

The arm holding the towel flexed, showing off a bicep that could surely lift her off the ground. She pursed her lips. She wouldn't make a peep.

But it was close. Her eyes were drawn back down, and after

one wistful glance at his tight briefs, she took in strong, bulging thighs and sculpted calves. He looked like a damn Calvin Klein underwear model, but with a man's muscles from work rather than built in the gym.

She'd clearly lost her mind. Of all the thoughts she should be occupying her brain with right now, that wasn't one of them.

Moonlight filtering in through lace curtains highlighted the muscles of his back, which were sculpted like those of a Greek statue. She'd never been particularly interested in Greek art or history before, but perhaps she'd better look into it a little more.

She couldn't look away as he pulled on a pair of jeans and dragged the chair over to the window. After sinking into it, he gazed out into the night, his eyes intense. But when *weren't* his eyes intense?

God, she would be so embarrassed if someone could read her mind. She'd never dedicated this much synapse activity to a mere man before. It was beyond embarrassing.

But he wasn't just any man, and it would be so easy to roll over and crook her finger at him.

A SHARP CRY broke through the early dawn stillness. Cadan sat bolt upright in the chair by the window and was at Diana's side in seconds. She tossed weakly in her sleep, her face twisted with fear. A terrible trapped-animal noise came from her throat.

"Let go," she cried.

Her fist made contact with the side of his head when he tried to keep her from thrashing. Definitely a nightmare.

Cadan gently gripped her shoulders and shook her lightly. "Diana, wake up."

She thrashed, trying to lash out again. His hand trembled as he stroked her head. What was she dreaming of that terrified her so much?

"Please, lassie, wake up." When she did nothing, he shook her again, slightly harder this time.

Diana gasped, and her eyes flew open in confusion. "What happened? Where am I?"

"Shhh, shhh." He gathered her into his arms. "It's all right. You just had a nightmare."

She trembled in his arms. She seemed smaller than she ever had, and protectiveness welled within him, which turned to panic when she started to cry.

"Come on now, lassie, what is it? Doona cry."

She began to gasp through her sobs.

Oh, shite. He didn't know how to make this better, so he cradled her and stroked her hair. He'd do anything to keep her safe. But how was he supposed to protect her from dreams?

He sat up and gathered her closer to him, tucking her head underneath his chin. It felt so *right* to hold her. "It was a dream about your past." There was no question in his mind.

"Yes," she said, hiccupping, exhaustion tingeing her voice.

"Tell me about it." He hoped dread didn't color his. He couldn't stifle the fear of what she might have dreamed. "Why were you upset?"

"I was her again, but I wasn't dying this time. I've always been dying in the dream. I've felt everything—the pain, the horror—and I thought that was the worst feeling in the world. But I was wrong."

His stomach turned. She'd *felt* Boudica's death? "How many times have you felt it?"

"More than I can count since I was a child. But it's always the same dream—an overwhelming sense of betrayal. And the knife."

The knife. He swallowed. "What was the dream now? What could be worse than dying so many times?"

His stomach turned. He had no doubt that she remembered it all accurately—the feelings, both physical and emotional. They wouldn't be normal dreams, created from imagination and suggestion. They would be ingrained memories, which in Boudica's case were full of tragedy and misery.

"I'm tied up and being carried over the shoulder of the same man who holds me while I die. I couldn't... I couldn't control any of it." She pushed away from him and climbed out of bed. It was cold in the room, but she didn't seem to notice as she began to pace, her eyes distant, with the waxy look of a person about to be ill.

"It was cold. Raining in a never-ending drizzle. I was so angry with him, probably because he was abducting me, and I was screaming at him, trying to reason with him. But he wouldn't listen, and carried me to a small round house in the middle of the woods. I could only think, *Not now. He can't keep me from this. I must be there. Everything depends upon this.*" She stopped by the window, her hands tightly gripping the stone sill as she gazed out.

"But he left me there. Tied up and alone." She drew in a ragged breath. "While my daughters needed me. God, I was scared. And mad. Maybe that's why I felt betrayed when I died."

"You won't die again. I'm going to protect you, lassie." His voice, his vow, was fierce.

She turned and gave him a wan but appreciative smile. Then her gaze turned questioning. "But why did he lock me up? Make me a prisoner?"

Cadan looked away.

"Tell me. This is something you know, isn't it? Who are the girls? Did I really have daughters?"

"You know that I canna say, lassie." Would he if he could? He knew now how much her dreams must bother her, how much she hated being out of control. This was the worst iteration yet of her nightmares.

"No, I know that you *won't* say."

12

Esha tapped her foot and scowled at the zero that popped up next to *Missed Calls* on her phone. As if he could sense her anger, the Chairman stalked around her workspace, tail twitching. It had been two days since she had gone to Warren with her information about the underground. She hadn't heard from him, and who knew what could be happening down there?

"Doesn't he realize this is important?" she asked the Chairman as she paced.

He hissed absently, as if he were saying *bastard*. At least, that's what she liked to think. He was probably just sweetening her up for potential tuna.

"That was the biggest mess of evil I've ever seen."

She was fed up. Fed up with not being taken seriously, fed up with being an outcast, and fed up with Warren. She was done playing Little Miss Nice Soulceress, and she was going to do something about it. The Chairman looked at her balefully.

"All right. I guess I've never been Little Miss Nice Soulceress. But let's go. I want to check out the underground again."

She was feeling good today. She'd passed by a huge contingent of witches this afternoon—off to some party she hadn't been invited to, probably—and she'd picked up an enormous burst of power from them. They would barely notice the lack, and it would regenerate anyway, but she was ready for anything that came at her. She was almost drunk with the power.

"Get a move on, Chairman, we're blowing this lemonade stand."

She grabbed her keys off the table near the door and sailed out of the room, heading for her car. She didn't want aetherwalking to burn off some of her power and the Chairman loved the ride, often standing with his front paws on the dash while he stared intently out the front window.

Soon, they were creeping through the underground gloom once again. Only this time, they knew where they were headed. The Chairman stalked ahead of her, not bothering with minor scents scattered here and there. He was hunting big game, and this mysterious evil was the biggest they'd ever found. They reached the large chamber in less than thirty minutes, anxious to see if it had changed.

"Slow down, Chairman," Esha whispered.

They hovered in the entrance, peering into the darkness as she made her fireball glow brighter. It smelled just as stale and rancid as it had the other night. Once again, she had to amp up the power to the orb of light in her hand. A flashlight would have worked as well, but it wasn't nearly as cool. Apparently she only cared about wasting power when it came to things that made her look less like a badass. Oh well, a girl had to have her priorities.

As the light expanded, Esha made out the edges of writhing shadows. The Chairman hissed when one leapt out toward them, but they were still a good twenty feet away. Hadn't the shadows been farther from the entrance the other night? Yes, definitely.

Yet these shadows were big and strong enough that she could almost get a feeling for the nature of the evil. She breathed deeply and exhaled with a shudder.

"Chairman, come here." Contact with her familiar would amplify her powers and possibly allow her to figure out where the shadows were from.

The Chairman wound himself around her legs, staring intently, ceaselessly, at the shadows. His citrine eyes glowed, and when Esha closed hers, images and feelings began to fly at her from the tangle of shadows. Desperation, fear, rage, and a sick kind of joy made her stomach turn. Souls gathered and writhed around one stronger force.

Images began to form behind her eyelids—not of a person, as she expected, but of a place that was gloomy gray, broken only by details of black and red. A river. A boat, with a ferryman standing in the bow, punting his way across the river. People— no, souls—huddled behind him in the boat.

She focused harder and her effort drew her farther into the world her vision had entered. A great beast rose before her, like a dog with three heads. It guarded a gate, allowing some souls through, but keeping others from leaving. A great force had gathered behind him, pushing to escape, the souls reaching out to her, almost touching her with cold and clammy claws of misery and desperation.

She sucked in a bracing breath and went deeper into the vision, passing wandering souls and desolate trees. She caught a glimpse of fields and made it into a copse of trees before a shock of power hit her.

She stumbled backward, gasping, desperate to leave the vision. She was near the source, but the power was too great. If she stayed until she was too weak, she'd be trapped. Forever.

Trembling, she focused her power with an effort that felt like she was crushing her organs, and ripped herself from the vision.

She stumbled back into the wall. Screamed. A huge figure bore down upon her, humanoid in shape, but details of its form were indistinguishable from the endless dark that surrounded it.

Terrified, she threw her fireball at the figure. As it glanced off its cheek, it illuminated his face.

"Warren? What are you doing here?" she cried.

Had he come from the shadows? What the hell had he been doing there? She hadn't seen him when she'd gone in.

"Gods damn it, Esha. I told you no' to come back here." A red welt streaked across a glass-sharp cheekbone where the fireball had grazed him. His face was all hard angles, a beautiful composition of living sculpture animated by rage.

When he reached her, he grabbed her arm and jerked her toward him, forcing her to look up to meet his eyes. She hated the vulnerability of the stance, particularly with him. She rarely had to tilt her head to look at anyone. She stood nearly six feet tall, but Warren towered over her by at least six inches.

"Why did you come back here?" He all but growled the words, his full lips curving in a snarl.

Heart thundering in her chest, she pushed him, her hand making no dent in the firm muscle of his chest. He didn't budge an inch, so she shoved harder.

"To do what you were supposed to. Damn it, Warren, you didn't even—" Her words were swallowed by the fear that leapt into her throat when the shadows expand and pulsed menacingly behind Warren's back. She swore that a great black claw reached out. "We need to go, Warren, now."

"No' until I'm done with you." He shook her arm, sounding like he wanted to punish her.

What did he intend to do? Turn her over his knee? She wouldn't necessarily argue, but now was *so* not the time. The portal was expanding and shrinking repeatedly, its energy growing by the second.

"Warren, this is bad. We need to go. Now." She looked around for the Chairman. "Come here, Chairman, we're getting out of here."

The cat was at her side in an instant. Strongest together, he never left her side in times of trouble. The Chairman twined himself around her ankles.

"Warren, wrap your arm around my waist." She shot him a look that said, *Do it or regret it.*

"You want to aetherwalk," he said, wariness in his voice.

"Yeah, trust me, I'm the fastest way out of here and you *really* want to get out of here *right now.*"

Warren hesitated, but once again, her face must have spoken volumes and he wrapped his arm around her waist in a kind of embrace. Trying to ignore the feel of his arm around her because it would break her concentration, she closed her eyes and focused on her flat.

When her eyes snapped open, they were standing in the middle of the room. The Chairman untwined himself and sauntered off. Warren's eyes were still closed and she took a second to appreciate the feel of his arm wrapped around her. Strong, but not bulky with too much muscle. Perfect. It felt so good just to be held.

Regretfully, she tapped his shoulder.

He stiffened and looked down at her but didn't remove his arm from around her waist.

"Damn it, Esha, you scared the shite out of me." His brow was creased, his eyes worried.

Concern? For her? Her chest warmed while her head reeled. But nay, that couldn't possibly be right. He couldn't be concerned for her. He didn't even like her. She frowned up at him, confused.

∿

Esha's frown snapped Warren back to reality and he jerked his hand away from her waist, regretful and yet relieved to break the contact. He had been worried and having his arm wrapped around her made it all seem so much more real. So much worse, the risk she'd taken.

But his arm still burned with the memory of her. She had a long, lean, supple kind of strength, one that was suited to her work as a mercenary. Despite the feeling of being sucked through a straw while aetherwalking, the soft press of her breasts against his chest caught his mind in a snare. Their softness was a contrast to her lean, muscular form. The feel of them would follow him, of that he was sure. Straight into his dreams.

When he met her eyes, there was fear bright within. She worried her bottom lip with white teeth that contrasted with the red of her mouth. Her garnet lips and amber eyes were the only flashes of color in an otherwise pale face.

She looked like a sin he wanted to commit.

Bloody hell, celibacy had never been this hard. He hadn't been truly interested in a woman in centuries. Why this one? She had the ability to really see him, and it freaked him the hell out. And on the whole, soulceresses shouldn't be trusted. If only he could make himself remember that.

"Why did you go back there alone?"

"I already told you that." The confusion cleared from her face and annoyance rang in her tone. "You weren't doing your damned job. You were supposed to check out the tunnel, but I didn't hear back from you for days."

His mind buzzed with anger. "That's what you think? That's why you disobeyed me and went back to the underground?"

"Disobeyed?" She laughed. "I'm not yours to command. And you didn't do anything about my warning, so I *had* to go back."

He dragged a hand down his face. "Damn it, that's no' what I meant. I just doona want you getting hurt. I sent two guardians to the chamber to guard it and asked Lea to check if something like this has happened before. We haven't learned anything yet, so I dinna call you. You're jumping the damn gun on this."

"I didn't see the guards."

"How do you think I knew you were there?"

"So they were hiding?"

"Of course. Do you think we advertise our presence when performing reconnaissance?"

"Fine. Whatever. You tried, but they can't see what I can." She inhaled deeply, then said, "It's a partial portal to the fucking Roman afterworld."

"As in, hell?" he asked.

She nodded. "Probably Erebus. It was pretty depressing, but it didn't look as torturous as Tartarus or as nice as Elysium." She described what she'd seen and he had to agree.

"Well, shit."

She wouldn't joke about this. Portals to the afterworlds opened rarely and were always bad news. Maintaining peace between the afterworlds was a primary reason the university had been founded. A big part of that involved keeping the denizens of the afterworlds where they ought to be.

Now that an afterworld was threatening to open onto earth, they had a real problem. It might have been easier if it had been a heaven, or even one of the middle-of-the-road afterworlds, but a godsdamned hell? Souls would flood out as soon as the portal was strong enough to carry them through the aether.

"Someone in Erebus wants out, and they've almost figured out a way to do it," she said.

"How long?" He shoved a hand through his hair, and spun around to pace.

She threw her hands up, the international symbol for *I don't fucking know*. The soulceress didn't internalize her stress. "The barrier between earth and Erebus is much weaker than before, which is why there are more shadows of evil, but I don't know how much longer it will take before it opens. Or what the final key is to open it."

Mind whirring, he watched the cat settle on the rug in front of the hearth and look pointedly at Esha.

"Oh, all right," she murmured, and directed an open palm at the fireplace. She blew lightly and it burst into flame. Logs had already been laid, so the fire had something to consume.

"Erebus, you say?" Roman. Then realization dawned and words spilled from his lips before he could stop them. "A Celtic warrior has been reincarnated. Diana, she's called. She fought the Romans in her first life. She could have been reborn to deal with this."

Esha looked at him sharply. "That's got to be it, right?"

"Could be. But if we're wrong, and we tell her, it could be disaster."

"Damn it, Warren, we might not have that kind of time. The barrier is weakening and I don't know how to fix it. Do you?"

"Nay, but I'm no' joking when I say that giving the reincarnate the wrong hint could be disastrous." And he knew. Doing so once before had been the first of many fuckups in his long life.

"As disastrous as this portal breaking open? This Celtic warrior is too much of a coincidence to be ignored. She's got to be the answer."

"I'm serious, Esha," Warren said. "Meddling with a reincarnate's memory can be disastrous. You are forbidden to tell her anything."

She glared at him. "Forbidden? You can't order me around!"

He sighed. "Maybe no', because gods know you'll do whatever the hell you want." Which he liked about her, actually. "But maybe I can convince you."

She walked to the kitchen island and leaned against it,

crossed her arms over her chest, and gave him a *give it your best shot* look.

"I doona suppose you know about the plague that swept Edinburgh in 1645?" Horrifying visions of it still haunted him.

"The bubonic plague? Spread by rats and all that?"

"Fleas carried by rats, though we weren't aware of that at the time. Had a lot of theories about how it was spread, but never the right one."

The Immortal University might have the power of magic and the supernatural, but science had progressed no more quickly for them than it had for the mortals. Slower, even, since they'd tended to look down upon mortals.

"A reincarnate came into his consciousness right around then," he said. "First one since I'd joined the university. We knew he'd been of the Beaton clan in his first life. Healers. But we didn't tell him who he'd been, no' at first. Even back then it was considered a poor idea to tell a reincarnate about his past. People older and wiser than I knew it. We waited, hoping he would discover his task on his own or experience a catalyzing event. But after two weeks of watching more and more mortals die of the plague, we became convinced that he'd been reborn to heal them. To put an end to it. It made perfect sense at the time. So bloody obvious to us."

The angry light had begun to fade from her eyes as a hint of understanding crept in. Dread followed. Good. Horror was the only thing that had made him learn.

"I discussed it with his guardian and we decided to tell him our suspicions. He took to it like a fly to trash. And why would he no'? Reborn as a savior to the masses. What's no' to like? He strolled right into the worst of Old Town, down into the depths of Mary King's Close, where the most direly ill were put."

Her eyes widened as she waited, lips just slightly parted in horrified anticipation.

"Dead a week later."

She blanched, but he could tell she'd expected it. "Maybe he did help."

"With what? He had no magic, no antibiotics. Nay, it was meant to run its course without us."

"Then what was he reborn to do?"

He laughed bitterly. "A couple of months later, a portal was created from an afterworld whose name we'd long forgotten. The university was attacked by demons. Poison arrows took a dozen of our men and women, some of our most powerful Mytheans. Mytheans with potential for the future. But no one recognized the poison, and within twenty-four hours, they were dead. Our reincarnate? He was an herbalist in his new life, a growing science at the time. Mortal, but gifted in his work. He was reborn to heal, aye, but not with skills from his past life."

Esha tipped her head back and squeezed her eyes tight. "Damn it."

Frustration surged through his veins as well, every time he thought of that awful year. He wanted to kiss her, to bury that pain and frustration deep inside once more and think only of the feeling of her against him.

Instead, he started counting backward in his head.

"Say I agree with you." Her words stopped him at sixty-two. "How long would we wait before deciding to tell her?"

"As long as it takes," he said. "I'll call her guardian and warn him of this. Immediately. But we won't interfere. We canna. Can I trust you no' to jump on this too soon?"

She frowned at him, but eventually nodded. Whether or not he believed her, he wasn't sure.

13

The moon was barely peeking through the clouds when the ferry finally docked at the Isle of Mull. Their car had been the only one, for which Cadan was grateful. They saw no living beings as they drove along the empty roads, save for another group of sheep huddled on the pavement to soak up the remaining heat from the day, their eyes reflecting an eerie green in the shine of the car's headlights.

"We've been on Mull for ages. Are we getting close to your house?" They were the first words Diana had spoken in hours.

"Aye. There's a left turn, about a mile up. My home is at the end of it. No one can see the road unless they know it's there." He squinted out of the window. Were there figures in the middle of the road? They looked to be about half a mile ahead, two of them standing in the middle of the pavement, like they were waiting for something.

Waiting for them.

"You do like your privacy, don't—" She leaned forward to peer out the window at the figures. "What—what are they doing?"

"Waiting for us. Must know where I live, but they canna get

past the barriers that protect my house. I've got to deal with them or they'll lurk out here until they get you. And mortals use this road. We canna have demons hanging out on it."

Her head whipped toward him, face stark. The dark landscape flashed by, barely discernible mountains rolling past like ocean waves. It was too late to slow down and stop far enough from them, so he barreled toward them. They scattered and he pulled to a stop thirty yards ahead.

"Lock the doors. The car's reinforced, so they canna get in. If something happens to me, my house is the next left. Go there. Dial two on any phone and it will direct you to the university."

"But—"

"Stay here," Cadan said as he leapt from the driver's seat.

DIANA'S STOMACH dropped to her feet when Cadan's car door slammed. She twisted to watch him lope toward a body lying prone on the ground, his hand gripping a sword that he must have grabbed from the floor of the car.

A demon stood in the road, the other one missing. Cadan reached it and their swords clashed. She flinched when Cadan's blade cut through the demon's forearm and it dropped to the ground.

Gone was the man who'd held her after her nightmare, and in his place stood a warrior, aggressive and terrifyingly beautiful.

There was one more demon out there. But where? Was it lurking in the shadows?

Don't be such a coward—get out and help him.

But her limbs were frozen in place. How was she ever supposed to accomplish some great task if she couldn't even get out of the car to try?

Diana squinted into the night. There, she was almost sure. A figure was approaching Cadan from behind. But he didn't see the demon.

Turn around. Please, please, turn around. But he wouldn't.

Protectiveness surged within her. Was there another weapon in the car? She glanced around frantically. *There.* A small sword lay on the floorboard. She reached for it, but jerked her hand back at the last second.

She glanced up to see Cadan wiping his sword on the dead demon's clothes, seemingly unaware of the figure at his back. She started to call out, but Cadan whirled around. She swore she could hear the clang of weapons as they clashed.

Cadan was fast, but his opponent had an incredibly long reach. Just as the demon's sword carved a deep slice across Cadan's chest, two other demons crept out from behind a cluster of bushes.

Shit. They'd been hiding. And Cadan was wounded and outnumbered. Diana sucked in a breath and reached to grab the sword out of the back seat. It felt natural in her hands. Too natural for someone who'd never held a sword, but she wouldn't worry about it now. She'd use it instead.

The unnatural confidence the sword gave her helped to propel her out of the car. Despite the yawning chasm of fear in her stomach, she had to do this. To take control of her destiny before it spun out of her hands. She couldn't leave Cadan alone to fight them, just watching like a stupid sheep.

Diana yanked the blade out of its leather sheath, the hilt heavy and hard in her hand, and ran toward the two demons that were nearly upon Cadan, who still fought off the other demon.

"Hey, over here," she shouted, hoping to distract it.

They glanced at her, dismissed her, and continued toward Cadan.

Oh hell, what have I done?

Apparently, nothing. It pissed her off. She cursed, then ran up to the demon closest to her. At the sound of her footsteps, it spun around. She swung her sword, the motion more graceful than it should have been, and carved a gash in the demon's arm. The harsh, birdlike features twisted as the demon screamed. It withdrew a long knife from a sheath at its side and they clashed, steel ringing.

With her sword now in motion, instinct took over and that otherworldly sense of purpose and knowledge rushed through her. As she swung the sword, she was herself, but not. Three swipes and two jabs later, the demon was dead at her feet, long black hair spread over the pavement.

Diana stood, her mouth agape, and stared at the body. She'd just done that. She'd killed her second demon and all she had to show for it was a shallow cut on her forearm. Again, it had felt a little like her body had taken control of her mind and accomplished the deed, but she'd done it.

She shook away the shock at her success and ran for Cadan. By the time she reached him, Cadan was beheading the smaller demon. But while his arm was outstretched, the larger assailant managed to sink its sword into Cadan's side and twist the blade.

Covered in blood from a dozen wounds, Cadan turned on the demon and sank his blade straight through its neck. The figure crumpled, and with a quick jerk of his sword, the head was nearly severed from the body.

Cadan fell to his knees. He swayed, but didn't collapse. She ran to him, felt the gravel bite into her knees as she fell to his side on the wet road, and reached out to brush his hair off his face.

"Cadan, come on, you have to get up." He groaned and opened his eyes. She glanced down at his body and gasped. The wounds were terrible—slices all over his torso and legs that were seeping blood. The last stab wound just blended in with the rest. "We have to go. What if there are more of them?"

"Go on, lassie...to the house. I'll be fine...I'll follow." He coughed.

"No, I'm not leaving you." She already hated herself for cowering in the car. She wasn't going to leave him here when clearly he couldn't walk.

"Go, Diana."

She ignored him and raced across the wet pavement to the car. The door handle was slick beneath her trembling hands, but she finally managed to yank it open and get the car started. After a brief prayer that she'd be able to operate a car with a steering wheel on the wrong side, she revved it into reverse and backed up close to the spot where he lay. She scrambled out of the car and struggled to help him up.

"Come on, you have to get up so we can go to the hospital." Could there possibly be a hospital on this small island? Was the ferry still running?

"No hospital." He clenched his teeth, his face twisted with pain. "I'll heal."

He'd heal? Magically? That was something she didn't want to ponder, not now.

He pushed himself up, and between the two of them, they managed to get him into the back seat. Then she hurled herself into the driver's seat and took off, foot pressed hard on the gas. Squinting, she peered out the windshield and tried to make out the road that was supposed to be ahead. Left turn, left turn. Where was it?

There. A small road, nothing more than a dirt path, shimmered in the wet grass. The temperamental moon provided barely enough light to see it. She pulled the wheel left and the tires spun on the gravel.

The drive went on forever, gradually leading up toward the

sea, until a large stone manor house appeared. The land just beyond it dropped off abruptly. The house sat on a cliff. She got the impression of a sprawling old building with as many secrets as its master.

She pulled up to the front steps and climbed out of the car. With shaking hands, she yanked the car door open.

"Cadan?" He was slumped in the seat, but he looked up at the sound of her voice. "Come on, I'll help you up. We need to get inside."

She glanced around her at the land surrounding the house, grateful to see no ominous figures stalking the night. Just tree branches whipping in the wind. He groaned as he climbed out of the car, but was already moving a bit more easily.

"I'm fine," he said brusquely, but stumbled.

"You're not." Stupid man. She wedged herself under his arm again and led him up the worn stone steps that had been trod upon by countless feet. Or perhaps the same feet, just countless times. She looked up at the man leaning heavily on her.

He seemed to be dragging himself up toward the door. How many times in his long life had he crawled away from battle, barely alive? She was just glad she'd been here to help him this time.

"The key, Cadan, where is it?" She patted at his pockets, desperate to get both of them to safety behind closed doors.

"Doona need it." His voice was breathless with pain.

He leaned against one of the wide wooden doors and it swung open slowly, silently. Clearly, either no one would dare enter his home uninvited, or it was hidden by magic.

The foyer within was high ceilinged and dark. She led him across the wooden floor toward the wide stairway.

"Where's your bed? Is anyone else here?"

"Upstairs, left." He stopped to draw a ragged breath. "And nay."

They stumbled up the stairs together, his weight feeling like Sisyphus's boulder on her shoulder. He nodded toward a doorway at the end of the hall, and they staggered through it. As they passed over the threshold she stuck her hand out, hoping to find a light switch. Sheer luck led her fingers to it quickly, and she flipped it on. Windows covered one wall that would probably look out to the sea, and against the adjacent wall sat a large four-poster bed.

She steered Cadan toward it and he collapsed onto the bed, groaning heavily as he settled onto the comforter. Soft, dark cloth covered a sea of mattress set into a heavy wooden frame.

"Cadan, listen to me. Do you have any medical supplies? Extra towels?" The idea of stitching his wounds made her stomach heave, but some of them were deep and miserable. "You need stitches."

"Bathroom. No stitches. I'll heal."

Relief rushed through her. No sewing through flesh today, thank God. But she could still help him, so she turned, scanning the different doors that led from the room, looking for a bathroom. One, near the wall of windows, looked like the most likely candidate.

Inside, she found a large, modern bathroom. After rifling through the cabinets, she found a box of medical supplies and a large bowl beneath the sink and dragged them out. She filled the bowl with water and grabbed some towels. Arms loaded, she headed into the bedroom.

Most of the color had faded from his skin and his paleness stood out starkly against the dark bedspread. Closer inspection revealed that Cadan had drifted into an uneasy sleep, and though he was breathing evenly, his face was tense.

She dipped a cloth into the bowl of water and ran it over his face. It grated roughly over the stubble of his beard, but she managed to remove most of the sweat and blood. Cleaned of it, his features were strong and symmetrical. Handsome, there was no other way to put it.

Diana blew out a breath. She needed to quit ogling. But it was hard, particularly when the man had leapt out of the car to defend her and had received these injuries on her behalf. He'd been so fierce. He'd protect her with his life, but push her away because it was against the rules. He wouldn't kiss her, not once he remembered that he shouldn't, and he wouldn't give her any clues about her identity.

But then, she understood about following rules.

She sighed, then reached into the First Aid kit and withdrew a pair of shears. Carefully, she cut away his tattered and blood-soaked shirt. She bit her lip as she spread it open to reveal his wounds, wincing when it stuck to dried blood.

His sculpted chest was coated in streaks of sweat and crimson, cuts and gashes marring the otherwise flawless skin. As she ran the towel over his chest, she felt each swell of muscle beneath the wet cloth. She wiped blood from the slowly weeping wounds, some of which appeared to be knitting together in front of her eyes.

With the speed that he was recovering, she'd probably just have to put a few of the large butterfly bandages on the more serious gashes. The plastic backs peeled off easily and she put three over the largest wound under his right pectoral muscle, stroking the undamaged skin for a little too long.

Cadan's hand closed over her wrist in an iron grip. Diana jumped, barely suppressing a scream. He glared at her, shadows haunting his eyes.

"What're you doing?" he said through gritted teeth.

"I'm trying—" She winced as his grip tightened. "I'm trying to help you."

"Doona need your help." Cadan's voice was harsh and dark with pain. His gaze dropped to her wrist. Scowling, he removed his hand and sat up. "Leave me alone, I doona want your help."

"Fine." She rose to leave.

"There's a bedroom across the hall." He gestured to the door as he limped around his bed and headed toward the windows. "You can sleep there, but leave the door open. There's a spell on this house that makes it invisible to most who pass by, but better safe than sorry."

14

Vivienne Lawrence accepted the last test from a grinning student. All the others had left within the last fifteen minutes, but this smiling girl who'd sat in the front row was the last to turn hers in.

"Good?" Vivienne asked.

"Great." The girl's eyes gleamed with satisfaction. She turned and headed back to her desk to grab her bag. On her way out of the classroom she asked, "When will Dr. Laughton be back?"

Vivienne tried to play it cool. "Next week, I think. She's a little under the weather."

"Cool. 'Night."

Vivienne stacked the tests and idly watched the girl walk out of the classroom that Diana's department used for Intro to Medieval History. She'd only covered Diana's classes for a few days, so she didn't really know the student, but she knew her type. Sat front row, smart, dedicated, and always turned the test in last because she always had something extra to say on the essay portions.

Vivienne had been that girl. Diana as well, probably. Most

archaeology and history professors had been that girl. Vivienne had always been clever, but in truth, it had been her work ethic and sense of urgency that put her ahead of her colleagues.

She tucked the tests in her bag, then reached for her laptop to close it. She'd been analyzing remote sensing data from her last field project in Egypt and she was just flying through it. Normally she struggled with learning a new program for analyzing data, but this one had been a breeze. Her colleagues had been complaining about the interface all summer as they'd gathered the data, but for some reason Vivienne was having no problems.

It was the weirdest thing, but she was reading exponentially faster, too. And grading tests faster. She was just getting smarter in general. She'd considered talking to Diana about it, especially with all the crazy stuff that had been happening to her friend. But she was just too scared. What if she had a tumor? Sure, she was leaping to the worst possible conclusions, but she couldn't help it. And ignoring it meant that it wasn't real. Right?

A disgusted sigh escaped her as she tucked the laptop into her bag. She swung the bag onto her shoulder and headed for the door, wondering about Diana. A text from Diana had arrived a couple of days ago. It hadn't been long, just a note that she was safe.

Hopefully she'd figure out what was going on and be back soon. Her department would figure out that Diana wasn't teaching her classes and then they'd really have to do some fast talking.

It was crazy, though, what had happened to Diana. Vivienne believed her, of course. Not just because she was her friend and one of the most rational people she'd ever met. She'd been raised by her father to believe that all wasn't as it seemed. He'd been an Egyptologist too, and one year while on a project in Egypt, he'd met Vivienne's mother. Vivienne had showed up ten months later, though her mother had died in childbirth. Her father had tried to make her mother seem real to her by sharing the fairy tales and myths of her culture. Ever since she was a little girl, Vivienne had felt a strong affinity for them.

But she almost wished now that she hadn't believed Diana. Hallucinations were definitely better than what had happened to her. God, she hoped she got out of this safely.

Vivienne flicked the light switch as she stepped out into the dim hallway of the history building. The test had run a bit over, so it was after seven. Across the hall, waiting right near the building's main exit, a tall figure leaned against the wall. A long leather coat hung off incredibly slim shoulders and a wide-brimmed hat shielded a face that was tilted toward the ground.

Before she could take another step, the head rose. Eerie features, sharp and almost birdlike, glanced up at her and back down. Vivienne's heart thrummed like a butterfly's wings.

There was something wrong with the figure. She spun on her heel to hightail it toward the other exit. She had taken only a couple of steps down the linoleum-covered corridor when the chill-inducing sound of leaden footsteps sounded at her back. She picked up her pace, but hard arms gripped her from behind. The scream was crushed from her lungs.

"Not getting away this time, Diana," the rough voice said in her ear.

Suddenly, all she could see was blackness and it felt like she was being thrown from a rollercoaster. She had no breath to gasp. Hard ground appeared beneath her feet and she opened her eyes, her stomach pitching when she saw three figures standing in front of her, all spindly and harsh-featured like the one who held her. Cold rain sprinkled her face.

She was in a city, and it wasn't one she recognized. The buildings were all made of old gray stone or muted red brick, far older and larger than anything in Clayton. There were no people except for the monsters who held her.

"Got her," the voice said from behind her.

Vivienne's scream was cut off by a blow to the head. A flash of pain, then unconsciousness.

15

The screams of dying men and terrified horses echoed in her ears as she glared at the boy cowering at her feet. She'd cut through dozens of men on the battlefield to reach him. Now that she had, victory and vengeance sang through her. Finally.

She raised her sword and brought it slicing down across his neck.

DIANA SHOT awake as if she'd been plunged into a vat of freezing water. She gasped and pressed her hand to her stomach, struggling to keep from throwing up.

Oh God. It had been the worst dream yet. Fragments swam in the corners of her mind, too vivid for her sanity. She lost the fight and ran to the bathroom.

Twenty minutes later she walked into the kitchen, still queasy and shaky. Cadan leaned against the counter with a steaming mug in his hand. Her eyes were drawn to his hair, slightly tousled from sleep, and the simple shirt that stretched over his broad shoulders. She could see no bulky bandages beneath the shirt.

Wow, he must really have healed overnight. He'd been a jerk

when she'd tried to help him, but then, she couldn't blame him for being moody when he was covered in stab wounds. He didn't accept help easily, but perhaps that was because he so rarely needed it.

"Coffee?" His voice was still slightly rough from sleep and she hated what it did to her insides, especially after the dream she'd had.

"Um, yeah."

His brow furrowed. "Are you all right? You look...unhappy."

"Give me a moment." Shakily, she took a sip of the coffee he offered her. Normally she would appreciate the big, beautiful kitchen with windows open to the fresh sea air. This morning, it taunted her. It was so normal in the face of all that was so strange in her life.

She stared out at the overcast sky that hung over an iron-gray sea and focused on her breathing. After a while, the soothing sight of waves crashing against huge boulders at the base of the curving cliffs pushed the pain of the dream away. The horror and guilt as well, though it was something that would never fully disappear.

"I was a bad person, Cadan," she said when the worst of the pain was gone. With every new fact she learned, it felt like she was losing control of who she was.

He reached out to her, then pulled back. "Ah, lassie, why would you say that?"

"I dreamed that I killed a boy. A teenager. It was so quick, but as I cut his throat with my sword I just kept thinking, *I'll take what you love.* I was so angry. So hurt." The pain had bubbled like acid beneath her skin. "But it was horrible. *I* was horrible. Tell me you know what I'm talking about."

She *needed* to know if she'd really killed that boy. Could she live with herself if she had? But she looked up at his face to see genuine shock. Her shoulders fell. This was one thing he didn't know.

"Lassie, you weren't a bad person. You may have made mistakes, but you weren't evil."

"There's no excuse." And there wasn't, but she couldn't help but appreciate his attempts to comfort her.

"Maybe no'. But it doesn't sound like he suffered."

A bitter laugh strangled in her throat. "It doesn't matter how quick the death. It's still my fault."

"*No'* yours." He gripped her arms gently, but his face was fierce. His eyes burned into hers. "You aren't the same as your past soul. You have some of her characteristics and memories. But you *aren't* her. This isn't your fault."

"It sure feels like it. Every new thing that I learn about her life is more horrible than the last. I feel like I'm losing control of my life." Her eyes burned. Damn it, she would not cry.

He rubbed her arms, concern darkening his eyes. "You're no'. You killed a demon last night. You specifically disobeyed my orders—you're too damn important to take such risks in the future, so doona do it again—but you are taking control."

"I suppose. I didn't feel entirely like me when I did it, though. I felt the same unfamiliar skill take over my body. It's like my body remembers something my mind doesn't."

"I'm no' surprised, and you'll figure out what it means. But I'm serious. Doona take risks like that again. What you were reborn to do is too important to risk for some demons out on the road."

"You would have been killed."

"I'd have been fine. But thanks for the help." She met his eyes, dark and deep beneath his furrowed brow. This aspect of her past might have thrown him for a loop, but he still knew more than she did. And was keeping it from her.

"Sure. Will you show me where the library is now? I'd like to start researching." And maybe she could weasel some more information out of him if she could find any clues in the library.

CADAN NODDED, relieved that the devastated look had faded from her face. He walked to the windows to shut out the sharp scent of sea air and the oncoming storm and then led her out of the kitchen and down the hall toward the library. Though he'd had a home here for most of his long life, he'd razed and rebuilt the main house every hundred years or so, attempting to erase memories as the years tolled on. By the thirteenth house, he'd finally figured out that he was trying to rebuild the home he'd lost so many years ago to the Romans.

He'd stopped building after that, choosing instead to modernize the thirteenth house, built in the early nineteenth century. The ridiculousness of it all had him spending most of his time at his flat in Edinburgh these last two hundred years.

He pushed open the door to the library and she preceded him inside. She stopped in the middle of the expansive room and looked around at the towering shelves of books that had kept him company for centuries. Her shoulders relaxed.

"You like it here," he said.

She nodded. "I've always loved books. They gave me a way to temporarily escape my nightmares." A shelf of particularly old tomes caught her eye and she walked toward it.

"Use your mornings here to research your past. But in the afternoons, we'll be in the gym on the other side of the house."

"All right." She turned to face him and held up her wrist. "Do you think this tattoo could be a clue to my identity?"

"No' likely. I think the tattoo was meant to draw you to Edinburgh." *To me.*

"Well, I wouldn't have been drawn here if my former soul wasn't British, right?"

"Aye, you were British. Arthur's Seat has the strongest magical energy of any place in Great Britain. Reincarnates are often led there by their catalyzing events."

She sighed. "Research it is, then."

"How will you start?" He looked around the room, brows drawn. What could she find here? He'd stay with her, help her, and hopefully discover her task before she did. She was braver than he'd originally thought, but the idea of her risking her life made him ill. It was unacceptable.

Tonight, he'd come down and hide the texts that were more likely to give her answers. Then, when he had a moment, he'd see if they held anything useful.

"I'll flip through books and see if anything reminds me of my dreams. Clothes, weapons, tools, furniture. With history, you can never tell what little piece of evidence will put the whole picture together. Hopefully something will jog my memory."

Jog her memory? Of his own face, perhaps?

CLOTHES AND WEAPONS were only a few of the clues her dreams provided. The man who had held her as she died was the other part of the mystery. But it had all happened so long ago that she couldn't remember his face or even his hair color.

"How much do you remember of your past?" she asked. And how much harder would it be for her to remember hers when it was so much older than his?

"All of it. No' all in great detail, but I remember more than I care to." He sounded weary, as if the weight of the past bore down upon him. He was so strong, so steady that she couldn't imagine anything hurting him. But muscle and bone couldn't protect the heart and the mind.

She didn't know how to respond, so instead she watched silently as he walked across the soft carpet toward one of the shelves. He reached up and withdrew a delicate volume, then settled himself in a chair in front of the windows that looked out upon the sea, an air of lethal grace about him despite the delicate book he cradled in his hard warrior's hands.

Her gaze jerked away from him. She needed to stay focused on her own past if she had any hope of getting out of this, not on the devastatingly sexy and very possibly damaged man sitting across from her. But it was hard not to think of him when she liked everything that she learned. She shook the thoughts away and got to work.

Four hours later, after looking through countless texts, her heart sped up with the thrill of discovery. This was why she liked studying history. For the moment when a puzzle piece fell into place and her mind ran a mile a minute while her lungs and heart tried to keep up.

But this was even bigger than that. It felt like a lightning strike. She'd found something. She was dead certain of it. "Cadan." Her voice trembled. "Come look at this."

Within moments, he was standing behind her. "What—what's that?"

"Verulamium." She read the text beneath the picture of the tumbling stone ruin. "I don't know why it's important, but it is, I can feel it, and we have to go there."

"Nay. Absolutely no'. Too dangerous."

"Look at what it says beneath the picture. It's a first-century Roman settlement that was destroyed by the Celts. That falls within the period of my dreams. And it feels familiar. Just like I'd hoped."

"Feels? That's no' very scientific."

She twisted in her chair and scowled up at him. "Seriously? A magical tattoo and the appearance of demons sent me across the ocean to discover that I've been reincarnated and you're harping on science? Having a feeling that Verulamium is important is no less crazy than that."

"It's all the way in the south of England. I'm no' taking you all the way down there. Demons would be all over you as soon as we stepped off my property. Now, it's well past lunch and almost time for your self-defense lessons." He spun on his heel and walked toward the door and she hopped up to follow.

"This is the first clue I've had, and you're making me ignore it? I am one hundred percent sure that this is important. I really do feel it."

"It's no'," he said. "Verulamium is a Roman fort. You weren't a Roman, I'll tell you that much. Going there is too dangerous. It's my job to keep you safe and going to Verulamium is no' going to happen."

Her brow creased as she looked at him. If his face was hard, his eyes were diamond. Why was he so resistant to go to Verulamium when she was sure it would help? Was it really just about keeping her safe...or was there more to it?

16

"That's what you're wearing to learn to fight?" The husky voice announced Cadan's entry to the arsenal that he called a gym.

Bracing herself to turn around to face him, Diana stared blindly at the honey-colored wood of the walls that would have been inviting if they hadn't been a backdrop for gleaming weapons of copper, iron, and steel. Wicked and threatening, even in this lovely room.

But then, they were what she'd come here to learn about now that the late lunch she'd shared with Cadan was finished. Finished, but not before she'd confirmed that she was actually starting to like him, despite his shiftiness about her past.

Now she was here, wearing too-tight yoga pants and a tank top—both had seemed like a good idea when she'd pulled them out of her bag. Due to the fact that planets could orbit around her butt, she didn't normally wear things like this outside of gardening in her very private yard. But she didn't have much else in her bag because of her hasty packing. And it hadn't seemed like the worst idea, considering that she liked him. But now that she was here, and she had to turn and face him.... Well, it didn't seem so clever anymore.

To buy time, she pointed to the wall hung with weapons made of brightly colored metals or stone and without turning around, asked, "What are those?"

His footsteps sounded behind her as he approached. "They're weapons that I've collected from other Mytheans over the years. They doona mean too much to mortals."

Her gaze passed over the crosses, pendants, talismans, and other less identifiable items that hung below the weapons on copper hangers, and landed on fine leather straps looped over another copper spike. "And those?"

"Maoin straps. They're like magical handcuffs. They're enchanted to negate the strength of whoever is bound."

"Interesting." Knowing that she was past a reasonable amount of delay, she turned to face him.

He coughed, rubbed a hand across his mouth.

"It's all I had," she said, surprised and gratified at his response and the heat in his eyes as they swept up and down her form.

It had still been a stupid idea, but at least she didn't feel like an idiot, especially considering how flawless he looked. She couldn't decide if she wanted to look more at the breadth of his chest or at the hint of stubble shadowing his strong chin.

"Well—" His gaze shifted around the room like he wanted it to land anywhere but on her. But inevitably it was drawn back. "Are you ready to start?"

"Yes. After what happened out on the road, I want to know if I really do have a knack for this."

"You were supposed to stay in the car."

"And you need to stop being so protective. I can do this. I have to do this. There's something within me, something new that likes violence—that's very good at violence. I want to get used to it, to be able to control it when it does come out."

He nodded, his expression approving.

"So, what will we start with—small weapons?" she asked.

"Hand-to-hand, then move on to weapons later, depending on how naturally proficient you are. You won't always have a weapon when you are attacked. Better be prepared to use your fists." He lifted her hands, and her breath caught in her lungs. "Your feet." He tapped one of her feet with his. "And your brain." He tapped her forehead with a finger.

She scowled, but a grin followed.

His big hand enveloped hers and a shiver raced up her arm. He drew her to the center of the mat. "Because of your size, you're going to have to rely on speed and cleverness."

Standing so close, she couldn't help but notice how much taller he was than she, and broader. And that there was a faint scar right at the bridge of his nose where it had once been broken.

"I know you'll have no trouble with cleverness, but the speed? I'm no' so sure."

She wasn't either, but decided to keep her mouth shut.

"You won't be able to do much damage through brute strength, so you'll have to focus on doing the most damage possible with what you've got. Use your opponent's body against him."

"Or her."

"Or her. Aim for sensitive areas—knees or groin—or if you can reach his face, go for the neck, eyes, nose, or ears."

Her hand flashed up quickly, smacking him in the ear.

He jerked. "Damn it."

She stifled a grin. "Sorry."

He rubbed his ear and glowered at her, then gave her

another approving nod. "Good. You used surprise. And doona apologize. You canna hurt me."

"Not yet."

"No' ever," he corrected, making her grit her teeth.

That's what you think. She felt her competitive streak—normally reserved for academic endeavors—coming out.

"Even though you're small, you can use your weight to your advantage. With the right leverage and a bit of physics, there are ways to bring even large opponents to their knees."

She nodded, then lunged at him, thrusting her elbow into his throat. He caught on barely in time, sidestepping to take the blow to the side of his throat instead of the center where she'd aimed. He staggered backward, coughing. Before she could revel in her success and consider a second move, he grabbed her and spun her around, jerking her back against his chest.

"Ah, ah, lassie. Mythean Guardian here, remember? I like that you fight dirty, but it's going to be harder to pull one over on me now. But points for sneakiness."

His voice, rough from the blow, sent shivers down her spine. She was surrounded by his arms and chest, hot as a flame. *Was he flirting with her?*

Yes, she decided. Yes, he was.

"How did you learn to do that?" he asked.

She swallowed, tried to focus on her answer and not on the feel of him. "I didn't. You said *leverage and physics*, so I put the force of my body behind my elbow, ensuring that the force would be focused on a small surface area and act upon you most strongly. Then I aimed for a delicate area."

"Like I thought, no problem with cleverness." He released her.

"Okay, now what?" She was eager to continue the lessons. There were scarier things out there than the trees that scratched at the windows. With each new skill, each new bit of information, the helplessness leached away and she felt her courage growing.

"I have a feeling you're a natural. Let's practice," Cadan said. "I'm going to come at you like an assailant. Try to fend me off."

They practiced for hours, until Diana was tired but certain her skill in combat wasn't a fluke. It was totally weird, but she *was* a natural. Maybe her body really did remember things that her mind didn't. More than that, she couldn't shake the flashes of recognition when she looked at Cadan.

Especially now that she'd tackled him to the ground and sat astride him. Normally, she'd have hopped up and he'd have issued another challenge. But she couldn't make herself move.

"Why do you seem so familiar?" she asked, unable to take her eyes off his face. So handsome. But so strangely familiar, even though she was certain she'd never met him before.

"We've been around each other a lot. Now get off." His voice was tight.

She shook her head. His body was huge and hard beneath hers, and he looked up at her with surprised heat in his eyes.

"I really do think there is a lot you aren't telling me," she said, then tentatively ran her hands down his chest to see what he would do.

His jaw tensed and his hands shot up to grip her thighs, almost reflexively, as if he would stop her but didn't quite want to. She decided that distracting him from his objections would be an excellent way to get him relaxed enough to answer her questions about Verulamium, which she couldn't get off her mind.

And being on top, in control, sent a wild and heady power streaking through her veins. The proof of his attraction—the hard shaft now pressed against her, the light mist of sweat at his brow, his shallow breaths—gave her courage. So she braced herself for rejection, clung to hope, and said, "I have a question."

"You have a lot of questions," he said, his voice pained and his gaze racing over her form.

"True. I'm a historian, after all. Which leads me to my question. Why is it," she asked, as she ran a hand over his hard chest, "that you are so very large?"

He could push her off him at any moment, but from the way he looked at her, eyes fierce, he wouldn't be doing so anytime soon. "What do you mean?"

"Well, you're over three hundred years old. And you're nearly six and a half feet tall. You shouldn't be this tall. Three hundred years ago, hardly anyone had your height. Were you *really* this big back then?" She ached to put her hands on the bronzed flesh she'd revealed, but resisted.

"Wisely noted," he said as he squeezed her thighs.

Had he spread them slightly apart? She shivered.

"I wasn't always this tall. But as a guardian, we're meant to protect. To be the strongest in this world." He paused to draw in a deep breath. "So we grow. As the average mortal height increases, so does ours."

"Ah, I see." She bit her lip, her gaze drawn once again to the expanse of his chest, and gave in to temptation. She ran both hands over his pecs, nearly sighing at the feel of hot, hard muscles beneath her palms. A small noise strangled in his throat.

"And why is it that you're so, well, muscular? Were you always this strong?" She was buttering him up with compliments, but she *was* genuinely interested. She'd get to the real questions soon enough.

He shrugged. "Aye."

Wow, so this is how he had looked three hundred years ago? Three hundred years. Or older? Much, much older? The idea was so terrifying and so insane that her mind backed away from it immediately. It couldn't be, and with him here to distract her, it was easy to force something so awful to the back of her mind.

He was a dead man.

Cadan stared at Diana perched above him and all his good intentions to maintain his distance for her safety fled his mind. He knew, *knew*, that if his judgment was compromised again as it had been so many years ago, she would suffer an equally horrific fate.

But everything about her clouded his senses. The feel of her, the look of her, the smell of her, and the sound of her all reminded him that it had been a long time since he'd been with a woman. Even longer since he'd been with one who made him feel more than simple lust. Two thousand years, to be precise. And Diana was turning out to be more than he'd thought. Much more.

Now he was pinned beneath her, the heat of her making his cock twitch. He had to get up, push her off, but she immobilized him. Not with her strength—hers was nothing compared to his —but with her will. Just a minute longer. Then he would move.

But she leaned down then, pressing herself against his chest, and whispered close to his ear, "Are *all* the guardians built like you?"

The feel of her warm breath, the brush of her lips, made a shudder run down his spine. Unable to stop himself from experiencing this pleasure just once, he ground himself against her. He forced himself to still, but not before he heard the small noise of surprised approval at his ear.

Fuck, what was her game? But he nodded once in answer to her question, surprised to hear her laugh low in her throat.

"Oh, I don't think so," she purred as she rubbed herself

against him. "I think that you—" She ran her hands down his sides and his muscles tensed at her touch. "—are unique."

She began to press small, hot kisses along the side of his neck, lightning shooting through him to his cock every time he felt her mouth. He groaned when her tongue darted out, tasting him.

"Make me yours, Cadan."

Aye. Mine. Always mine.

"Who *are* you?" His voice was raspy, nearly broken. He'd have been embarrassed if he'd had any blood left in his brain to keep it operational.

"I'm afraid I don't know what you mean." Her voice was husky, desire thick in her tone. She glanced down at his mouth.

"You're different—" He nearly groaned when her small pink tongue darted out and wetted her top lip. "—than you were before."

She smiled and raised a hand to run it through his hair. "You caught me by surprise, then, that's all. This time—" She fisted her hand in his hair. "—I'm in control."

The warrior in him, the leader, the commander, boiled at the idea, but the man in him, the one trapped beneath the temptress who licked and bit and stared at him with endless eyes, thought, *Aye.*

The internal battle tore at him, one side determined to throw her off and tear her clothes away, pounding into her until she begged, the other desperate to stay beneath her and see what she did next. A small voice, that of reason and logic, told him to get away from her, quickly, before this went too far.

"And I suppose that I want to know something now," she said.

"What do you want to know?" Alarm pushed at the edges of his desire.

"What is it about you that's so familiar to me?"

And with that, he remembered his reservations. She'd remember who he was. Who she was. And then everything would be over. Diana—his hope of atoning for his sins—everything would be destroyed because he couldn't keep his cock in his pants.

"Nothing. There's nothing about me. And this is over." He used guilt to crush his regret as he dragged his hands from her full hips up to her waist and lifted her off him.

"What?" Surprise was clear in her voice as he set her on the ground next to him and surged to his feet.

"I doona want you." His heart tore at the sight of her looking up at him, shock in her eyes, but he forced himself to spin on his heel and walk out of the gym.

17

L ightning struck for Diana again three days later. She'd come to the gym a bit early today because she just had to get out of the library. The books had revealed no clues, and worse, she was almost certain that some of them were missing from the shelves. The only person who could have moved them was Cadan.

The idea that he might be hiding things from her stressed her to the point that physical activity seemed like a really good idea. So she'd come here to practice with the small sword he'd loaned her a couple of days ago. She was a natural. Not like someone with unusual skill. Like someone who'd had other-worldly powers handed down from a past life.

She was certain now that her body remembered things that her mind didn't. As she stared up at the wall of weapons that had distracted her from her practice, she was having the same feeling she'd had when she'd looked upon the image of Verulamium.

"What are you doing here so early?" Cadan asked from behind her.

She jumped, startled out of her trance. She hadn't seen him

since this morning in the library. They'd circled each other the last three days. He, probably wary that she'd jump him again, and she, scared of falling for him when she knew there was more that he wasn't telling her. He'd kissed her twice now. He wanted her, yet he kept pushing her away. Maybe it was because of university rules, as he'd said. But she couldn't shake the feeling that he was hiding something.

"I'm looking at that sword," she said.

She pointed up at a blade high on the wall. It was in a cluster of the oldest weapons in the room. Its dented and scratched iron blade spoke of the lives it must have taken, though the hilt, with its swirling scrollwork, was still in fairly good condition. More than that, the decoration could be used to date the weapon.

"I recognize that sword," she said. "I know I do. Where is it from?"

DARE HE TELL her the truth? It was a distinctive blade; it wouldn't take her long to catch him if he lied. And after the lie about Verulamium, Cadan couldn't risk another. Yet, the idea of telling another lie made his stomach turn. He told himself he was doing it to protect her, that she wasn't ready to face Boudica's challenges. But it still made him ill to lie to her repeatedly.

"It's a sword from southern Britain." He settled on truth and hoped she wouldn't make the connection.

"Can I hold it?" Her voice was quiet, thoughtful.

Nay. "Aye."

He strode over and reached up, carefully drawing the old sword away from the wall. It was a typical Celtic sword from Boudica's homeland, one that she would have seen her men use on the battlefield. Her blade had been different, suited to her size and status, but this simple implement told tales of her past life as well.

He placed it gently in her palm, and she gasped slightly when it touched her skin. Her fingers closed tightly around the hilt.

"It's familiar," she said, awe in her voice as she slowly twirled a figure eight in the air. "I recognize this type of sword."

"This type of blade was used for a long stretch of time."

"Yes, but not as long as the stretch of time I've been researching. A few hundred years, no more."

"More or less."

"What's the date on it?" Her gaze was clear and penetrating as she looked at him.

Gods, what should he say? Telling her could lead her closer to her identity, but the sword was so distinctive that twenty minutes with a weapons book and she'd know. If she ferreted out the truth, she'd never trust him again. Hell, she barely trusted him as it was.

"No' sure, exactly." It slipped off his tongue. *Coward.*

She arched an eyebrow. "Really? I have a hard time believing that. Everything in here is organized by type, and from the looks of the styles and conditions of the weapons, by date as well."

Damn it. He glanced hastily up at the wall as if to check for a date. If he lied now, she'd know he was up to something. "Ah, around one hundred AD, give or take a century."

She looked up at him sharply. "One hundred AD?"

He jerked his head in assent.

She flipped the sword and turned it around on him until the blade pressed into his stomach. He froze. If she wanted to pierce him, fine. It wouldn't kill him, and maybe he deserved it. For lying—or hell, for telling the truth and putting her that much closer.

"You're going to take me to Verulamium. I know it's important, and you're going to take me."

"Nay, I'm no'."

She pushed the blade harder, glancing down at it apprehensively before glaring back up at him. It didn't break the skin, but it was close.

"You are, or I swear to God I'm going by myself."

"And how would do that?"

"Steal your car. Call your boss. Walk out the front door and hope for the best. I'd figure it out."

She was bluffing. That was it. But her eyes gleamed with a slightly crazed, desperate look. He shifted uncomfortably. The lassie was trouble. "You would no'."

"Try me. I'm not going to sit around here while you hide things from me. And don't think I'm not aware that's what you're doing. That's twice you've refused to take me, and twice I've found something that points me in the direction of the first century AD. I'd bet tenure on the fact that I was a Celt, but there were a hell of a lot of Celts. I want to know why I'm drawn to a Roman fort."

"Well, you weren't Roman."

"Don't try to distract me. Why are you keeping things from me? Are you on my side or not?"

He'd have been angry that she questioned his loyalty if he wasn't already burning with the deceit. "I'm just trying to keep you safe."

He knocked the dull-edged sword aside and pulled her to him. She was delicate under his hands and it made his stomach churn with fear for her. "Do you no' get it? That's the most important thing. *Keeping you safe.*"

"I get that." Her breath was short, her eyes wide. "And I appreciate it. I do. But it can't be at the expense of me making my own decisions. If we're careful getting there, then the demons won't know to follow us. I don't have a death wish. But I do want answers and this sword and Verulamium are the closest I've come to getting them."

"Fine," he said. There was no way around it now. "I'll take you if I can get my colleague Esha to create a portal to take us directly there. That way the demons canna track us. It's the safest way. Her power level fluctuates. If she doesn't have enough, we wait. I won't risk you over this."

18

E sha stared at the text on her phone, puzzling over the note from Warren.

"A meeting?" she said to the cat, not particularly concerned that he was paying her absolutely no attention. "Warren wants to have a *meeting* with me? Like, we're trying to nail down the problems with the budget before the end of the quarter type meeting?"

Too weird. No one ever asked her to a group gathering, and his message had specifically said *join us in a meeting.* Her job never involved meetings, primarily because fueling her own power meant taking it from the souls of others. Not that she could help it, but still, they didn't like it.

Despite her flaws—which she didn't actually agree were flaws—the university had given her a place to live and a pretty nice salary when they'd figured out the extent of her power. She could manifest her every desire, so long as she was fueled up on borrowed power. Once she'd proven herself trustworthy, her unique ability to see true evil had given her a *carte blanche* license to kill the super baddies whenever she came across them.

She'd initially thought that Warren avoided her because of the way she refueled her power. But then she'd realized that she didn't affect him. Now she had no idea why he avoided her. He was the only Mythean she'd ever met who wasn't affected by her powers. She could actually get close to him. It was probably half the reason she was interested in him. Hell, who was she kidding? She'd probably be mooning after him no matter what.

Frowning, she glanced down at the text message. It must be about Erebus, though she was surprised he hadn't texted her the news to avoid having to see her.

"Well, Chairman, it looks like we're going to our first-ever business meeting."

With disgust, she suppressed the thrill of delight she felt at being asked—by Warren—to come to the meeting.

Idiot.

An hour later, Esha strode through the open door of Warren's office. He and an unknown woman sat at the small round table in the corner.

"So, what's up?" she asked as she walked over to the table.

Warren stood to greet her, but rather than shake her hand, he gestured toward the woman. "Esha, this is Aerten. She's a goddess of fate and head of the Praesidium."

Whoa. Goddess was right. Esha reeled from the hit of power she got off Aerten. It felt like the hit she got off her only friend Andrasta, the Celtic goddess of war. She didn't get to see her much, but when she did, boy, was it something.

Esha smiled somewhat drunkenly at the serene figure who'd also risen to greet her. "Hi," she said, holding out her hand. "Celtic, right?"

The woman nodded as she sat. Esha took the chair next to her. "Well done of you to know. Sometimes it seems there are so many of us from various faiths that it can be hard to keep straight."

That was the truth. "I studied up once I got to the university and realized how much there was to the world."

And you're colleagues with my friend, which I'm not allowed to tell you since it would ruin her trips sneaking out of Otherworld .

Aerten nodded. "The Mythean Guardians are supposed to protect those who are important to the fate of humanity. My sight allows me to see who those individuals might be, and to select the Mythean Guardians from the bravest mortals. But my name does mean *renowned in battle* for a reason." She smiled wryly. "That was a long time ago, though. Now I'm a bureaucrat, and Warren is the real head of the Praesidium."

"I see. But you don't come around here often. At least not when I'm here. I'd feel it." Hoo boy, was she feeling it.

"Celtic gods don't really leave Otherworld. I'm an exception because of my duties to the Mythean Guard, but even I can only come for very important reasons. And you are a very important reason."

"Me?" She squashed a tiny flush of pride. Wasn't this about Erebus?

"Aye," Warren said, and she had to work a little harder to crush the burst of happiness. "As you know, we invited you to the university because of your power. But because of the way you reap your power, we weren't exactly sure how to use you other than as a mercenary."

"Now you have?"

"With your discoveries in the underground, and recent complications, we have," Warren said.

"Complications?" Esha asked.

"We'll get to that in a minute," Aerten said.

Esha frowned, but nodded at them to continue.

"Warren has proposed that we add you to the Praesidium."

Esha tried to keep her jaw from slackening. Why would

Warren do this for her? She liked her badass solo merc status, but if she were honest, she'd longed to be part of a team. Just once, to see what it felt like. But it was too weird.

"Oh, hey, thanks, but I'm not a team player," she said.

"You doona need to be," Warren said. "You'd be a consultant. Your discovery in the underground highlights your skill, and we've recently determined we need some of your other talents. I've never spoken to you much before this recent problem, but I realized that you don't drain my powers."

He really wanted her to join the Praesidium?

"What do you think?" the goddess asked.

She must be here to make the whole deal official, Esha thought.

"Could you work with us on a consultant basis? You'd retain your current duties, but we want to ensure that you come to our department when you find something strange, as you did in the underground. Or that you'll work for us when we need you to," Aerten said.

Esha mulled it over. It would be nice to be part of a team. Not that she needed them, or anything. "What's in it for me?"

"We'll pay you more," Warren said.

"Triple?" They already paid her pretty damn well, but why not shoot high?

"Double." Warren's voice was firm.

"All right, good deal. I'd have settled for half again, anyway." She smiled and held out her hand, first to Aerten since she was the big boss, and then to Warren. Her palm tingled where it touched his.

"You mentioned recent complications with the underground?" she asked.

Aerten nodded, her face grim. "The two Mythean Guardians that Warren stationed at the portal to Erebus intercepted four demons abducting a mortal female. They tried to save her, and Lorne, one of the guardians, was killed. Three of the demons were destroyed, but one took the soul of the mortal into Erebus. The mortal's body is in a coma here in the infirmary."

"Shit. Are you sure she's mortal?"

"Honestly, we're not. A mortal body normally wouldn't survive going through a portal to an afterworld. If she's a Mythean, there's no sign of what kind. We're not even sure if she's a victim or an accomplice who went willingly. We'd like you to take a look at her to see if any shadows of evil remain with her body."

"Sure, I can try. But even if she was evil, it's not a given that the shadows would stay behind with the body. Most often they follow the soul."

"Give it your best shot," Warren said.

Esha nodded and followed them out the door. Warren led her and Aerten across campus to the infirmary. The day had turned rainy and miserable and Esha used the power she got off Aerten to create a dry space around herself and the Chairman. He sulked for hours if he had to get wet.

Out of the corner of her eye, she noticed that the goddess hadn't created a dry spot for herself to walk through and wondered about it. Surely she had the power to do so. As Esha looked closer, she realized that the goddess was looking at the raindrops on the back of her hand and smiling. Weird.

Esha glanced at Warren. He'd popped up the collar of his jacket to keep his neck dry and had his head bent. She waved a hand and created a dry space over him as well.

He jerked, then looked at her. A rusty and tentative smile pulled up one corner of his mouth. "Thanks."

She nodded, then looked back at the rolling hills of campus and the big gray building that housed the infirmary on the first floor. They hurried up the steps, through the big wooden door, and down the hall into a long room with a dozen beds. Only one bed had an occupant and they walked up to it.

"What's her name?" Esha said as she looked down at the body of the beautiful, dark-haired woman. She was hooked up to machines to monitor her vitals, but she looked peaceful. Esha could already tell that there was no evil attached to the woman.

"Vivienne Lawrence. American," Warren said. "She had a driving license in her bag. It's hard to say where they got her from, but I think they aetherwalked her straight from America to the portal because she dinna have a passport to get through Customs."

"Well, I don't see any shadows," Esha said. "Either they followed the soul, or she's a good person," Esha said.

"I was afraid you'd say that," Aerten said. "If they've abducted a mortal nonbeliever, there'll be hell to pay. And now there's a scared mortal trapped in the wrong hell."

Esha nodded, still staring at the woman and puzzling over the mystery. But Aerten was right. Abducting living mortals to an afterworld, especially mortals who didn't believe in said afterworld, was hugely against the rules. The university would have to get involved.

With a last look at the woman, they walked out of the infirmary and out under the covered porte cochere at the front of the building.

"I appreciate your help with this. And I'm glad you'll be joining us," Aerten said. She smiled, then disappeared to return to Otherworld.

WARREN LOOKED out at the rain. Esha had made a magical umbrella over his head on the walk here. It made his chest feel warm, which worried him. With good feelings came bad. He'd heard a saying once that the bad things in life allowed you to appreciate the good things. For him, it was the opposite. The good things reminded him how bad things were, both in his past and in his soulless future.

Esha was becoming a good thing in his life, as complicated as she was. A soulceress, for gods' sake. Of all the species to feel something for, he'd chosen the type who had gotten him into his soulless state, which he despised. He was no longer mortal, but neither was he Mythean, and he despised it.

He should leave now. Staying around Esha was bad for his sanity. He'd never before seen her so frequently or in such proximity, and the contact was only heightening his fascination with her. His past wariness and avoidance of her species had been wise. Now, it was impossible.

She'd crept into his dreams these last days, slipping away as the sun rose, leaving him hot, hard, and disgusted with himself. Yet he couldn't get his stupid mind off her. He bit the inside of his cheek hard and focused on the pain and the present.

"Thank you for agreeing to this arrangement," he said to her. "It's a very good move for the Praesidium. We've been underutilizing you by having you work solo. I'll call on you when I need you for something."

She nodded, then said, "Hey, what about the portal in the underground? This isn't a coincidence. Have you put any more thought toward telling the reincarnate? I know you said it's dangerous, but this is just too much to ignore."

He stifled a frustrated groan. "You've got to trust me, Esha. It's a dangerous idea. I called her guardian and warned him. Maybe once she remembers who she was, we can suggest the portal to her. Maybe. Until then, our meddling will only make things worse."

"I really think it would help," she said. "This has to be it."

"Nay." His voice was hard and she flinched. He almost apologized, but didn't want to soften the warning. "I'm serious. It would be bad to tell her anything before she remembers who she is. Tell me you won't."

She shot him a suspicious look and nodded.

Hell, that could go either way.

19

"Watch out, lassie."

Cadan's warning came soon enough for Diana to dodge a puddle in the damp grass that stretched between the tumbling ruins. He'd upheld the agreement he'd made last night to take her to Verulamium, and they now walked amongst the stone walls.

He'd called his colleague Esha on the phone last night to ask if she could make a portal for them to travel through. Diana could tell he'd been surprised when Esha had agreed. Apparently she was a type of Mythean who could only perform her magic when she had enough power stocked up. The portal spell was a big one, so big that she rarely had that kind of juice.

Fortunately for Diana, this morning she had. Esha was able to create the portal without coming to Cadan's house. Diana and Cadan had stepped through it in Cadan's kitchen and out into Verulamium a second later. They had eight hours in which to get back through. This world got weirder with every day she spent in it.

"Be quick, Diana. It's no' safe for you here," he said from

behind her as they wove their way around collapsed stone walls and piles of rock.

"I'll be fine. Quit being so overprotective and keep an eye out for anything unusual." She glanced around at the ruins that looked like an old fortress with broken-down walls.

She shivered when the chill morning air cut through her thin jacket. Or perhaps it was the creepy feeling of the ruins that had her shivering. A fine English drizzle turned the sky into a gray, dreary backdrop for their adventure. With the soft grass beneath their feet, even footsteps couldn't be heard in the silence.

Cadan followed close behind her, so near that she could almost feel the heat of him. She'd felt his eyes on her since they'd stepped out of the portal. Even when he scanned their surroundings, he was always sure to have her in his line of sight.

"Nothing to be found here, lassie. It's been four hours."

No, damn it. She would find something here. Except that she was starting to fear that the secrets of this place weren't on the surface. Perhaps they were underground, but she was a historian, not an archaeologist.

"Just a few more minutes, because I don't get it. I really recognized this place in the photo. I could *feel* it."

But now that she was actually here, the view was entirely unfamiliar. Perhaps she'd once looked upon this place rather than actually been inside it? The photo had been a long-range shot from the nearby hill. Maybe that was it.

"Let's climb up that hill." She pointed toward the only rise.

He scowled, scanning their surroundings for danger. His broad shoulders were tense, the muscles of his arms in sharp relief. Cadan clearly liked things to go his way, and this wasn't what he'd have chosen.

"Really, lassie? Isn't it bad enough we're out here with only these bloody tiny walls for cover? You want to climb up that hill there, in the open for all to see?"

"Which all? We're alone here. Come on." She headed off toward the hill. He'd catch up.

He did. Too soon. She hadn't made it a few feet before he swept her up in his arms and swung her around to press her against one of the stone walls. His big body was hot against hers while the cold stone pressed into her back.

"Have a care, lassie. I'm this close to swinging you over my shoulder and carrying you back to my home. Doona be charging off like that again. You'll stay near me."

Though his tone was harsh, his grip on her arms gradually loosened. As he stared down at her, his dark brows drew together and something fierce flashed in his eyes.

"Either kiss me or let go." She couldn't believe she'd said that, but she meant it. He had to make up his damned mind.

He scowled at her, but she almost—*almost*—thought she saw longing. Then he released her and looked away as if the moment that had passed between them had flown away on the wind, or never existed at all.

Her heart didn't sink. Not even a little.

"To the hill, lassie."

She turned from him and headed toward the hill. If she could get to the top and look down—

A small sign caught her attention and made her breath catch in her throat. There, nestled against the western edge of the fort with a bit of bright green grass tufted at the base, was a sign that read Watling Street. In a daze, she walked up to it, the big hill in the distance forgotten. She could vaguely make out the sound of Cadan calling her name, but the buzzing in her ears drowned it out.

Watling Street. How had she not noticed this before from the books?

"The hill, lassie?"

"No, Cadan." She reached out with a trembling hand to touch the sign. It wasn't old, just a tourist marker, and one she'd never seen before, but it marked the remnants of a road that was two thousand years old. "You've got to see this."

She looked over to see him striding through the ruins toward her, his big body moving gracefully among the tumbled stones. She caught sight of his eyes when his gaze landed on the sign. Surprise and also something like dread? But it was gone in a flash.

"You recognize Watling Street, don't you?" She certainly did. Any scholar in her field worth their tweed coat would recognize Watling Street.

"It's a historic road."

"Not just any historic road. A Roman road. Scholars think that the last big battle between the Celts and Romans took place near Watling Street."

There—it flashed across his face again. She was definitely on to something. And he'd definitely been lying.

"A warrior queen led the battle, but she lost." A chill ran over her skin. "That battle was famous for having women as the last line of defense. They fought with the men."

She looked around the place with new eyes. She *had* seen this place, then, but she'd probably never been inside. To go inside as a Celtic woman would have spelled disaster, the kind that she'd now feel if she'd been there. No, she'd probably looked upon it from afar, maybe even from on the hill.

"I was one of those women, Cadan. But which one?"

20

Diana trudged up the wide wooden stairs to the second floor of Cadan's house. They'd just returned from the ruined Roman fort and she was beyond ready to fall into bed. Even the wind had more energy than she did; it roared as it hit the house and dragged along crevices formed by windows and eaves. It would carry a storm, she was almost certain, and that suited her mood perfectly. Maybe it would drown out the chaos in her mind.

She finally had a lead. If she hadn't been the warrior queen —which she wasn't, since there was nothing regal or particularly warriorlike about her—she must have been one of the soldier women who'd chosen to make up the last line of defense between the Romans and the Celtic children and homes. She did have that dream about protecting her daughters, after all. She could almost see it. It...fit. A bit like an awkwardly large coat, but it fit.

Diana flicked on the light switch as she walked into her room. Just as she reached the bathroom door, a voice from behind said, "Nice sword."

Shock dropped her stomach to her toes as her fist tightened

on the sword she'd taken to Verulamium. She whirled around to see a lanky, dark-haired woman reclining in the big wing chair in the corner. The chair had been out of her line of sight when she'd entered the room. A scruffy black cat lounged by her side.

"Who are you? How did you get in here?" She worked to make her voice brave.

"I'm Esha. And this—" She pointed to the cat who'd started to clean himself shamelessly. "—is Chairman Meow."

Diana's heart slowed its gallop. "You're the one who made the portal for Cadan and me to go to Verulamium."

"Yep."

"Why are you here?"

"I wanted to talk to you."

"Not Cadan?"

"No. You, specifically. He's not going to come up here anytime soon, right?"

At her words, the cat lowered the leg he'd stuck up into the air while grooming and sauntered toward the door to peer out. *Double weird.*

"I don't think so, but you never know." Diana decided not to be afraid of the woman who'd done nothing but help her. And who, most important, wanted to speak to her specifically. As if she had information. "Why did you want to talk to me? Do you know who I was?"

"I don't know any details, and even if I did, I've been warned against giving you too much information. But I think I have some clues about your task. And those, I am gut certain you need to know."

"How? And why are you telling only me and not Cadan?"

Esha eased the door closed. "Cadan and Warren—that's Cadan's boss, by the way—both know who you were. Cadan won't tell you, Warren won't tell me. The only other people who know are Aerten, Warren's boss, and Lea, the Historian. You met her when you first came to the university, remember? Anyway, Aerten is too high ranking for me to contact, but Lea is my friend and gave me a few pertinent details."

Diana felt a scowl crease her forehead at the confirmation that Cadan and this Warren guy were keeping things from her. Any control she tried to exert over her life was slipping through her fingers and they weren't helping. "Why?"

"Because I asked her."

"No, I mean why do you care who I was?" Diana doubted that Esha was a Good Samaritan intent on helping her discover herself.

"Something in the Edinburgh underground has gone wrong. Really wrong."

Diana listened with a growing *oh shit* feeling as Esha explained her ability to sense evil and the afterworld hell that was trying to break loose from somewhere in Edinburgh's underground.

"What hell did you say it is?" Diana asked.

"Erebus. I think that fixing the portal could be your task, and that you should come to me as soon as you remember who you were."

"Why do you think it's my task?"

"Because of which hell it is, and because of what Lea told me about your life. She said you're a professor from America."

"What does that have to do with anything?" Diana asked.

Concern shone in Esha's amber eyes. "I'm sorry, Diana. I don't know if you actually knew her or not, but your colleague Vivienne Lawrence was abducted to Erebus a few days ago."

The air rushed out of the room in a great gust, leaving Diana to sway on her feet. Vi? Abducted to the Roman afterworld?

"What?" Diana pressed her hand to her chest, trying to calm the sense that she was drowning.

"You knew her? I'm so sorry. Her soul was taken to hell while her body stopped at the portal. Her body couldn't cross over because she's mortal. She's in a coma."

"No. A coma? She can't be. She's safe in America, teaching my classes."

"Maybe that's where they nabbed her. They thought she was you, perhaps."

Oh, God. She was directly responsible for Vi's abduction. And her *coma.*

"She won't wake up?" Diana asked.

"Not unless her soul is returned. And even then, I don't know if it's possible to revive her. Most mortals wouldn't have survived. They'd die immediately at the portal."

Diana stumbled backward to the bed. Sat. The sword tumbled from her loose fingers.

"I can get her back. How do I get her back?" A panicked sob strangled in Diana's throat at the idea of Vi's soul trapped in hell.

"I don't know if you can. I don't know why they took her, but it's a clear link to you and suggests that this is your task. If it is, maybe there is some way you can save her."

Diana nodded blindly. She could do this. She had to do this.

"If you can figure out who you were," Esha said, "and if it turns out that the portal is your task, I can help you with it. I would bet a million pounds that this is why you were brought back. I shouldn't be helping you, but I've never liked following the rules."

Diana drew in a shuddering breath and looked Esha in the eyes. She looked tough, and she looked serious. And she had some major connections in this crazy new world. She'd need her. Vi would need her.

Especially if Cadan and this Warren guy were going to go all alpha male on her and stand in her way. She was going to need an ally.

"All right." Diana forced her voice to be level as she held out her hand. "Deal. And...thank you for telling me. For helping me. For trusting me."

"It was shitty news. I'm sorry." Esha looked down at the Chairman, who'd nudged her with his head. He was looking pointedly at the door. "Someone is coming up the stairs. I've got to go. But hurry. This is only getting worse. Do whatever you can to figure this out. Whatever you can."

Esha pressed a card into Diana's palm. Then they disappeared.

Diana was staring blindly at the floor when Cadan knocked on the door a minute later.

"Everything all right?" he said as he walked through the doorway. "I thought I heard something."

Diana raised her head to meet his eyes, knowing that her face reflected the bleakness within her.

"Ah, Diana, what's wrong?" There was something in his eyes, some pain or longing she couldn't recognize, that made her breath catch in her lungs. Like he hurt for her or wanted to fix her. Maybe both. But the way he stared at her, as if she were *someone*, could steal the very heart from her. She'd never been the recipient of such a stare, or of such intensity.

Yet he hid things from her. Things that were so vital they'd killed her friend. Or as good as.

"Why did you hide the importance of Verulamium from me?" she asked.

"I dinna."

She had no idea if she should believe him or not. "But you're trying to keep me from discovering who I was. I'm certain of it. It's because of my past, isn't it? You've got a stake in this whole thing, but I've got no idea what it is."

He dragged a hand across his face, then spun around and stalked toward the window. His big hand gripped the wooden sill so tightly that the tension radiated down his arm, making the muscles and veins stand out in harsh relief.

He's hiding something. She was certain of it now. But what it might be terrified her. She cared for him, hated that he pulled away from her, but was afraid she knew the reason why.

She approached him, determined to force the truth from him if necessary. So much depended on it. She wanted to tell him about Vivienne, but didn't think she should reveal her connection to Esha. If he was working against her, she'd need Esha more than ever.

She laid a hand on the bunched muscles of his shoulder, all too aware of the latent strength of the man she was cornering. "You're becoming someone to me, Cadan. And you know the answers that I'm seeking. I'm running out of time to discover them on my own. You've got to tell me what you're hiding. *Why* you're hiding it."

"Leave it, Diana." Cadan turned and took a step toward the door, desperate to get out of there before he did something he regretted, but she grabbed his arm and jerked him to a stop in front of her.

"No." She glared up at him, her hands tightening their grip on his arm. "Tell me why you've lied, damn it. Tell me why you get close to me, kiss me, then stop and storm off. It's because of what you know, isn't it?"

She wanted to know the whole, horrible story? That she tempted him with every move she made, reminded him of all that he'd lost? Made him think that everything could be better with her, except that if he went for it, it would all crumble to dust around him with her death?

Nay. These things he would not tell her. But helpless to stop himself, he cupped the back of her head and drew her to him, so close that he could almost feel her. The scant inch of air between their bodies vibrated with tension. Her scent washed over him, arresting and familiar, and the feel of her, the heat of her, stole the caution from his mind and tore the words from his throat.

"You want to know why I've lied?"

She nodded, her cheeks flushed and her eyes wide. Desperation and fear glimmered in their depths.

"Because I want you, damn it. I care for you. I've never been able to stop, no' for thousands of years. But I can *never* have you."

Desperate and crazed, he pulled her to him and crushed his mouth to hers. He kissed her with the fierceness and desperation of a man who had everything to lose and knew that it was already gone.

When she threw her arms about his neck, he clutched her closer, sinking his hand into her hair and wrapping his arm about her waist.

Just a moment more.

Just a moment of this thing he could never have. This person. He thrust his tongue between her lips, desperate to imprint her taste upon his mind. She was sweet and soft beneath his lips, everything he'd longed for and more than he'd ever expected. More than he could have. Three times he'd failed to keep his distance. Three times, yet it would have to be enough. He'd have to make it enough.

He pulled away, leaving her flushed.

He couldn't resist her.

It was ridiculous to have thought he could. Yet the proof of his weakness was still hot on his lips, beneath his hands. One more encounter like this, and he wouldn't be able to stop. And she would remember her past.

He made up his mind. He'd call Warren, have another Mythean Guardian assigned to her.

He stepped back. "No more." He shook his head, then turned to stride out of the room. "No more."

But only he could hear the words.

21

Diana barely restrained herself from chucking the book at the wall. It was the last of the books in Cadan's library that might have something to do with her past. And it had been useless.

Which had come as no surprise, by this point. Books wouldn't work, and visiting Verulamium had only told her that she had been one of the female warriors at the battle of Watling Street, but not which one. To ancient written history, they were nobodies. Her answers weren't in books, as she'd proven today in a last-ditch effort to find something.

She leaned back in the chair and glared at the clock. Nearly nine at night and she was no closer to figuring out who she'd been or to saving Vivienne.

She'd only seen Cadan once today, when they'd trained in his gym for several hours. He'd excelled at acting like everything was normal when it so obviously was not. She'd tried to ask him questions about what he'd said last night, but he'd deflected them, ignoring her. Ignoring everything.

But he wasn't just her protector. He was a link to her past. He was *part* of her past. And there was a very good chance that he was the man from her dream.

The idea that the man she'd come to care for was the same one who'd betrayed her sent a cold shiver through her. But if it was him—which she wasn't entirely sure of—why had he locked her up like that? And did it have anything to do with why she'd been reborn?

Diana set the book down on the table and leaned back in the chair to think. She had to find out, but when she'd asked earlier today, he'd deflected her questions like she was a fly on his arm. He'd been avoiding her, and it seemed like he was going to keep it up. Letting him do so wouldn't save Vivienne or get herself out of this mess.

But her previous approaches to figuring this all out weren't working. She tapped her fingers against her chin. If only there was a way to get Cadan to willingly tell her everything that he knew.

And then a horrible, wonderful, terrifying idea popped into her mind. No, it was idiotic. Crazy.

But he did want her. And she wanted him. More importantly, she was desperate and at the end of her options. Insane as it was, it might work.

22

Cadan felt himself surface from a sleep as deep as death. As his eyes adjusted in the dark, he reached up to rub them, but his arms jerked to a halt.

Leather straps bit into his wrists.

The fog of sleep dissipated immediately and he jerked on the bonds. They held tight.

Why the fuck was he chained to his bed? More importantly, where was Diana? Had she been kidnapped?

Shite. Heart pounding in his chest, he roared, "Diana!"

"Oh, you're awake." The voice came from the side of the bed. He wasn't alone, and though it sounded like Diana, the voice was throatier, sexier. She sounded like a woman who had just awakened after being fucked long and hard during the night. He wanted to be the one making her sound like that.

Cadan turned his head toward the voice and nearly swallowed his tongue when Diana rose from a chair by the bed, clad in nothing but scraps of lace that cupped supple flesh. The pale pink covered her breasts, giving him a tantalizing glimpse of large pink nipples. A thousand times better than he'd imagined.

His eyes were dragged downward and his breath caught. The

curls at the juncture of her thighs were the same beautiful shade as those on her head. He ached to touch her there. To taste.

He jerked his gaze up to hers. "Diana," he whispered hoarsely. "Come here. Untie me."

Let me put my hands on you.

How had he thought to resist her? He strained against the bonds, desperate to have his hands, his mouth, on her. To tear away the scraps of lace and make her his in a way that she would never forget.

Nay. Resist her.

She just shook her head. "No, don't struggle. They're the Maoin straps, so you can't get out."

She placed one knee on the bed, then began to crawl toward him, her heavy hair hanging over her shoulder and her eyes hot. Dark deeds flashed in her eyes and his cock leapt.

Was he dreaming? This was straight out of his fantasies, but when he jerked on the straps that bound him to the bed, it became clear that this was very much real life. Diana reached him then, the sultry smell of her skin, her hair, her pussy reaching inside him to squeeze.

She straddled his stomach and looked down at him. The heat of her sex burned him.

She rested her hands on his chest and began to rub her thumbs across his nipples. Goosebumps broke out on his flesh where she touched him, lightly trailing her fingers over his chest.

To have her so close and not be able to touch and taste? *Torture.*

Focus, Cadan. "What in the hell are you doing, lassie? How the hell did you get me tied up?"

"I called Esha. She gave me a sleeping spell for you. Some powder, like pixie dust, that I had to blow into your room after you'd fallen asleep. I didn't want you waking up while I fastened the straps."

He tried to keep his eyes on hers, but they were drawn down her body once again. She was ethereally pale, with small breasts and a trim waist that flared into beautiful hips. Freckles dotted her shoulders and chest.

Who was this woman? "What in the hell are you doin'?"

His cock was painfully stiff, so hard that it strained against her ass. He yanked at the bonds again, but they didn't budge.

"I'll tell you, but first, I want to know something."

"Aye?"

"You like me, right?"

"Nay, lassie, this hard-on has nothing to do with you."

"You know what I mean." She looked down at him uncertainly.

Ah, his lassie needed reassurance. As much as he knew he shouldn't admit it, that he should be cruel to end this game, he couldn't bear to see the hesitant smile slip off her face. His brain had flown straight out of his head.

Knowing that he would regret it, he said, "Aye, lassie, I do. There's no' another like you."

Her smile brightened. "Likewise."

"Now tell me what this is about." He had a pretty good idea, even though it shocked the hell out of him.

"You know who I was in a past life. I don't. And I really, really need to know. I've run out of time and options, so I think you should tell me."

Shite. That wasn't what he was expecting. "And how do you plan for that to happen?"

"I think you know." She smiled. "Have you ever been tortured, Cadan?"

His jaw clenched when she rubbed her sex against him. "No' like this."

She smiled. "Well, you get the gist of it anyway. I'm going to bring you to the brink so many times your eyes will cross. When you tell me who I was, you can have *anything* you want."

She reached behind her and grasped his cock in her small hand. He nearly shouted with pleasure, then desperately clenched his teeth to stifle himself.

"I doona want you." Gods, he was lying. He wanted her more than anything in the world. He wanted her in every way possible, pinned beneath him, his to take.

But more than anything, he wanted her now, this way. With him tied to the bed and her on top of him, taking whatever she wanted from his body. *Use me. Take your pleasure from me.* His hips jerked at the thought and she ran her soft palm up and down his length.

"You, Cadan, are a terrible liar. And you're *my* terrible liar."

Aye, yours. As you are mine. He wanted her to take her pleasure from him, untie him, and then he would show her what it meant to be his. But he couldn't, could never, and for everything in the past and future, he had to resist. But how?

And where had this temptress come from?

When Diana laughed he realized he'd spoken aloud. "I was always here. You saw me—young and a professor, reserved in my manners—and drew your own conclusions. They just weren't necessarily true. You're dating yourself again, Cadan. True, I've never tied up a man and had my way with him before, so I'm no expert, but I think I can figure it out."

With those words, she bent down and began to kiss his neck, her soft, hot tongue running across the tendons as he strained. Only now did he realize that the room was lit by dozens of candles.

She rubbed her breasts against his chest and he strained at the bonds. He wanted just one touch. To put his hands on her smooth skin and run them over the curves and hollows of her body.

She ran her warm lips down his chest, rising up on all fours as she did so, curved and soft in the light. She was careful not to touch his cock now, though it desperately reached for her.

"You have the most amazing muscles," she murmured against his clenched abs.

With a lick, she continued to kiss her way down his body, her mouth hot and avid on him. He tensed as she neared his cock, but she skipped over, raining soft kisses over his thighs and within inches of his balls. He groaned when he felt her breath feather over him and looked down to see her staring up at him.

Take me in your mouth. He wanted to see his cock slide between her pink lips.

She hovered just over his shaft, her face all but glowing in the candlelight. She knelt on all fours with her head bent down to his cock and the curve of her ass rising above her head. Her eyes burned into his and there was nothing but desire in them.

"I've been wanting this for a long time." She licked her lips and looked down with heat in her gaze.

He couldn't take his eyes off her. She was a vision of innocence and sin. Her pink tongue sneaked out of her mouth and licked the bottom of his crown. He groaned low in his throat, and when she opened her mouth and enveloped him, he jerked as the heat and softness closed around him. She sucked once, lightly, then took him deeper inside of her mouth.

His hips jerked. She began to work her hand up and down his shaft in time with her mouth. He wasn't going to last. His body tightened and tension coiled within him.

So close. He was so bloody close he was shaking with it.

She raised her head and licked her lips, then crawled back up his body and kissed him full on the mouth. "That was fun.

But if I do too much of that now, we might be moving a bit fast for my end goal."

End goal? Gods, he wanted to be her end goal.

This had to stop. He wouldn't make it through tonight, and his brain was getting whiplash from his conflicting desires.

"Diana, you have to let me go." *Please listen to me, I canna last through this.* "This won't work—it's dangerous. What if someone breaks in?"

She just looked down at him, knowledge and power and determination in her eyes.

"I'll release you if someone breaks in." Then she smiled. "Or I'll just kill them myself." She kissed him again, and then sat back up on his stomach. She reached up and caressed her breasts. "I think I should take this off. What do you think?"

The sight of her stroking herself made his cock twitch. He wanted her to slip a hand beneath her panties while she fondled her breasts. He glanced down at them, unable to resist. She was hot and wet on his stomach where she sat, and when he looked down, she laughed. "Those too. Eventually."

Diana reached behind her and unclasped her bra. She slowly peeled it from her shoulders and tossed it aside. Her breasts were small and perfect, topped with pink nipples that his tongue ached to caress.

"Would you like to taste?"

Aye, please. He should jerk his head to the side, away from her, but he'd rather die than look away.

She smiled and leaned over him, running one nipple over his closed lips. He tried to resist, but the feel of her soft flesh running across his lips was torture. He could hear her breath above his head, heavy and wanting. His woman wanted, and he ached to provide.

He broke, opening his lips so that his tongue could lave her nipple. She moaned and began to tremble.

"Untie me, lassie. I'll make it good for you." He honestly didn't know if he'd pin her to the bed and fuck her senseless or if he'd have the honor to walk away. He could control himself if he really tried. He'd give her pleasure, and aye, take his own, but he'd have the control not to take it all the way.

She dragged herself away from him. "Not unless you're ready to tell me what I want to know."

He shook his head.

"Fine. I'm not nearly done with you anyway."

But this time she turned away from him, rising on all fours so that her knees were placed on either side of his head and she hovered above him.

Christ, no' this. Anything but this.

Her sex, glistening and pink behind the transparent lace of her panties, hovered just over his mouth. He stared, riveted, and strained harder at his bonds. Cadan inhaled deeply of her scent and felt his cock throb. She smelled of woman and sex and happiness.

The bonds cutting into his wrists didn't register. *So close.* His fantasy was so close that he could have reached up and peeled the lace away from her body with his teeth if he hadn't been tied up. He wanted to lick her, taste her, feel her come against his mouth—and yet she hovered, just out of reach.

"Please." He groaned. She had to stop this. He ached. His tongue ached to taste her, his mind ached from resisting, and his cock ached for her to take him into her mouth and put him out of his misery.

Then her breathing changed. His own caught in his throat as he felt the heat of her against his cock. He shouted as his shaft sank into her hot mouth.

The pleasure. Excruciating.

Her hand closed over his balls, caressing them as she worked her mouth over his shaft. *Just a bit more.* It would take almost nothing for him to come like this. *Just a bit more.*

But she stopped, as if she knew how close he was.

He gasped as she slowly withdrew her mouth from his cock. "Ah, be a good lassie and finish what you started."

Diana gave his balls one last light squeeze before she removed her hand and straddled him once again.

"Maybe...if you've changed your mind about telling me what I want to know." She looked down at him, her eyes almost hypnotic.

His cock begged him to tell her.

"Nay." He had barely a thought left in his head, but this was something he couldn't do. No matter how much he wanted her.

"As I feared." But she didn't look disappointed. "Tell me, Cadan, is it true what I read in the library? That your kind are impervious to illness? And you don't carry it?" She drifted a hand down her stomach and slipped it into her panties. He couldn't tear his eyes away as he answered.

"Aye." He didn't care why she asked. He just had to keep his eyes on her hand slowly stroking herself. She was moving her hand more quickly now, her breath coming in shallow gasps. He wanted to see her come, to see pleasure wash over her. Already her pale skin was pinkening, her cheeks flushed and her eyes wild.

"Good, I'm clean too. And I'm on birth control. So I suppose that I don't need these." She slipped her hand out of her panties and snapped her thumb in the waistband. His brain fought a battle.

Please, take them off.

No, doona, I canna take it.

23

Diana crawled off Cadan and stood beside the bed in nothing but her panties. God, she felt powerful. This, without a doubt, was the best thing she'd ever done. From the moment he'd awakened and seen her, the desire and want in his eyes made her feel like a goddess. All her nerves, her fear, had disappeared. She could do anything, as long as he looked at her like that.

It had helped to suppress the fear that he might be the man from her dreams. Though it lingered under the surface, she couldn't help but continue. She wanted answers. She wanted him. The fear only added an edge.

He lay sprawled on the bed now, arms and legs splayed and fixed to the bedposts. Every muscle was taut as he strained at the bonds, desperate to get to her. He was magnificent. All tense muscle and hot male.

Her gaze fell on his shaft again. She couldn't stop looking at it. It was beautiful, more so than she'd ever imagined. It thrust upward from his rippled abdomen, veined, with a red crown topped by a shining pearl of fluid.

Diana looked back at his face and smiled, then turned around. She looked over her shoulder as she inched her panties down, teasing him. His gaze followed their movement, and when they'd finally reached her ankles, she straightened and turned to face him.

"Beautiful."

She could barely hear him, but saw his mouth form the word. She felt a smile stretch across her face and climbed back on top of him.

Diana aligned her body with his once more, with her face directly over his and her knees on either side of his hips. She held his eyes as she positioned his shaft so that it rested against her sex. She gasped at the feel of him, hot and hard against her.

Cadan was staring at her with the strangest expression of tenderness and something she couldn't recognize. Was this more than just sex to him? Was it more to her?

There was no time to think about that now, so she shook the thought off. "What about now, Cadan? Who was I?"

He shook his head and tried to pull his right arm out of the bindings. "Release me, Diana."

Excited fear rippled down her spine. Even though she knew he'd throw her to the bed and be inside her within moments, she wanted to release him.

"Would you be gentle with me?"

"Aye, lassie. At first. Then you'd beg me no' to be. I'll fuck you until you scream my name."

A moan escaped her throat before she could cut it off. If she didn't stay in control, she'd never get the answers she wanted. She had to retake the reins, so she gripped the thin silver chain that he wore around his neck. She'd never noticed it before because he wore it inside his shirt, but it worked well for her purposes.

"Tell me," she whispered as she tugged on the chain.

He moaned, but didn't answer, so she began to slowly work her hips up and down so that his shaft slid along her pussy. She'd have to be careful that he didn't come, but it was so hard to still her motions. While trying to make him desperate enough to reveal her identity, she was doing the same to herself. Diana leaned down to Cadan's ear and gently bit the lobe.

"I want you inside me," she whispered. His hips jerked uncontrollably upward at the words and she smiled. "I want to feel you moving inside me, first slow and gentle, so that I feel every inch of you, and then hard and fast. I want to come around your shaft, to feel you every time my muscles tighten."

She'd never imagined such words would flow so easily from her mouth, but he made it easy. The sounds he made, hot and desperate, made power streak through her veins.

Soon they were both sweating, slick and hot as she writhed on top of him. The feel of his shaft between the lips of her sex had her on the verge of orgasm. She wanted so badly to come with him between her legs, wanted to feel his orgasm splash upon her.

But if she was close, likely so was he.

She tore herself away from him, once again over his stomach but kneeling so that she didn't touch him. When she looked down at his face, she realized that she'd done the right thing. His breath was short and hard; he strained at the bindings until his muscles stood out in powerful relief.

Wild warrior. My *wild warrior.*

"Tell me," she demanded. "And I will untie you. You can do whatever you want with me."

"Nay." He groaned. "I will no' bend in this."

Damn it! She wanted to scream with frustration. She'd used up all her best tricks and he hadn't broken. "Tell me who I was. I need you, Cadan."

He jerked his head.

She made a wordless noise of frustration. She'd never been so turned on before, and literally, right between her legs, was the sexiest man she'd ever seen and she couldn't do a thing about it. She hadn't expected this night to be as torturous for her as it was for him.

She glared down at him. "Damn you, Cadan."

She'd have to regroup and rethink, and to do so, she'd have to take care of some of this dreadful desire.

EVERY INCH of Cadan's body ached with lust, his cock a rod of agony and pleasure. Diana's body rose above him, her pale skin shining in the candlelight. Her honey red hair was wild around her head, her lips swollen from kisses and her eyes heavy with lust. She was like nothing he'd ever seen. A pagan goddess intent on pleasure, her only thought to achieve her ends by any means necessary.

He'd never felt such desire before; it was almost pain. He strained against the bonds, desperate to reach her, to feel her skin on his again.

He wanted to sink into her soft flesh. To hold her hips and pound into her until he felt her pussy clenching around his shaft. He wanted to tie her up and kiss her and lick her until she came on his tongue over and over and she begged him to stop.

Thoughts of duty slipped further from his mind, and when she drifted a hand between her legs, he had to bite his tongue to keep from asking her to let him have a taste. She began to rub slow circles on the glistening pink flesh. What he wouldn't give to have his mouth there.

She circled her fingers faster, her breath coming more quickly as her breasts rose and fell. He glanced at her face, the look of pained concentration indicating that she was close. Gods, she was going to make herself come right above him so that he could watch every expression on her face, every motion of her hand.

"Put two fingers inside yourself." *Do it. So that I can imagine it's me.*

She obeyed, slipping two fingers inside her pussy. She reached down with her other hand to rub her clitoris. He looked up at her face to find her watching him, eyes locked on his.

"Pretend they're me."

At his words, she gasped and her head dropped back. Diana collapsed on top of him, still sitting upright but no longer on her knees. Her fingers began moving faster on her clit. Her back arched and she clenched her shaking thighs around his chest as her orgasm hit. She was silent as she came, as though consumed in a vacuum of pleasure that allowed for nothing but feeling.

"I will fuck you one day, Diana, so hard that this orgasm will feel like nothing in comparison. I will make you come so long and so hard that you won't remember any that came before me."

She cried out then, quietly as another orgasm wracked her body and she arched above him in the candlelight, the most beautiful thing he'd ever seen.

Finally, she collapsed on top of him, resting her head against his chest. She hummed happily, but when she began to toy with the chain about his neck, he stiffened.

"I'm not finished with you yet," she said as she ran the chain between her fingers. "What's this?"

Her words made his heart stutter. He couldn't see her face, but he knew she was inspecting the key he kept strung on the chain.

"I didn't realize there was anything on this chain," she said. "It slipped behind your neck."

"It's nothing."

She leaned up and searched his eyes. "It's not nothing. Why would you wear something that is nothing?"

"Because I like it." But he could hear the half-truth in his voice.

And so could she.

24

Diana stumbled down the hallway to her room several hours later. She was exhausted and sweaty and sore and it had been the best night of her life.

But he hadn't said a word about her past. Damn, he was determined. She sighed and stared at the key in her hand. He'd acted nonchalant as she'd unclasped the chain, but his eyes had told a different story. This key wasn't nothing.

He might not have talked, but her seduction hadn't been useless. She now had a key that might lead to clues. And an angry, painfully aroused male tied up across the hall. That part made her nervous. She'd have to free him eventually, but he was royally pissed off now so it would be best to wait.

She forced him out of her mind and stared hard at the key, willing it to reveal its secrets. Considering that signs pointed to his being the man from her dreams, it could be important to her. But what did it fit? The doors in the house didn't have locks. A chest or armoire, perhaps?

She mulled over possible hiding places while she showered and quickly dressed, then began her search. The two main floors of the house revealed no matches for the key. But then she found a door that led to an attic at the end of the hall. It would be up there. It had to be.

The attic was a museum. The old armor, paintings, sculptures, and trinkets made her fingertips itch to explore. But no chest.

Then she spied a crumpled tapestry that looked like it was draped over something, and with nowhere else to look, she pulled at it. Dust billowed. Her coughing turned to a gasp.

There it was. The chest was big and old, made of dark and beautifully carved wood. It was much older than the lock that had been fitted to it. She knelt reverently next to the chest, goose bumps pricking on her arms as she laid her hands on the cool wood that covered the top.

A low buzz sounded in her head. What was in here could change everything. It could be nothing more than an illegal collection of antiquities or his family's old hunting rifles, but she doubted it. Her hand shook as she fitted the key to the lock. It caught slightly, but finally opened with a *snick*.

Her breath came short and hard, dragging into her lungs but not filling them as she lifted the lid. With sweaty palms, she reached in and clasped the hilt of a sword. The moment she gripped the smooth handle, an unseen force punched her in the chest.

She tumbled onto her back, and the little air she had rushed out of her lungs as she hit the floor. The vacuum that stole her breath took her vision and hearing as well. The real world faded away.

Memories assailed her, one after another jumbling into her mind and fighting for supremacy. A woman clothed in a plain brown dress stood over a fire built into the middle of a roundhouse, smiling at her and beckoning her closer. *Mother*.

Warmth billowed from the fire and the smoke stung her

eyes. A baby wailed in a crib near the wall and the woman turned from her to hurry over. *I had a brother.*

Diana lay helpless as the scene changed. She stood outside in a glen, dressed in a fine wool cloak fastened with a straight bronze pin, looking up at the man who would be her husband. He smiled down at her, his eyes crinkling at the corners and mist gathering in his hair as he encouraged her to step forward. She didn't love him, was too young to love such an old man, but he would make her queen of her people. And she wanted to lead. Oh, how her young heart yearned to be a good queen to her people, the Iceni.

She was Boudica.

Time shifted forward and she sat on a grassy knoll, watching two girls of perhaps twelve playing in a stream. Her *daughters.* The bright sun warmed her face, but she and her husband, now a truly old man, spoke furtively of the future as their daughters splashed in the water. The world was closing in on them.

"It will never succeed, Prasutagus," she hissed to her husband. "We must fight them! The Romans will never honor your will."

"No, my queen." He shook his head slowly, white hair flowing around his shoulders. "You are brave and wise, but in this you are wrong. My daughters will succeed me on the throne. The Roman emperor will be satisfied to be co-heir. They are so far away."

"No! Rome encroaches farther every year. We agreed to their terms when they came to our borders the first time, as did the neighboring kingdoms. Our line shall hold only until your death, then our kingdom is Rome's. By law, the emperor becomes your heir. They will not accept this move and will come down upon our heads." She shook him to make her point, glancing at her daughters to see if they noticed. "We must attack first, and drive them from Britain. It is our only hope. Or remove our daughters as co-heir to the throne so that Rome will not atta—"

Diana realized that the scene had moved forward when a shadow of pain lashed across her back. Roman legionnaires held her by the arms, pinned to the ground in front of her people, as their leader swung a whip at her back. Her husband was dead of old age, and the Romans were at their doorstep intent on collecting on her husband's debt.

She heard her daughters' screams, and strain as she might, all she could see were the feet of the bastards who held her to the ground. Though the pain burned through her, she fought to hear her daughters, to know they were alive. But when their screams stopped abruptly and the Roman legion cheered, she knew.

Dead.

Diana curled onto her side in the dusty attic and vomited. Dry heaves wracked her body and tried to pull her soul from her. She'd never felt such pain. It was as if her heart were a glass bottle smashed to bits.

She lay, curled on her side in the attic, tears streaking down her face and into her hair, as memories continued to flash in front of her near-comatose eyes. The Romans departed, retreated after making an example of the Iceni by killing her daughters, the illegal heirs to the throne, and left her in the mud with the bodies of her children and the ruins of her tribe.

But they had erred. Diana's hand tightened unconsciously around the hilt of the sword. Oh, how they had erred.

She'd risen that day, with nothing left to lose and the burn of rage in her soul, to exact her vengeance upon the dogs who had dared trespass upon what was hers. Had *taken* what was hers.

The woman she had been—mother, wife—was no more. That woman had burned to ash in Rome's fires, but had not risen as a phoenix. Instead, she had risen as destruction, bent on vengeance. The man responsible would die by her hand alone. Rome's efforts in Britain would be crushed. Her people would have their freedom back. She rallied the neighboring Celtic kingdoms and, with her army, cut a swath of destruction through the Roman cities and legions of southern Britain.

It was then, during the months of the deadly and mobile revolt, that she had met Cadan of the Trinovantes, the son of the king of a southern tribe and a general in his army. A general in her army.

Diana curled in on herself and a cry tore from her throat as she was hit by memories of Cadan.

He had loved her, in his way. Though she'd had no love left in her heart, she'd trusted him above all others. He'd become her rock.

Their army had struck strong and true, driving the Romans back until everything depended on one battle. The man whose death she sought, their leader, was amongst them. The scene that coalesced before Diana's eyes was fraught with tension. She and Cadan stood over a table of maps within a large tent, arguing. The next day's battle would determine whether the Celts of Britain lived free or beneath the yoke of Rome.

"You will lead the Trinovantes from the south at dawn." The words scratched at her throat, stress and exhaustion her constant companions. "I shall take the rest from the north."

Cadan gripped the back of her head and glared into her eyes. "No. You will stay behind the front lines. Have Bran lead from the north."

"You forget yourself, Cadan." She shook him off. "I lead this army and will not stay behind."

They'd fought over this for months. She had rallied the troops, led them in battle, but once Cadan had lost his heart to her, he'd fought her before battle every time, attempting to get her to stay behind in a position of safety. He'd not cared that she was his queen, that she fought for something other than duty. That her fight was her everything.

Unable to look at him, she turned, never imagining that to do so would be her doom. He was on her before she could scream, had gagged her and bound her and tossed her into the hut that had haunted her dreams. The scenes before Diana's eyes and the dreams that had plagued her began to combine into one memory.

She escaped the hut and fought at the head of her people with single minded intent. Though she found her prey, had taken his head and that of the one he loved most, it had done no good. Her rage had remained unabated. The sense of loss and failure that had haunted her these last months did not lessen. As she'd lost her daughters, she stood to lose the battle as well. Her troops were outnumbered by the Romans, their position one of weakness. Defeat was inevitable.

She stood then, on the battlefield, surrounded by the bodies of her people, and realized that it was over. With her army decimated, they had no hope of routing the Romans. As their sole leader, a woman whose name had spread across the continent, she would be hunted as a dog and taken to Rome as a symbol of Celtic barbarism. At best they would drag her through the streets and behead her, mounting her head on a spike. At worst they would use her as leverage against her people, holding their hero hostage in return for something they couldn't afford to pay.

With her daughters dead and her people scattered, and Cadan's betrayal burning in her breast, there only one option. She didn't want to fight anymore and at least she could take the honorable way out.

Cadan had found her there, in the hut where he'd imprisoned her the previous night. She shouldn't have returned; she could have finished it on the battlefield. But she hadn't been able to fight the part of herself that hoped to see him one last time.

And then it was over, the last of her blood dripping onto the floor. His face, that of her betrayer and her lover, was the last thing she saw.

In the attic, Diana's hand tightened once again on the hilt of the sword. *Her sword.* This had been her sword. She had been Boudica, Celtic Queen of the Iceni, and Cadan the betrayer from her dream. She had wielded this blade in battle two thousand years ago and she would wield it again.

The attic floor was cold and hard beneath her. She lay, so emotionally and physically exhausted that she could barely move. But she *had* to move.

Sick with grief, she pushed herself upright, her muscles screaming in protest. *Focus, Diana. You have to get out of here.* She couldn't trust Cadan, had never been able to, apparently. When she'd been Boudica, he'd tried to take the most important thing she had: vengeance for her daughters and her clan. She'd *needed* it.

She crawled toward the chest, debris from the floor cutting into her palms. With the sword still gripped in her fist, she withdrew the remaining contents of the chest. A brooch and a thick gold necklace gleamed dully in her palms. The gold collar would have rested upon her collarbone. *A torc.* The quintessential Celtic jewelry. The heavy brooch would have fastened her cloak.

They had belonged to her, and Cadan had saved them all these years. Mourning her. She steeled her heart against the thought. Between hiding books and lying about Verulamium, he'd been hiding her past from her. He'd taken the decision from her, just as he had last time.

He left me locked up. I'll leave him locked up.

She rose shakily to her feet, her memories finally intact. She called Esha as soon as she reached her room, having to dial the numbers twice because her hands shook so badly. She'd barely begun throwing her clothes into a bag when the soulceress appeared.

"Damn," said Esha, her voice low. "You look like hell."

"I feel like it." Diana stuffed the rest of her clothes into her bag. "We need to get out of here. I know who I was, and I can't trust Cadan." *As I'd feared.* Why had she ignored that?

"Shouldn't we be quieter?" Esha whispered. "Don't want to wake the beast."

"Don't worry about it." Diana wished she could go over there and give him a good kick.

"So he gave it up?" Esha gave her an appraising look, raising her eyebrows.

"No. He had a key around his neck that unlocked a chest full of my old belongings. I found my old sword. Touching something that had belonged to me must have triggered my memories."

"Why would he have your old stuff?"

"We knew each other in my first life. I had my suspicions, but I didn't know for sure until now."

"Well fuck me, you must be pissed."

"You don't know the half of it." She was still shaking and just wanted to scream at Cadan until she was hoarse. "Actually, can you hang out here a second?" she asked Esha. Maybe this wasn't a good idea with her mind in turmoil, still split between two selves. Boudica's rage was influencing her, but she couldn't bring herself to care.

"Um, sure."

Diana stormed off toward Cadan's room, her footsteps echoing in the hallway. Scenes from her past played in her mind, fueling her rage until she didn't quite feel like herself. She had the same rage and energy running through her veins that

she got when she was fighting demons and her body remembered Boudica.

"Diana!" Cadan roared, clearly able to hear her coming and
probably wondering why she'd left him tied up.

She entered the room, dimly aware that she was herself, but
not. She was something different. Something more.

"Release me!" His eyes blazed and the tendons stood out on
his neck.

"Not a chance in hell. Why did you lie to me?" Her eyes
stung even as her fists shook and her mind seethed with rage.
She was being pulled in two directions—between Diana's pain
and Boudica's fury.

"What the hell do you mean? Untie these bloody straps!"

She laughed, not surprised to hear the bite of craziness in
her voice. "Why? So you can repeat yourself?"

"Stop talking in riddles, woman."

"Don't you mean *Boudica?*"

"What?" Cadan's brow furrowed, but something lit in his
eyes. A spark of recognition at the name. Or guilt?

"I know about my past, you bastard. And I know what you
did. And you're trying to do it again."

"Who are you?" His eyes searched her face, no doubt looking
for a change, something to tell him which woman he'd be
screwing over this time around. "Diana? Or Boudica?"

"Diana. Why? Disappointed?" Her heart twisted at the idea,
but her head continued to pound. She'd wondered if he was the
man from her dreams, but she'd pushed it aside. Idiot. Of course
he was.

"Nay."

She wanted to believe sincerity shone in his eyes. She might
have, if she had been just Diana. But she wasn't just Diana. Not
anymore. The control that her father had wrested from her in
the beginning of this life had been wrested from her before in

her past life, only worse. So much worse. And Cadan had been trying to do it again.

CADAN STARED at the woman in front of him. It was Diana, but her eyes glowed with the fierceness and determination of Boudica. She vibrated with the rage that he only now realized had followed Boudica like a shadow. It had simmered beneath the surface, banked coals that waited. Waited for battle. Waited for vengeance.

"Why did you hide who you are?" she asked.

"I told you who I was. That I'd known you."

"But you didn't tell me who you were *to me*. I thought I could trust you. But you're the one who betrayed me."

"I couldn't tell you." The breath strangled in his throat.

"Why? So I wouldn't figure out what you'd done to me?"

"What *I'd* done to you? All I did was try to protect you!"

"By locking me up on the eve of our final battle? I was fighting for my *daughters*. Their murderer was out there. After they were killed, that's all I lived for. You would have kept me from that?" Her eyes glittered with angry tears. "I was your queen. It wasn't your place to make that decision, especially when your reasoning was ridiculous."

His skin grew tight at the memory. "We knew we were outmanned. If you were at the front you'd have been a fucking beacon. They'd have gone for you right away. You'd never have survived. As it was, you fought your battle. And died anyway."

"By *my choice*. I knew that we were walking into possible slaughter, but it was the choice I made when I sent our warriors to their deaths. I was our symbol, our leader." She pounded a fist on her chest. "It was my place to go with them. What would I be if I were too cowardly to lead from the front?"

"You should have let me go instead! I couldn't lose you—I had to protect you." A beast raged within him. Anger, hurt, confusion all fought to be the victor. How could she not understand this voracious need to protect her?

"*That?* That is supposed to make me feel better? That you wanted to protect me?" she shrieked. Her face suffused with color and she trembled with rage. "The reason you did it doesn't make it right. It was my choice to risk my life in battle, my choice to die if that's what it called for, my choice to fight for my daughters. You tried to steal that from me. You say you loved me, but you didn't know me at all."

"Of course I loved you. I'd have done anything to protect you." The words were torn from his throat. He'd have done anything to keep from losing her.

"I didn't want you to protect me. I wanted you to love me. That's all." She slashed the air with her hand. "I wanted, and still want, to be able to make my own decisions! And you weren't trying to protect me—you were trying to protect *yourself*. You were too afraid to lose her!"

"That's no'—"

She whirled and stalked from the room before he could finish.

It wasn't true. That was ridiculous. Of course it was.

But something at the back of his mind wondered.

25

D iana woke that evening feeling groggy and disoriented.

"Hey, sleepyhead."

She turned her head toward the voice, blinking blindly at Esha, who stood next to the island counter that separated the kitchen from the living space. Her fluffy black cat sat next to her. Oh, right. After her confrontation with Cadan, which had been fueled by an unnatural rage that was still giving her a headache, Esha had aetherwalked them to her flat at the Immortal University. They'd arrived mere seconds after departing Mull in the early morning hours. The trip had sapped Diana's adrenaline-fueled energy and she'd collapsed onto the couch with barely a word.

She yawned and stretched. "What time is it?"

"Nearly nine—p.m., that is. You've been asleep since we got here twelve hours ago."

Diana sat up and rubbed her eyes. Most of the rage she'd felt the previous night was gone. Even the memories of her distant past had faded some. Though they would still be there if she called them up, she felt more like herself.

"Want coffee?" Esha gestured vaguely to the kitchen behind her. "I don't usually have guests, so the pantry is a little bare, but I'm sure we can find something."

"Yeah, that'd be great." She stumbled over to the big kitchen island and settled onto a barstool.

Esha put the kettle on for instant coffee, then rooted around in the fridge for milk. Diana caught sight of a multitude of strange glass jars jumbled on the shelves.

"For charms," Esha explained when she caught Diana's curious gaze. "Though most of those ingredients are expired. Charms aren't really my bag."

"No?"

Esha shook her head. "A hobby, mostly, since my power allows me to manifest my desires without aids."

That would be handy. Diana looked around the space. She was so on edge that she felt like someone might jump out at her at any moment, which made her want to search all the corners in the room. But the room had no corners. Large and round, the combined living room, dining room, and kitchen space had many windows.

"What is this place?" she asked.

"My flat, in a tower on the campus of the Immortal University." The round space was decorated sparsely, with a few pieces of simple, high-quality furniture that suited Esha's minimalist style.

Diana gratefully accepted the cup of coffee that Esha handed her and sipped, wrinkling her nose when it burned her tongue. She didn't slow down, though. She needed a clear head more than she needed working taste buds right now.

"How do I get to Vivienne?"

"Can you tell me who you were?"

Diana swallowed hard and stared down into the rapidly cooling coffee in her mug. "I was Boudica."

"No shit?" Esha looked Diana up and down with an expression of impressed respect.

Diana wished she could appreciate it, but it wasn't making a dent right now.

"That is badass. You are like the *original* badass. Cheers to you." Esha raised her coffee.

Diana raised her mug and cast Esha a strained smile. Sure, Boudica had been a renowned badass, but it had come at a cost. The title was little consolation, really.

"Oh, sorry." Esha grimaced. "Yeah, it didn't end so well for you."

"Nope. Pretty shit end."

"So, um, what's it like?"

Diana knew what she meant. *What's it like to remember all the really terrible stuff that happened to you in the past that led you to suicide?* "It sucks."

"Um, can I ask, how did it end?"

Oh, right. Historians still didn't know whether or not Boudica had died of illness or killed herself.

"I did it. There wasn't any other choice."

"Yep," she agreed, her brow wrinkled. "You'd have ended up like Vercingetorix, or worse."

Diana winced at the fate of France's greatest Celtic hero. He'd ended up on a pike in Rome, and that would have been the best she could have hoped for.

Esha paled, then set down her mug "Oh, Diana. What about your daughters?"

Diana's stomach pitched. "I remember them. Not well, just vague snippets here and there. Their death is one of those. When I first remembered, it felt like being stabbed. It's faded into memory now, and it's my memory, but it's not. I don't know. I know that it hurts even though it never actually happened to me." Her body ached, every part of her seeming to throb.

"Even if it didn't happen to you in this life, I think that it's something your soul would never forget."

Diana nodded, lost for words.

Esha changed the subject.

"So you found your sword and that's how you figured it out?"

"Basically. I'd been searching through books, but that's something the old Diana would do. Apparently I just had to get ahold of my old sword." And her new life. A crazy, violent one that she didn't know how to reconcile with her idea of what her life was supposed to be. Her gaze sought out her sword, which lay on the floor near the couch. The sight of it gave her conflicting sensations of security and horror.

"Anyway," Diana said. "I need to know more about the portal in the underground. I've got to save my friend."

"I think you've got to do more than that."

"Yeah," Diana said, knowing that she was right but unable to focus on anything but saving Vi.

"I can take you to the portal in the underground. There are a couple of Mythean Guardians watching it to make sure nothing escapes, but I can hide us from their sight while we look through the portal. I'm able to see in, and with my help, you can too. From there, we can figure out what the hell is going on. No pun intended."

Diana's skin prickled at the idea of getting so close to the danger, but she had to do it. For Vi, for Boudica, whose pain and rage still seethed under the surface of her skin. For herself. To take back control of her life.

"Excellent. I say we go now." Diana went to the couch to put her shoes on and grabbed her sword.

"Good thinking." Esha nodded at the sword. "We aren't actually going into the portal, but you never know what will jump out. We'll aetherwalk straight there, that way you don't have to walk down the street with it."

Diana nodded and rose to join Esha. Just before she reached her, someone pounded on the door.

Esha looked at her quizzically, then called out, "Yeah?"

"Open up, Esha."

"It's Warren." Esha smoothed her hair. "Let me get this real quick."

When she opened the door, Diana stepped backward in surprise. Cadan and Warren strode through. Who had released him from his bonds?

"You." Diana glared at Cadan.

"Aye, it's me."

Had anything she'd said last night made him see her perspective? His past actions angered her, but it was his unwillingness to agree that he'd done wrong that really got her. And the fact that he'd been trying to do the same thing all over again.

As herself, Diana, she didn't want to do all of this alone and could appreciate his desire to protect her. She wanted his help, but not at the expense of her agency. Her ability to choose her own fate was vital to her. She hadn't liked forfeiting it in her past life and she certainly didn't like it now.

"Why'd you come?" Diana asked, her gaze glued to Cadan.

Use this second chance, Cadan.

His eyes met hers, fire in their depths. "To keep you from doing something stupid and getting yourself hurt."

Her heart clutched. He clearly hadn't learned a thing. To trust him when he was like this was folly. If she was the only one who could save Vi and stop whatever was happening, she couldn't risk his trying to stop her.

Diana turned to Esha and said, "Let's go. I think I've heard enough."

"Where are you going?" Cadan demanded.

"To do what I was reborn for. And it's going to be *dangerous*. I might get hurt." She knew she poked at him at her peril, but couldn't help herself. She turned and cast Esha a let's-get-a-move-on look.

"Wait." Warren's voice was quiet. "You canna go alone."

"Oh, you, too? And why would that be?" First Cadan, now this Warren joker?

But Warren looked at Cadan instead of answering. "You dinna tell her, did you?"

Cadan cursed.

"Tell me what?" Diana asked.

"Nothing. It's no' important. It won't be an issue," Cadan said.

The hair rose on Diana's arms when she caught sight of the way Warren was looking at her. Sad, yet pitying?

"Cadan, she has to know," Warren said.

"What the hell are you talking about?" Diana demanded. The tension in the room prickled along her skin. Something was very wrong.

Warren was still looking at her weirdly, too. "You're destined to die as a result of the task."

"What?" She barely had the breath to form the word. He couldn't be serious. She'd thought it a possibility, but not a probability. Not a *fated* probability.

But from the way that Cadan was looking at her.... She grabbed for Esha's hand. Cadan took a step toward her, something unrecognizable in his eyes, but she backed up. He jerked to a halt, his fist clenched.

Damn you, Cadan.

"Why the hell did you keep that kind of information from me?" she asked him. "I don't know up from down anymore, and now I find this out?"

But it couldn't be true. She wouldn't let it be.

"You were never supposed to know!"

"Know what? Who I am, or what I'm supposed to do?"

"Both! Hell, I doona know. I just dinna want you facing this. If you never had to face it, you would no' be at risk." Cadan dragged a hand through his hair.

"Oh, well that's great. I wasn't supposed to find out who my soul belonged to. That's *who I am.* Don't you think I'd want to know that? That I'd need to know that? All so you can make make my decisions for me?"

"Aye. To save your damned arse." A muscle twitched in his jaw. The way he was looking at her... Like a possession he'd never be able to bear losing.

"Did you ever consider that I'm the *only one* who can do this?"

"The hell you are. You're no' going anywhere without me, lassie."

"You see, Cadan, the funny thing is, even though I've been reborn as a different person, I still don't like being lied to. Or being told what to do. That, I *really* don't like."

Diana squeezed Esha's hand to let her know that she wanted to leave. Just as she felt the familiar pulling sensation of aether-walking, she realized that she'd rather face hell alone than stay here with Cadan.

26

Fifteen minutes later, Diana picked her way through the tunnels of the underground behind Esha. The soulceress had sucked her through space and within moments, they were deep underneath the city. Rodent skeletons and other mysterious debris littered the ground.

Eyes up. Don't look down. But the creepy misery of it all dulled the mess of horrible emotions that bombarded her. Betrayal, rage, fear. They were still there, but she could vaguely recognize —as if she were standing outside of her own head—that her brain had attempted to preserve her sanity by tying them up in a big, knotted bundle and stowing them in the corner of her mind.

She stepped over a pile of tumbled stones and tried to push aside the image of Cadan's expression just before she'd disappeared with Esha. It had been confusion and...hurt? Diana rubbed her temple. Of course she'd hurt him. He'd done all this because he cared for her. Or he'd cared for Boudica.

Either way, he was so damned pigheaded. How could she ever convince him to meet her in the middle?

Did it even matter if she was supposed to die soon?

Ever since the first demon attack, dying had been a possibility that had weighed on her, but not a probability. Now that it was likely...

Her throat tightened, a hollow coldness pervading her chest. There'd be a way around it. Had to be. *Push it away.* She wrapped anger around her heart like a blanket, thrusting the fear away and embracing the rage and betrayal that kept her from collapsing.

Focus on your surroundings. Stay in the present. But there wasn't much to look at in the darkened tunnel, especially if she didn't want to see what was crunching beneath her feet. The best she could do was stick close behind Esha.

She flushed. She was supposed to share a soul with one of Britain's greatest warriors, and the best she could do was stick close behind her friend who led the way into danger?

But she had to do this. For herself—for Vivienne, who'd been dragged into this mess because of her. She had to do this. She *could* do this.

And she didn't want Cadan to think otherwise. More important, *she* didn't want to think otherwise. Being protected at the expense of her ability to make her own decisions was something she couldn't live with.

If she got to live. Either way, she'd be taking control now. Determining her own fate and doing what was necessary.

"We're here." Esha's hushed tone jerked Diana back to the present.

"We are?"

Diana squinted into the dark, but could see nothing out of the ordinary. Just a big black chamber that dripped water. The air had an unnatural chill that couldn't kill the reek of decay. Her nose wrinkled.

"Yeah, come closer." Esha beckoned her forward with a wave of her hand.

When Diana reached her, Esha wrapped a slim arm around

her waist. She mimicked the gesture until they stood side by side.

"All right, you need to close your eyes and focus on the feeling of my arm. I can't give you my sight, but I can let you see inside my head."

Diana squeezed her eyes shut and focused on the warmth of Esha's arm. She twitched when she felt the cat twine itself between her legs and Esha's.

"All right, I'm going in. Not my body, but my sight."

Diana gasped and stumbled back as a black cloud of shadows bombarded her mind.

"That's in front of us?" she whispered.

"Yep. Creepy, huh? Now focus and stop me when you recognize something. I'm going to try to find the source of the energy."

The black cloud began to dissipate as Esha's mind went farther into the new world. It was dark and gray with a sluggish black river snaking through marshes while mist crawled through the reeds and along the edge of the field upon which they stood. She couldn't tell where the dim light that illuminated the dismal scene came from, which made the surroundings extra creepy.

They began to move forward and a chill crept up her spine. Shadows of people, almost ghostlike, wandered along the river and through the mist toward a dark forest.

Esha led her after them. Diana shivered. All her big talk about taking control of her fate and doing what was necessary seemed a bit ridiculous now that she was actually seeing an ancient hell.

"Where are we exactly?" Diana whispered.

"Erebus. It's the largest region of Hades. Many of these souls were warriors."

"We're getting closer." Diana shivered. The air crackled with a malevolence that made her skin itch.

"I feel it too."

They entered the forest. The trees rose tall above the ground, claw-like branches reaching toward a moonless sky. A vague glow emanated from farther ahead, brightening as they drifted toward it.

"We can't be seen, right?" Diana glanced around, looking for glowing eyes that would suit this Halloween world perfectly.

"Should be fine, since it's just my sight and not our bodies that are here. Been here before and no one noticed."

At a clearing in the wood, they passed a solemn looking boy of perhaps twelve leaning against a tree. He looked vaguely familiar, but her attention was drawn by the sight of Vivienne. A fist squeezed her heart at the sight of her friend sitting with her back against a tree that was slightly behind the boy's tree. Her eyes were closed and her wrists bound in front of her. Instinctively, Diana started to pull away from Esha to approach her friend, but Esha tightened her grip on her hand.

"You can't help her because we aren't actually here. Don't break our bond." Esha's voice was strained.

Desperate to figure out what was going on and a way out of this, Diana dragged her gaze from Vivienne. Black roots pushed up through the dark soil and dead leaves. The ring of trees surrounding the clearing was nearly circular. A great platform carved from black stone stood in the center. Her gaze landed on a man standing behind the altar with a book in one hand.

A man that Diana recognized.

Shit. Her skin grew cold and clammy.

"We will avenge your death, Maximus." His deep voice vibrated with the intensity of a zealot, committed to telling the world it was about to end.

Diana started. He was speaking to the boy leaning against the tree. The boy merely looked up. His gaze was sullen and doubtful, the look that any teenager might shoot a parent they thought was stupid. It was out of place in this solemn world. So normal that it made her ache for the boy despite her fear.

"Who's there?" The man's head snapped up and his black eyes bored into Diana. Her heart. "Someone's there, I can sense you."

"Gotta go." Esha's voice shook.

Diana nodded emphatically despite her desire to stay with Vivienne, who'd now opened her eyes and was blindly searching the clearing. Diana's stomach soured at the sight of her friend, trapped and bound, but she couldn't help her if they were caught unawares.

"Come on, Esha," she whispered. Why weren't they leaving?

"I—I can't." Her voice trembled with strain.

"What can I do?"

"Imagine the chamber. Picture as many details as you can. It could help, since our minds are linked in this."

Diana struggled to bring the image to mind, but the man was getting closer. Her breath began to saw in and out of her lungs. He couldn't hurt them. Couldn't.

She squeezed her eyes shut and visualized the chamber. Their bodies still stood there; they just had to return their minds.

"That's it—it's working," Esha said.

When Diana opened her eyes, the scene in front of her began to fizzle out like a dying fog. A moment later, they were standing in the underground chamber.

"Hang onto me, I'm getting us out of here." Esha's grip tightened, Diana felt a brief tug, and they were back in Esha's flat. She reached out to steady herself against the couch, swallowing hard against her roiling stomach.

"What was that? Why were we trapped? Could he see us?"

"I—I don't know. That's never happened before." Esha sat on

the couch and buried her hands in her hair. "None of this has ever happened before."

27

"They had better be back here, damn it," Cadan said as he pounded on the door to Esha's flat.

He stood next to Warren, rage and confusion brewing a bubbling poison in his veins, waiting, hoping, for their knock to be answered. At Warren's suggestion, they'd tracked Diana and Esha to the underground. They hadn't seen them there, nor had the guards. Either they hadn't been there, or Esha had cast a spell to hide them.

It had taken them nearly twenty minutes to get from the chamber back to Esha's tower flat in hopes that they might have returned. They had no other leads. He hated this feeling.

Diana had run off alone. A sense of helplessness he hadn't felt in millennia fueled the anger vibrating through him. Ever since losing Boudica the first time, he'd become obsessed with controlling his environment and having a handle on things. Like her.

He'd tried to let go of Diana after she'd left him tied up in his own house. He hadn't wanted to come after her. But then Warren had arrived, sent by Esha to free him from the Maoin straps. He'd been bloody lucky the goddess Aerten had been in a meeting with Warren when Esha had told him about Cadan. She'd helped Warren get to him so quickly. When faced with a chance to return, Cadan had felt compelled to do so. When he'd stood across from Diana in Esha's flat earlier today, he'd realized why.

She was his heart.

He'd been stupid to ever think, no matter how briefly, that he could stay away from her. Diana drew him toward her like a dying man to his last sight of the sky. But the way she'd looked at him when he'd said that all he'd wanted to do was protect her...

"Gods damn it." He pounded on the door again. They'd been standing here five minutes and he was starting to wonder if this was hopeless when the door swung open to reveal a scowling Esha.

"Hold your horses, damn it," she said irritably. "What are you doing here?"

"Are you joking? I'm here for Diana," Cadan said.

Esha raised a brow. "Any idea how she feels about that?"

"Doona care." He pushed past her into the room. "Are you all right?" He directed the words at Diana, who stood near the couch.

She glared at him. He'd take that as a yes.

"What the hell do you think you're doing, running off?" He was at her side in a moment, running his hands over her, checking for injuries while she struggled to pull away. Relief that she was unhurt washed over him and he released her when she started to struggle.

"What I'm supposed to do! Trying to save Vivienne and stop that bastard Gaius Suetonius Paulinus." The gleam of battle lit her eyes as she squirmed out of his grip.

"What?" It had been centuries since he'd heard the name of the Roman general. Millennia, even. And who the hell was Vivienne?

"Who is Gaius Sue Whatever?" Esha asked.

"Gaius Suetonius Paulinus. The man who killed my daughters and destroyed my home. I killed him when I was Boudica."

Cadan's fist clenched. He remembered the bastard well. The one who'd taken everything from him. Not only Boudica, but his family too, years earlier when Paulinus had burned his village, Camulodunum.

"And the boy who sat against the tree? Maximus?" Esha asked.

"I killed him, too." Diana sat hard on the couch, a vacant look in her eyes.

"Oh." Esha blanched.

"I killed a lot of people." Her voice was scratchy. "The boy followed his father everywhere. He was being groomed to take over and he was there when Paulinus killed my daughters. He was also on the battlefield when Paulinus came for me. So I killed him when I killed his father. Now, he wants to get out of Erebus."

"What the hell do you have to do with that?" He didn't want her anywhere near Paulinus, and it shone in his voice.

Diana's eyes met his. "What *don't* I have to do with that? He. Killed. My. Daughters. And I'm the one who sent him to hell. With his son." She looked ill. "I killed anyone who got in my way after they killed Aela and Calea. I don't regret most of it."

"Just the boy," Esha said.

Diana nodded, looked down at her hands.

"That's it, then," Esha said. "Paulinus could sense you because you killed him. Or your soul, rather, sent his to hell when you killed him as Boudica. Souls are powerful. By killing him, you probably linked the two of you together. At least in a small way. You're his link to the outside world and I bet that's why he wants you. It's why we had a hard time leaving, too. Your soul was attracted to his."

"I don't get it," Diana said. "Why is the portal threatening to open here? Why not in Italy, if it's the Roman hell?"

"For the same reason that the university is here. Arthur's Seat has the most magical energy of anywhere in Europe. The boundaries between earth and the afterworlds are weakest here."

Diana buried her head in her hands. "What am I going to do? And why does he have Vivienne?"

"I don't know about Vivienne," Esha said. "She could be bait, a mistake, maybe even involved somehow."

"Vivienne?" Cadan asked.

Diana briefly explained her friend's abduction to him. "But she's not involved. She was teaching my classes. Maybe the demon abductors got confused. So you think he'll try to use me to get out?"

Esha nodded. "There was an altar."

"An altar?" Cadan asked, dread sinking his stomach.

"Yeah," Esha said. "Nothing says *blood sacrifice* like an altar."

Diana swallowed, her eyes stark. "They want to sacrifice me?"

"Yeah, sucks," Esha said.

"Eloquent, Esha," Warren said.

"Shut up, Warren—some dead guy wants to cut open my new friend here on a big black rock in hell. *Sucks* is one of the nicer words to describe it."

Diana nodded. "So, there's a spell—probably one that involves my death—that is the key to getting Paulinus out of Erebus?"

"Yes," Esha said. "I think it is supposed to be an equal exchange. One soul imprisoned so that another can escape. And because you're the one who put him in Erebus in the first place, your soul is the only one that can get him out. If any soul would work, then he'd have escaped long ago. Hell, most folks in there would be out."

"So what is Diana supposed to do about it? She has no magic, no way to get to Erebus to kill him. All she can do is look in with Esha's help," Cadan said.

"Don't talk about me like I'm not here! I'm not helpless. And I'm sick of you deciding for me." Her cheeks flushed red. "I killed him the first time—I can do it again if I have to. Which apparently I do."

"Nay." It was all Cadan said, but she jerked as if she'd been slapped, then turned to glare at him. He was getting her out of here, and they were going to talk.

"*No?*" She asked, her voice vibrating with rage. "You dare to tell me no? You have no say over what I do! I know better than to trust you after what you've done."

"What *I've* done?" He was at her side in a second, grasping her arms once again and staring down at her fiercely. She matched his gaze, the dead look in her eyes drowned by rage. "What about you? You're the one who left!"

He could hear Esha and Warren talking, but through the buzzing in his head couldn't make out their words.

"*Lef—*" Diana started to yell back at him, but before she could finish, Esha and her damned feline were at their side. Without warning, she sucked Cadan and Diana through the aether and within seconds. they were standing in his flat in Edinburgh's Old Town.

"You two have something to work out before we can get any further. Call me when you're done." She disappeared.

They stood, breathing heavily, still clasped together.

"Why, Cadan? Why did you lock me away? Why did you take my choice?" She gazed up at him, the questions hanging between them.

28

"I couldn't lose you." Pain hollowed out Cadan's voice, as if something vital had been carved free of his soul. "I'd lost too many. Was unable to protect too many."

It dawned on her then. *His family.* When the Romans had taken his village, they'd killed many of the Trinovantes and expelled the rest from their homes. She'd known the loss of his sisters and mother in the initial attack had affected him, but she'd had no idea how much. He'd carried that burden with him, blamed *himself,* though he'd barely been out of childhood when they'd attacked. As Boudica, she'd been too filled with her own pain to ask about his, to even wonder. Had that wound been festering all this time?

"You couldn't have protected them, Cadan. You were a boy. The Romans were an army with the support of the greatest empire on earth. You were lucky to survive when they burned your village."

"It *was* my fault. It was my responsibility to protect them."

"Not yours alone, and their deaths aren't on your shoulders."

"Yours is." His voice was bleak, his eyes dark with pain.

"No!" She wanted to stamp her foot. How could he not *get* this? "It's not. That's what you don't understand. It wasn't your job to protect me above all else. We were to look out for each other in battle, yes, as soldiers do."

"You were my woman. The woman I loved. The only person left alive who meant anything to me. When our homes were burned, our people killed, you were all that was left."

Oh God. What was she supposed to do? Her anger was just, his sins unjustifiable. But what could she do in the face of such pain? Continue to kick a man who'd committed his sin out of love? Because she had escaped his trap and fought in the final battle, his actions hadn't had long-ranging consequences other than killing Boudica's trust in him.

"And then you left me." His voice had the jagged edges of pain. "Without a word, without a good-bye, you plunged that dagger into your heart."

The sight of him standing tall and strong across from her made her feel like a piece of glass had just carved its way into her heart, not unlike the blade from so long ago.

"I missed," she said, recalling the pain of dying slowly, with the blade piercing her lung instead of her heart.

"Aye. If you hadn't, I'd never have come upon you while you were still alive. I'd lost so many. You, and vengeance, were what I'd lived for. And you, the woman I loved and the only good thing remaining on earth, left without a word. Would have snuck off into death."

"What was I supposed to do? I couldn't trust you to let me do the right thing—you'd have taken that choice from me as you'd done the previous night. Tied me up, thrown me over your horse, and taken me away to hide."

His jaw tightened; she could see in his eyes that it was true.

"I was not just the woman you loved. I was a warrior, the

leader of a lost people. We'd been crushed in that last battle—
the Romans even slaughtered the women who made up the last
line of defense. They'd have come for me, taken me to Rome to
be slowly executed as an example of our so-called barbarism, or
worse, ransomed back to the Iceni."

Her tribe would have paid a price they could ill afford, and
they'd already suffered so much. She hadn't wanted to fight
anymore. "I couldn't be either of those things. You'd have done
the same if you had been in my position. Why shouldn't I have
had that right?"

"We could have fled. Gone north."

She could admit that now, as Diana, she might have run with
him. Run with the man she loved when the battle was lost, and
hidden for the rest of their lives. But not Boudica.

"That's what you don't understand, Cadan. Boudica would
never have done that. After the death of her daughters and the
theft of her land, she saw no future for herself. Not even with
you."

"What?" He took a step back.

"She—no, I mean, *I* cared for you." It was becoming harder
to speak as Boudica once she realized that their choices might
have been different. "But she didn't have her whole heart to give
and what she had wasn't enough to change her path. Paulinus
took that when he took her daughters, when he took her home.
When she picked up her sword in vengeance, she never planned
to lay it down. There would be no life for her if she failed to
expel the Romans from her land. She knew that she stood for
her people, was a symbol for her cause. And her warriors were
dead." She could remember them, as she knew he could, too,
their bodies scattered across the fields in all directions.

"Had she fled, the people in the villages would have known.
The last armies would have known that their chosen leader, the

one who had sent them in to die in a near hopeless battle, had abandoned her honor and fled. Fleeing was never an option and there was no life that she wanted to flee to."

He said nothing, just stood strong and still in the middle of the room, and she watched as he tried to process what she'd told him. *The woman you loved didn't love you back in the same way. Couldn't love you back in the same way.*

She could see everything more clearly now that she remembered who she was. It was as if a fog had cleared from her mind. She felt more herself than ever. Boudica's memories gave her context for her own life, for the things she'd felt and missed and hadn't understood. They were clearer now; her whole life was clearer.

The feelings she'd had for Cadan—the mixed-up mess of attraction, mistrust, affection, hate, love, curiosity—had all begun to make sense when she regained her memories. She knew him now; knew his past and why he'd done the things he had.

They had both been broken by loss those many years ago. He by the slaughter of his family, and by the time he'd spent alone atoning for a sin he thought he'd committed. And she by the loss of her daughters and her home. But that didn't make him any less hers.

She realized now that she'd hurt him as much as he'd hurt her, perhaps more. He hadn't respected her will, but she had abandoned him without an explanation, leaving him to wonder and mourn for millennia.

I was selfish. Noble and well intentioned, and she wouldn't take back her actions, but selfish all the same. Though wasn't that always the way of it? Fighting for a great cause could lead one to neglect the details. Like the people around you who were still alive. Like the strong, beautiful man standing across from her. His bravery and self-sacrifice awed her.

With their wounds laid bare, their sins stood between them like an impassable lake of pain they continued to fill with buckets full of more. There was only one way across.

"I'm sorry, Cadan." Tears burned her eyes. "Truly. For what she took away from you by not saying good-bye. She was brave and her cause was just. But I'm sorry for not saying good-bye. For the hurt it caused you."

It FELT as if something large and hard was lodged in Cadan's throat. He hadn't thought he needed Diana's apology. Or that he would agree with her.

He was ashamed to admit it, but when he truly thought about it, when Diana *made* him think about it, he'd cared for Boudica, but not in the way he should have. He'd still been reeling from the pain of losing his own family, had been running toward redemption or forgiveness or death. Which it should be, he hadn't known or cared. Boudica had become his solace, a woman who'd been as betrayed by life as he had and had given him something to fight for again. *If he could just protect her.* On the eve of the final battle, he'd been overcome by the fear of losing her.

He scrubbed a hand over his face. Christ, she was right. He'd wanted to protect her, true, but more out of a desire to save himself. To prove that he could. He'd wanted to protect her, but she'd wanted to fight, wanted her vengeance. Wanted to protect her daughters, even if it was only their memories, by killing the man who had taken their young lives. As he wanted to do for her. Could he begrudge her that? His fear, which had made him take her choice from her, was the same fear that had driven her so many years ago.

He hadn't seen it then, had been blinded by his past. After

her death, he'd buried his head in the sand. Thinking about it had only made him ill. But he could see it, now that he'd heard her perspective. It had taken nearly two thousand years, and Diana, to make him see that it hadn't been his choice to make.

He'd been so caught up in his own pain that he hadn't thought about hers. She'd been their leader, their queen, but above that, she had been the woman he loved.

"I—" *Keep going.* "I'm sorry." He dragged a hand through his hair. "You're right. And it's something that I could only realize when I heard it from you. In my head, I just couldn't have that perspective. I was a product of my upbringing, and then of my own fear. I took your choice from you, and I shouldn't have. I'm —sorry."

Cadan stood, not daring to move, possibly unable to, as his words hung in the air. He'd never been able to think of the past in that way. She began to walk toward him, and his heartbeat drummed in his ears. Diana stopped inches from his chest and reached up and laid her palm on the side of his face.

"You'll never do that again, right? You'll let me fight my own battles, and never take the choice from me even when it's a hard one to make?"

"I won't." And as he said the words, he realized that they were true. "You're the only one who can do this, and I'm behind you. 'Til the end. I was so afraid to lose you again, but I realize now that I've got no control over it."

As much as it tortured him not to do everything in his power to protect her, taking the decision from her had been wrong. Looking down at her, he saw a woman who had changed drastically from the shy mouse he'd thought she was. A sense of assurance pervaded her being now. She had the courage and the skill needed to face her demons. And like Boudica, the wisdom to do what was right. They would fight side by side, and only fate could determine the outcome.

"We'll help each other," she said. "I'm not stupid and my pride isn't going to get in the way of my taking any help I can get. And it's your help I want."

He reached out and crushed her to him. "Thank you," he whispered into her hair. He lifted his head and asked, "Do you think Boudica would have forgiven me?"

"I don't know. But I do, and she is me. Maybe it's my life experiences that allow me to."

He squeezed her tight. It didn't take away the pain of the lost years, but it helped him now.

They stood, wrapped in each other, as rain began to patter on the roof above. His heart squeezed in his chest, but he spoke no words of love, and neither did she. What had formed between them was too new, too raw, and too much to process for more words. Something deep and intricate tied them together; forgiveness and understanding had created a bridge over the lake of pain.

"I need you." Her voice was ragged, desperate.

He groaned as he bent down to take her mouth, hauling her up against him until he could feel all the curves and hollows of her body pressed to his. Her lips were soft and sweet, warm beneath his as they parted on a sigh to accept his tongue.

He fisted his hand in her hair, holding her steady so that he could explore her mouth, half afraid that she would change her mind.

It was too late now. There was no saving himself the pain of losing her. If he lost her, he'd be broken, his heart finally torn apart once and for all. He gripped her tighter, running his tongue along hers and nipping her lower lip.

Her arms clutched him fiercely as a desperate energy drew them together.

She clouded his mind with her soft body, scent, and the

small noises she'd begun to make as he slipped his hand beneath the back of her shirt.

She tore her mouth away from his and whispered, "Your bed. Take me to your bed."

He swept her up into his arms. Her soft mouth found the side of his neck, her tongue dancing along his skin.

Thunder boomed. He strode across the wide wooden floor as lightning lit the interior of his flat from the windows and skylights above. Lightning continued to illuminate the room as the streetlamps from below cast a soft, steady glow through the windows.

He reached his bed and gently set her down. She rose to her knees on the mattress, the waves of honey-red hair falling from the band she'd tied around it. Her eyes were hot as she began to pull at his shirt.

"Take it *off*," she demanded.

"All right, my eager Diana." He smiled as he yanked the shirt over his head. He began to unbuckle his belt, pausing to watch appreciatively as she undid the buttons of her conservative blouse.

His breath caught as she peeled the cream silk back and revealed an expanse of lightly freckled skin. Her breasts swelled out of a pale bra, her nipples hard and visible through the lace. She slipped the silk blouse off her shoulders and it fluttered to the bed behind her.

His eyes were riveted on her as she unbuttoned her slacks to reveal matching lace. He caught sight of the fiery curls visible beneath the lace and his cock throbbed painfully against his pants. He dragged them over his aching shaft and was naked in seconds.

He wanted her. Needed her. Now.

Once she was clad in nothing but the lace, he stalked toward her, reaching around her waist and lifting her up so that he could lay her upon her back. He climbed atop her, settling himself between her thighs, and they both gasped at the contact.

She was hot and soft and made for him.

"You're more beautiful than anything I could imagine." He gazed at her in awe. She smiled tremulously, as if she were nervous. Good—she should be nervous. He bit her earlobe and growled low, "I am going to torture you, my love, the same way that you tortured me. Until you are hot and desperate and aching, I am going to torture you. And even when you beg me, I might no' give you what you desire. At least, no' then."

She gasped and he grinned at the sound, delighting in the way her eyes widened.

He began by tracing kisses down her neck, stopping briefly to bite her gently at the curve he knew excited her so much, and was rewarded by a moan and a shudder as he laved the spot with his tongue.

Impatient, she arched against him, rubbing her body along his to make him move faster. He chuckled low in his throat, content to let this game play out. This was their first time together, their *real* first time, and he was going to make her cry out and beg and tremble beneath him. He wanted her to come so many times she forgot who she was.

He needed to make this even. Needed to know that she wanted him as much as he wanted her.

He trailed his mouth lower, slowly massaging one lush hip with his hand and slipping his fingers beneath the waistband of her panties as he leaned on his other hand.

He pressed his mouth to the curve of her left breast. When she moaned and squirmed beneath him, he unclipped the bra and kissed each of her nipples, stroking them with his tongue until they were shining and wet.

"Please, Cadan."

"Please what?" His shaft dragged against the bed as he

moved lower, the friction from the bedding making him grit his
teeth and groan low in his throat. He didn't know how long he
could last in this little game, with her writhing and begging
beneath him.

"Please," she panted, arching her hips off the bed.

His face hovered above her center, and the rich, sweet scent
of her filled his nose.

"Please touch me."

"Here?" he asked, as he kissed her low on her stomach. He
stroked the soft skin with his tongue, nipping gently when she
squirmed beneath him. He reached up and grasped the low
waistband of her panties, dragging them down a mere inch so
that he could press kisses along the top of the curls that were
barely covered.

"Lower."

"Part your pretty thighs for me, Diana."

She didn't hesitate, letting her thighs fall apart.

"Farther," he rasped, and with both hands, he spread them
wide. He raised one hand and laid his thumb against her clitoris
and began to stroke, teasing her, and occasionally slipping
beneath the edge of her panties.

"Please," she cried out. "You're torturing me."

"That's the point, now, isn't it?"

Her pussy was wet now, the lace damp. He continued to
press kisses along the edges of her panties, but even that was
becoming too much for him. He had to taste her. Sink his tongue
into her flesh and feel her quiver against him as she had in his
fantasies.

His control was slipping.

Cadan yanked her panties down and threw them off the bed.
He gripped her ass in his hands and pulled her to him, draping
her thighs over his shoulders. He sank his tongue into her flesh,
parting the soft pink folds and dragging his tongue up to the

cluster of nerves at the apex. She was more than he'd dreamed she would be.

Perfect. She tasted perfect. She was his. He'd see to it. He'd mark her mind and her soul tonight so that she never forgot it.

DIANA'S HIPS arched up off the bed at the first touch of his mouth. Pleasure raced up her spine as his tongue stroked her.

Oh my God, oh my God, oh my God.

Diana squirmed beneath the onslaught of Cadan's mouth, his hands firm on her ass and his tongue plunging into her sex. She shuddered beneath him, overwhelmed by the vulnerability of being held so tightly by such a huge man while he played her body with his mouth.

Hot. So hot.

Not just the feeling of his tongue, which felt like magic running back up to her clitoris and making chills and heat break out alternately along her body, but the feeling of being helpless beneath him as he took her toward orgasm.

She could push him off and climb on top, but she didn't want to. Not now. She liked the feeling of him positioning her body, looking at her with hot eyes, and stroking his tongue along her sex.

"You're going to come for me," he growled against her, and she swore she could feel the vibration of his gravelly voice.

Yes. He flicked his tongue against her clitoris repeatedly and she fisted her hands in the sheets. She pressed herself against his mouth.

"Please." Her voice shuddered.

"Please what?" He gave one long lick. "You're going to have to tell me what you need."

Her cheeks burned briefly. She couldn't believe she was

doing this. But the need was too great to be ignored. "I need you," she panted, "inside me."

She looked down to see him grin up at her. "You'll come against my mouth," he told her, and then bent his head back to her.

This is happening. This is happening. She gasped as she felt his fingers against her. He slipped one inside her, gently but inexorably pushing forward, and her hips jerked as he curled his finger upward to rub against the sensitive pad of nerves. It was hot and rough and delicious, and as he laved her clitoris with his tongue, he began to push a second finger inside her.

"Gods, you feel good," he said.

He sounded pained, and she wanted to fix that, but more than anything she wanted him to put his mouth back on her.

All thought left her head when she felt his mouth again and he began to thrust his fingers. Her breath strangled in her throat as she felt the orgasm begin to coil in her core. Her thighs trembled uncontrollably as it broke through her.

She writhed, eyes blind, as it wracked her body and Cadan worked her through it. *Too much.* Her legs fell apart weakly when it was over, but rather than rise up away from her, Cadan set back in against her sex.

"No." She tried to push him away. "I want you inside me."

"You're no' finished."

He bent to her again, his tongue both rough and soft, and she jerked as it swept over her sex. He pinned her down until she began to clench around his fingers, this orgasm more powerful than the last. By the time it had faded, she was panting and desperate for him.

She needed him inside her. Now.

Diana grasped his hard shoulders and tried to pull him up toward her, but he wouldn't budge, his tongue continuing to swirl and stroke.

She tugged again and he looked up at her, his full lips gleaming from her wetness.

"Please." She felt like her soul was in that one word. "I need you."

He gave her one burning look and rose up along her body, dragging his well-muscled form against her softer one, and fit himself to her perfectly.

Finally.

Fear and excitement made her breath short as she looked at him above her, dark and strong, an angel of destruction and her salvation.

The hard, hot length of his cock pressed against her. She reached up and clasped his face. He pressed his mouth hard against hers until she could taste herself on his lips, then grinned down at her with a soul-stealing, beautiful smile.

She stared into his eyes as he reached down and positioned his cock at her entrance, the broad head pressing against her sensitive sex. He thrust gently and she gasped. He pushed farther in, his hot, hard flesh parting hers easily. She bit her lip and shifted beneath him, adjusting to accommodate his size. He hesitated, giving her time to adjust, but she thrust up to take more of him. She winced. Maybe that hadn't been the best idea.

He noticed the small movement and looked down at her with fierce concern in his eyes. "Are you sure this is okay?"

"Yes." She wanted this, wanted to know where it would go when it was with someone who mattered. He reached down between them and stroked her clitoris as he began to thrust slowly. Her flesh soon grew slicker and there was only pleasure.

More.

Cadan rose up above her on his knees and jerked her toward him. He was illuminated in the streetlights from below, his face a work of art cast in shadow and light as he gazed down at her. The muscles of his arms bulged as he worked her hips.

So close.

CADAN BIT back a groan as Diana writhed beneath him. He had her lush hips clamped between his palms and he feasted his eyes on her small form. A bolt of lightning highlighted her quivering breasts and the need in her eyes.

He wanted her to lose control. The feel of her, tight and wet around him, made him want to fuck her hard, pounding into her until he came in an explosive rush. He was so *close*. He bit his lip hard, hoping the feeling of his teeth sinking in would stave off the orgasm. She *would* come. He wanted her as wild and frenzied beneath him again as she had been before.

Diana had been more delicious than he'd imagined, her flesh warm and soft and sweet. When she'd clenched around his finger in orgasm he'd nearly lost himself on the sheets. She'd been tight when he'd first thrust into her and he'd tried to go slow, but it had been one of the most difficult things he'd ever done.

He needed her now, hard, and the sight of her stretched out before him was almost more than he could bear. He reached down and yanked her up against him so that she sat in his lap, he upon his knees.

"Faster," she demanded.

He growled as she gripped his hair and forced him to stare straight into her eyes.

"I need you faster. And harder."

He groaned at the command and began to pump her harder upon his cock, lifting her body with ease, his hands gripping her slick skin. He felt the pressure building in his balls and was desperate to make her come before he did.

He stared into her eyes as he reached down between them to

rub her clitoris once again. Her eyes began to darken and her breath came quicker.

"Come for me," he gritted, and his words made her cry out breathlessly. "You're *mine*."

Her eyes went shocked and blank and she cried out as her pussy began to clench around his cock, her thighs shaking and her breath coming in strangled gasps. She was the most beautiful thing he'd ever seen as she shook in his arms, her entire body quivering. He'd wanted to hold her through her orgasm and make her come again before he found his, but he couldn't.

His thrusts lost their grace as he felt the orgasm rip through him, his cock plunging into her clenching core as his seed shot from him. She continued to come around his shaft even after he'd finished, and when he finally felt her quiet and begin to breathe more normally, he cradled her in his arms and looked down at her. He felt like a god from the way she looked at him.

Then she collapsed in his arms. He laughed low in his throat as he slipped out of her and laid her back upon the bed.

"Oh, *wow*," she sighed, shifting so that she was more comfortable. "I mean..." She was still panting, trying to catch her breath, and he dragged her up against his side. "Just *wow*."

He swore he felt his chest puff up. He drew her closer to him, tucking her head under his chin.

He rolled over then, and looked down at her sprawled on the bed, skin flushed and her form lushly curved. She grinned up at him with a happily seductive smile.

"Why did you resist doing that for so long?" she asked.

He frowned. "A couple of reasons. Intimacy and trust between us could help you regain your memory. Because of our connection in the past. But mostly because I was afraid I'd fall for you."

He'd tried to save himself the pain. Gods, he couldn't lose her. She had become everything to him. Fear turned his contentment to a sick anxiety. But how could he keep her safe when she was the one who had to put her life in danger and he wasn't allowed to interfere?

He couldn't go back on his word, but would he be able to stop himself, when her life hung in the balance?

29

"Does anyone have any ideas about how to keep me from dying?" Diana asked Cadan, Esha, and Warren. They'd just assembled in Warren's office to discuss her options. It was still fairly early, but nerves made the idea of coffee or breakfast repulsive.

"Your task takes place in Erebus, a Roman afterworld. The only way for a mortal to enter an afterworld is through death," Warren said, his face grim.

Cadan's hand tightened around hers and she felt the tension that surrounded him as he fought to say nothing.

"I presume I have to kill Paulinus," Diana said. "If I was reborn for this, it makes sense that I would have to repeat past deeds."

"I think that I could possibly get you into Erebus," Esha said, her brow scrunched thoughtfully.

"Nay." Cadan bit out the word. Diana squeezed his hand.

"No, I mean, I think I can get you in without dying," Esha said. "You know how I can see into the portal and helped you do the same? Well, since you were reborn for this, it's possible that I can send part of your soul through the portal. Maybe it would be enough to allow you to do what's needed."

"How?" Diana asked.

"I can manipulate souls if I have permission from their owner. All soulceresses can. I couldn't send just anyone to an afterworld, but because your soul is linked to Paulinus's through death, then maybe I can project part of your soul into Erebus." She paused. "I think."

"You think?" Cadan's voice was cutting. "That's enough to send Diana's soul to hell? A hunch?"

Diana pushed away the dread that filled her mind like black muck and squeezed Cadan's hand to get him to shut up.

"Only part of her soul," Esha said. "Like an illusion. That's why it would be safe. Part of it would stay tethered to earth with her body."

"What are my odds of dying from this?" Diana asked.

Esha stroked the disheveled black cat who jumped onto the couch next to her. "Slim, I think. Since I'm just projecting part of your soul into Erebus, your body would stay at the entrance with us. So he can't kill your body. And he could only kill part of your soul."

"Honestly, that sounds terrible," Diana said.

"This is all terrible," Esha said. "And there's a very slim chance I wouldn't be able to call your soul back if you get in trouble. But that's never happened before. It really should be fine."

Diana swallowed hard. *Should be fine.* Her life expectancy was now *should be fine.* To think that only weeks ago, her biggest concern had been whether or not she got her promotion.

"Any one else have any ideas?" Diana asked. Because she certainly didn't.

"Aye," Cadan said. "Doona do this. Let the Praesidium handle it."

She scowled at him.

Cadan held up his hands. "Just giving other options here."

Ha. It was a subtler expression of his control issues. "I was reborn to do this. If anyone else on the planet could have, I wouldn't have been reincarnated. And it's my best friend trapped there. No matter what possible evil could come of ignoring this threat, there's *definite* evil in leaving Vi there."

"She's right," Warren said.

Diana nodded at him, grateful that he backed her up, yet annoyed that he'd had to. "I think we should try it. How am I supposed to get Vi back?"

Esha bit her lip. "Well, she's not supposed to be there in the first place, since she doesn't practice that religion. Presumably. It's been dead a couple thousand years, after all. So I think it's the spell that's holding her there. I can't guarantee that when Paulinus dies and the spell is broken that she'll wake from her coma. But at least her soul will escape. Try to grab her arm or something if you can, see if you can drag her out with you and back to earth. That way her soul could maybe reunite with her body. Otherwise her soul will go to whatever kind of afterworld she believes in. And mind you, this is just me guessing. It's the best I can do."

Diana nodded. She had to believe it would work.

"I want to go with her," Cadan said.

Esha shook her head. "I can't send two. It's too difficult."

"Then—"

Diana's glare cut Cadan off. She wouldn't object to him coming with her, but she wanted him to talk to her about it first. But it seemed it didn't matter. She'd be going into hell alone.

Two hours later, the four of them stood in the chamber that

held the portal. Two Mythean Guardians who'd been stationed
in the chamber to guard the portal stood with them. Diana eyed
Cadan suspiciously. He was shifting back and forth on his feet,
clearly anxious and wanting to take control of the situation.

She wanted his help. She wasn't stupid. With him, her odds
of success were higher. But only if he didn't try to take control
and do this for her. She really believed that she was the only one
who could do this. She had to believe it in order to go through
with it. And she didn't want him dying for her, especially if it
wouldn't accomplish the end goal. He'd had thousands of years
being himself, living according to his code of ethics. He wouldn't
change overnight. But he was trying.

"Are you ready?" Esha asked.

Diana gripped her sword and nodded. Esha had needed to
make a stop at a Mythean bar to refuel her power from other
Mytheans' souls. If this was ever going to work, it would be now,
when Esha had as much power as possible.

Esha approached her and took her hand. Cadan and Warren
stood to the side and Diana could almost feel Cadan's anxiety.

"Don't let go of my hand," Esha said. "I'll link our vision, so
you can see what I see. Then I'll try to project part of your soul."

"Will I feel it when it splits?" Why hadn't she thought to ask
that before?

"No, because it's not really tearing in half or anything,
because it's not a physical object. I'm just sending part of it in,
and you shouldn't feel it."

Diana nodded. It sounded so simple in theory. But when
Esha squeezed her hand and a cold frisson shot up her arm, she
realized that it wasn't simple at all. The frisson turned to heat.
Then darkness. She shook her head, and realized that it wasn't
darkness, but shadows. She had to stop herself from stepping
backward as they pushed out, writhing and clawing from a
space at the edge of the chamber.

Their minds passed through it, and again they passed by the river Styx, through the fields, and into the forest. At some point, she felt Esha's presence fade. She was alone. The sword felt almost natural in her hand, and for that she was grateful. It was an extra sharp security blanket. Her fist clenched around the hilt and she crept through the woods, certain that she was near the clearing that held Paulinus and Vivienne.

"What have we here?" The rough feminine voice cut through the silence.

Diana jumped and spun around to see one of the red demons bearing down on her with a sadistic grin on its birdlike face. Great wings flared from its back. Recognition dawned.

A harpy. Of course. This was the Roman underworld. On earth, they must hide their wings with magic to avoid attention.

She lunged at it with her sword and caught it in the arm below the fall of dark hair.

It shrieked and yanked a sword free of the sheath at its belt. "You'll pay for that."

The harpy swung and she parried, knocking its sword aside. They circled, trading blows, until her arm sang from the effort. Exhausted, she tripped over a root and fell on her back. The harpy leapt for her. She thrust her sword up and managed to catch it in the stomach. The sword sank grotesquely into flesh, then slid out when the harpy fell to the side, gasping.

She stumbled to her feet, but before she could rise fully, felt a slender arm wrap around her torso.

"That wasn't very nice, was it?" The harsh voice in her ear was that of another harpy.

Clumsily, she managed to flip her sword backward and stab the thing in the stomach. It grunted and released her. She stumbled, but regained her feet and spun around to swipe her sword across its throat. It collapsed to the ground and she looked around frantically.

No more. Good.

And thank God she had Boudica's talent with a sword.

She set off in the direction of the clearing until she reached the edge of the woods and crouched behind a bush. In front of her, about fifty yards away, the altar rose black and menacing out of the ground. A vision of herself bleeding atop it flashed into her mind and she flinched, her muscles tightening.

She was here for vengeance, here to stop something monstrous from opening into Edinburgh; but in the end, she was also here to save her friend and her own life from the man who now stood above the altar reading from his book. He wore the armor he'd died in, though it was tattered and stained with the shadows of old blood.

He was but a shadow of the Roman general she remembered, but enough of him was there to make her skin tighten with ancient rage. Her daughters' murders, her own brutal beating, the destruction of her village. Now he'd threatened her life and that of her friend. Her jaw tightened.

As quietly as she could, she crept through the forest at the edge of the clearing, ears and eyes alert for any sign of harpies on guard. Finally, she reached the tree line directly behind Paulinus. Vivienne was only a dozen feet from her, but Diana resisted the urge to go to her friend. She needed the element of surprise.

She crept forward on quiet mouse feet and raised her sword to strike. As much as she wanted to gloat, to lord it over him that she'd defeated him again, it would be stupid. Instead, she'd finish this quickly. But as she brought the sword down, he spun and stepped backward. Her sword sliced ineffectually through the air.

"You," he said. The crazed light in his eyes gleamed and made a shiver run down her spine.

She lunged for him again, managed to swipe his arm with

the tip of her blade. But no blood welled. As if she'd never touched him. He reached for his own blade, but not before she landed another swipe across his middle. Still, no blood.

Vivienne's cry echoed across the clearing, distracting her. Suddenly, she felt two strong hands grip her arms. Her sword fell to the ground. In her peripheral vision, she caught sight of harpies on either side of her. Damn it. They were so fast.

Paulinus laughed, a deranged chuckle that made the hair on the back of her neck stand up. "You've come to me, then," he said.

"To destroy you forever."

"That's not how this will go, Boudica."

She didn't bother to correct him. For his purposes, she *was* Boudica.

"Let my friend go," she demanded, thrashing in the arms of her captors.

"No."

"You don't need her. Why take her?"

He shrugged. "Mistake. But she was very good bait."

Diana flailed in the arms of her captors, reaching back to claw at the face of one. It shrieked when she gouged its eye and loosened its grip. She dropped her weight to the ground, then kicked up and broke the hold of the other.

"Get her," Paulinus roared.

She scrambled to her feet and snatched up her blade from where it had fallen. She swung it wildly at one of the demons, but managed only to draw a shallow cut upon its chest.

"Let my friend go," she gasped, unsure of her ability to finish this and get Vi out as well. There were too many harpies. Two more approached from across the clearing. Paulinus's laugh cut through the sounds of clashing swords and she knew he'd never let Vi go.

"Go, Diana, get out of here," Vivienne cried.

Diana ignored her, pivoting on her heel to land a fatal blow to one of the harpy's neck. Suddenly, pain blossomed at her own back. It burned through her, stealing her breath, and she fell to her knees. She struggled to rise, but before she could gain her footing, she felt herself being dragged backward through Erebus.

No. Esha was pulling her out. But she hadn't finished yet. Paulinus was still alive. Vivienne was still trapped. Diana clawed at the ground to stay in Erebus, but the pull was too strong.

30

"I wasn't ready," Diana cried as soon as she stood in the chamber. It was even darker than the forest in Erebus and it took her eyes a moment to adjust. Cadan was running his hands over her body. He cupped her face.

"The hell you weren't," he said.

Diana felt Esha's hands at her back. "She looks okay," Esha said. "I can see the mark on her soul, but it will fade since it isn't physical."

She pulled away from them both. "You should have let me stay."

"Your sword dinna affect Paulinus," Warren said. "And you dinna have a chance against five harpies."

"I had no idea there'd be so many. We didn't see them when we went in the first time," Esha said.

"Damn it." Diana stomped her foot. "I just really wanted to finish this, especially if it could be done without me dying."

"That was no guarantee, not once their blades cut so deep and there were so many of them. You couldn't get to Vivienne, and your blade wouldn't work on Paulinus when only part of your soul was there. This plan gave you a greater chance of living. Not a certain one."

Diana scowled. Esha was right. She'd held her own, but she'd been outnumbered. More importantly, her blade hadn't affected Paulinus. But the sight of Vivienne, bound at the foot of the tree, stuck in her mind like a burr. She had to save her.

"We need a new plan. Fast. Can we talk about it in your office?" Diana asked Warren.

He nodded and they departed the chamber, making their way through the underground until they reached the entrance near Edinburgh castle. Diana realized they were close to Cadan's flat.

"Can we swing by your place so I can get cleaned up? I know my body didn't go in, but I feel filthy from that place," Diana asked him.

"Sure."

Esha looked up from where she stood nearby and said, "We can meet at Cadan's if he doesn't mind. It's closer."

"Aye, it's fine," Cadan said.

It was a short drive to his flat. Esha rode with them since she had aetherwalked to the underground.

"I won't be long," Diana said as she carried her bag of clothes to the bathroom.

She showered quickly, more to wash away the memories of the demons' hands on her than to actually get clean. As she was rifling through her bag for clean clothes, her hands closed on the book at the bottom of her bag.

The treatise with the picture of Arthur's Seat that had led her here. She'd read it on the plane, but hadn't found anything useful. But now that she knew who she was...

Diana dressed quickly and carried the book out of the bathroom and into the living room. Cadan sat on the couch, while Esha and Warren had taken the two chairs at either end.

She held up the book and said, "A month ago, I ordered this book off the Internet because I thought it might have something to do with the manuscript I'm working on back home. But there's a drawing inside of Arthur's Seat that led me here. Did you send it to me?"

Warren shook his head. "Dinna send you anything. We dinna know exactly who Boudica's soul would be reborn to, so we couldn't. Could be coincidence, or fate that you picked that one. Perhaps Aerten sent it to you."

He reached out and she handed the treatise to him. It was a compendium of Celtic myths recorded during the Celtic Revival period in the eighteenth century, when academics and antiquarians had become interested in what they perceived to be Britain's misty and romantic past. It had appealed to her a month ago when she'd found it for sale on a used books site. Her attraction to it made even more sense now.

Warren frowned down at the book. "I'll be damned. Mary Anderson."

"Who was she?" Diana asked.

"A mortal who came to the university in the mid eighteenth century when I first joined the Praesidium." He looked at Cadan. "You would no' remember. I think you were off somewhere else that century."

"West Indies," Cadan answered.

"Aye, well, and Esha would no' be here for another three centuries. Anyway, she was a seer, and while she was here, she wrote three volumes of prophecy. They were presented in the form of myths or fairytales, but she was certain they would come true."

"That's the second volume—a collection of Celtic myths," Diana said.

"Well, shite. That makes sense, then. She saw backward as well as forward."

"Whoa," Diana said, excitement thrumming through her. "If she really could see the past, then her myths are true. We know so little about Celtic beliefs, but she did, because she could actually see it."

She held out her hand for the book. Warren passed it to her and she sat next to Cadan and began to skim through the pages, glancing at the chapter headings for something familiar.

Within minutes, a shiver skittered up her spine at the sight of chapter title she recognized. She hadn't noticed it before, but now that she had Boudica's memories, it stood out. Quickly, she skimmed the story. Visions from her childhood, the first one, flashed across her mind. Their Druid priestess had loved to tell this tale, and it had been her favorite as well.

But now, with the idea of embodying the role of the heroine, her blood ran cold. When Warren had said she was destined to die as part of her reincarnation, she hadn't really believed him. But this story... Her stomach clutched as she looked up at Cadan.

"I think the answer is in the story of Andrasta—how she became a goddess." Her voice trembled only slightly, but she could take no joy in her show of bravery as she looked up to meet the eyes that had been watching her for the last few minutes.

"Your patron goddess?" Cadan asked.

Diana nodded. Andrasta was the Celtic goddess of victory, the one that Boudica had called upon during her revolt—the one she had made a symbol of her campaign. It was all coming full circle, but she had the sick feeling that the circle was going to close all too soon.

"You don't remember how she became a goddess?" she asked Cadan.

"Bits and pieces. No' enough to say so."

Diana swallowed to force the boulder down her throat. "She was born mortal, but her skill with a bow attracted the attentions of Camulos, the god of war. He didn't like the idea of a mortal sharing his skill, and so he sought to kill her. But Andrasta got lucky when he came after her. He was arrogant and didn't think she was a real match for him, and she killed his mortal form.

"His soul was sent to Otherworld, the Celtic land of the gods and deceased mortals, where he plotted to regain his physical form so that he could come after Andrasta and her family. She knew he would succeed. He was a god, after all. To protect her family, she knew that she had to kill him once and for all. Killing him in the land of the gods, where she could destroy his soul and not just his body, would ensure that he could never come back again. And she was the only one who could do it, since she had sent his soul there in the first place." She stopped speaking for a moment, remembering what Esha had said about the power of souls and her connection with Paulinus.

"But the only way to get to the land of souls is to die." She saw Cadan's knuckles whiten on the arms of the chair, but he didn't say anything, and let her continue. "So she killed herself, knowing it would free her soul to pass over."

Blackness started to creep in on the edges of her vision, forcing her to close her eyes and focus on breathing carefully to keep herself upright.

"And it worked," Esha said.

Diana nodded, unable to speak, and was relieved when Cadan continued to speak for her.

"Aye, it worked. In thanks for ridding them of an unwise god, the other gods allowed her to take his place, for she was wise and just, two qualities a war god required if the world was going to thrive rather than be dragged into endless strife."

The room was silent for a minute and Diana's empty stomach heaved.

Esha broke the silence. "Damn it. It's not a coincidence. Your blade couldn't hurt Paulinus. You could hurt the demons, because of their ability to go back and forth between earth and Erebus means they straddle both realms, as you did when I projected part of your soul. But Paulinus is fully within the afterworld. For you to hurt him, he must be able to hurt you, too. The universe wants equality that way. You have to lay it all on the line. You'll have to do as Andrasta did."

It was too much for Diana. Bile burned in her throat and she stumbled for the bathroom. The hard floor bit into her knees as she heaved. Cadan wrapped an arm around her shoulders and held her hair back.

When the dry heaving finally ceased, and with her throat burning, she raised her head and stared blankly into space. Something buzzed faintly in her ears, and as if from outside of herself, she felt Cadan scoop her up into his arms.

"We'll speak to you soon." Esha's voice echoed. The sound of the door shutting behind Esha and Warren as they departed the flat barely made a dent in the buzzing that was sounding in Diana's head.

Cadan gave her water to wash out her mouth and carried her through the flat to the bedroom and placed her gently in a big chair in the corner of the room. He grabbed a throw blanked from the back and wrapped it around her, but no matter how cozy the wool, the chill in her bones remained.

"I'll be back."

She nodded, unable to speak. This was so real. She was going to die to get into hell. The idea raced in circles around her mind until Cadan returned to the room with a steaming mug of tea. He put it into her hands, and though the warmth made her sigh, she didn't drink.

Cadan sank down onto the floor next to the chair. After a while, when some of the shock had worn off, she noticed that he'd laid his hand on the arm of the chair. After a moment, she reached down to lace her fingers with his.

AFTER A WHILE – minutes or hours, she had no idea – Diana put the cold tea mug on the ground. The chill in her heart threatened to shatter her into a million pieces. She'd tried to reconcile the future that was before her with the one that she'd envisioned for herself. There was no overlap. Even when she'd first arrived in this world, she hadn't imagined that she might never return to her own.

She looked down and met Cadan's gaze. His eyes searched hers, worry creasing his forehead.

"I need you," she murmured, then stood and tugged on his hand until he rose.

"Aye." He lifted her into his arms and carried her to the bed.

His big body followed hers down as she sank into the mattress. She needed him to fill the void within her.

"Please." She moaned, beyond being embarrassed. "I need you. Make me forget what's coming."

"Anything," he rasped. He caught her eyes as he settled between her thighs. His gaze was intense, searching. "You're mine, Diana, and we'll get you through this."

Please be right.

She shivered as he ran his hot tongue along the side of her neck.

"Gods, you taste sweet," he whispered in her ear. He nipped the lobe and her hips bucked up slightly at the pleasure.

Too much. Not enough.

She clutched at his shirt. "Faster. I need you now."

She didn't want to think, didn't want time to process what

her fate might be. She wanted him. Wanted Cadan. He would make her forget.

He must have heard the desperation in her voice. While she struggled out of her clothes, he reared up and jerked the shirt over his head. His jeans were gone, then hers, and she stared up at the magnificent form rising above her on the bed. She reached up toward him and ran her hands along the rigid beauty of his abs. Then she yanked him down to her.

"Now," she demanded, running her arms over his sculpted back. She sank her nails into his ass and jerked him toward her. "I need you *now*."

She wanted him pounding into her so hard that she could only feel him. Could only think of him.

"Hang on," he grated, his breath harsh at her ear. He wanted her as much as she wanted him, she knew it. She jerked at his hips again.

He resisted, pulling back enough to slip a hand between them. "I want to make sure you're ready."

He stroked his thumb over her clitoris. *Yes.* She squirmed beneath him.

"More." She moaned when he pushed a finger inside her.

"A demanding one, aren't you?" He grinned down at her, but it didn't quite reach his eyes. They were still haunted.

She closed her eyes and focused on the feel of him.

When his fingertips pressed against the pad of flesh that was so sensitive, her hips arched off the bed.

"Yes." She moaned as he began to thrust inside her while circling her clitoris with his thumb.

His breath was hot on her neck as he worked her toward orgasm. He thrust his erection against her thigh, mirroring the rhythm of his fingers inside her. She reveled in the hard heat of him against her.

A tingling suffused her as the pleasure built toward its peak.

Just as the tension began to coil at her core, he withdrew his hand.

"No, please, I'm—"

He thrust his cock into her, stretching her. Filling her almost unbearably. Light burst in front of her eyes as the orgasm crashed over her in waves.

"*Fuck*." He groaned. "I can feel you clenching around me."

He shuddered atop her as he rocked into her. His strong hands grasped her legs and pushed them up, spreading them wider and thrusting harder.

Her back arched as a second orgasm seared through her. She opened her eyes in time to see him throw back his head, tendons at his neck straining and his eyes squeezed shut as he poured himself into her.

31

I t was near dusk when they rolled apart and lay side by side staring at the ceiling. Only the sound of their breathing broke the silence.

I might love him.

She swallowed. He made her...*belong*. After so many years of trying to find a place in her small family that would never fit, and then trying to make one on her own, she'd found it with him. He accepted her for what she was. He cared for her, knowing everything about her. Even the worst of her past. As she knew his. Maybe he even...*loved her?*

She shook the thought away. It wouldn't matter, if she couldn't get herself out of this mess. As much as part of her wanted him to take over and save her, a far larger part, a far more important part, needed to see this through herself. Paulinus was the man who'd killed her daughters, burned her lands, abducted her friend. Now he threatened her again?

This, she would deal with. Then, maybe, she could make things work with Cadan.

"This is awful," Diana said. All the risks she thought she would face had just doubled.

Cadan squeezed her close to his side. "There's got to be another way for you to get to Erebus. Or leave him. The biggest threat to you right now is the demons he keeps sending out. We'll keep killing them as they come and you'll stay on earth."

Sounds good to me. She had to *kill herself* to gain access to the Roman underworld in order to have her vengeance? Seriously?

"You know it's not that simple. Vi is there. I can't leave her."

He nodded and heaved out a great sigh.

"Something has been bothering me about what Esha said." It had been tickling her mind and she only now realized what it was. She reached out to lace his fingers in hers, wanting to feel his skin against hers as much as she could. The contact warmed something cold inside her.

"Aye?"

"She said the soul was a one-for-one deal. If he kills me, it will only give life to one soul, presumably his."

"That's right."

"Well, what about his son? He said in the forest that he wants to avenge his son. But he would leave him there in Erebus?" Just thinking about the misty gloom of Erebus made her shiver.

"He's a right bastard, Diana."

She thought about her daughters. "Yes. But not about his son. There's no way he'd leave Maximus there."

She wouldn't have left her daughters in the misty gloom and misery of Erebus. She'd have done *anything* to get them out. Cadan squeezed her hand as though he knew her dark musings.

"So what do you think he's planning, then?"

"Well, either he's got something else up his sleeve, or he's only planning to save his son. Because he can't use Vi's soul, right?"

"Aye. She had nothing to do with his death and putting him

in Erebus. Yours is the only soul that has the power to free them, and maybe you're right. He'll use it for his son."

That was something she could understand, empathize with. But what could his other options be? What could *her* other options be? With something—no, someone—like Cadan to fight for, she couldn't come out of this battle on the losing side. Especially not with Vi's life on the line. She had to believe there was a way out.

"Cadan, I need to see Andrasta. I'm going to ask Esha to send me south."

"I just got you back. Doona be runnin' away from me now."

"I've got to see her—she's my patron goddess. I called her to me once before. It was the night before the battle. Right before you abducted me." She turned her head in time to see him grimace. "I have to ask her what's to become of me. And she might have ideas."

"All right. What do you need?"

"A hare. And I need to go alone."

32

_____

Warren leaned against the kitchen counter in Esha's flat, trying to keep his eyes off her where she stood talking to Cadan. They'd sent Diana through Esha's portal just moments ago and she would be returning here once her mission was complete.

In the meantime, he'd be staying here with Esha to await her return. Memories of their last encounter and the dreams that she haunted had kept him awake at night.

Gods knew he'd tried to ignore her these last ten years, but with her appearance in his office last week, now he couldn't stop noticing her. He'd suggested her addition to the Praesidium because it was a wise tactical move for the organization. But it wasn't something that he should have done for his own sake.

He'd done it anyway.

He watched Esha squeeze Cadan's shoulder in comfort and the gesture made him grit his teeth. Jealousy? It was ridiculous.

"I'll be back soon," Cadan said. "Call me if Diana returns before I do."

Esha turned back to the room and her gaze stopped on him.

"Why are you looking at Cadan like you want to tear his head off?"

He scrubbed a hand over his face. Gods, now she was noticing that he was acting crazy. "I wasn't. Where'd he go?"

"To check something at the university. He didn't explain." She strolled into the kitchen and hopped up onto the counter across from him.

It was bloody hard to keep his eyes on her face. Not only would he be alone with her now, she was sitting so close he could smell her. Damn it. He really needed to get himself together. He was a mess over her. A soulceress.

Her kind were dangerous. He had every right to be wary of them. In fact, he should be staying the hell away from her. The hell he'd gone through as a result of tangling with another soulceress was directly responsible for the celibacy that she was threatening. He could only imagine what a mess he'd be in if he actually slept with her.

"Can I ask you something, Warren?" She swung her long legs. Back and forth, back and forth. Like a metronome to which he wanted to keep his eyes glued.

He dragged his gaze up to hers. "Is it about going to Diana and interfering?"

"Damn it, you know I had to do that. And I didn't screw anything up!"

He frowned, then flattened his mouth to wipe it away. "Nay, you dinna."

"That's right. And that wasn't my question." She hopped down off the counter and stepped toward him so that she stood right in front of him.

Her eyes glinted gold in the light and her lips were a red that drew his eyes. He swore his mouth actually watered at the scent of her, so close and so lovely. His mind was starting to fog.

"Your question?" His voice was rough, embarrassingly so.

"Why are you hot and cold with me?"

"Hot and cold?" He swore his brain was shutting down and it was making a ball of panic rise in his throat.

"You know, you used to avoid me on campus, but then you invited me to join the Praesidium."

"That's just good business. You're good at what you do." It reminded him of what she was. Of why he needed to be wary. He felt his face harden.

"See," she said. "There it is. Your face changed. You were looking at me like you liked me, like you wanted me, and now you're looking at me like I'm a snake in your garden."

"I doona know what you mean." But he did. She'd nailed him. The hot and cold of what he wanted from her and what he knew he couldn't have. She made him want to chuck his celibacy out the window.

"I think you do. I think you like me." She raised a hand to his neck and a shudder wracked him.

"You like that. I can feel it," she said.

A woman hadn't touched him like that in centuries. He wanted it so badly he ached. Touch, warmth, a release from the self-imposed iron cage of control that kept his demons at bay. She offered it all.

His cock swelled and punched against his pants and that fog fell across his brain again. She was so warm and soft and close. He reached up to cup the back of her neck to draw her to him.

The heat of her skin against his fingertips shocked some sense into him. He jerked his hand away and stepped backward until he bumped into the counter. Gods, that was so close. He'd been so damn close to losing it. And he would, with her. One touch, one taste, and he'd be lost.

To a damn soulceress.

"What?" she asked, confusion and hurt on her face. She moved toward him.

He sidestepped. This had to stop. He couldn't fight it.

"I doona want you."

"Yes, you do. I'm not an idiot. I see the way you look at me."

"I doona bloody want you. You're a soulceress, for gods' sakes." It was a godsdamned lie, but it came out easy, pushed by the panic.

Her eyes stopped shining and took on a leaden cast. She stepped backward.

"Ugh. Boring. Always with the soulcery business." Her words were light but her tone wasn't. She strolled over to the couch but didn't sit. "Like I have the fucking plague or something. I really thought you were different, Warren. What's your problem, anyway? You're a damned mystery monster. I don't drain your power, so what have you got against me?"

Her tone was acid, but he swore he could hear a note of vulnerability in it. It made him feel even worse, which only exacerbated the crazy panic within him. He didn't know how to deal with this kind of situation.

"Canna trust them," he said.

"Ugh, you're just like everyone else. A stupid bigot. What, you get screwed by a soulceress once?"

He started to speak, but wasn't sure what he would say. *Aye, she made me the monster that I am?*

She didn't give him a chance. "You know what? Forget I asked. My mistake. And I don't care, anyway. I don't need you. I don't need anybody."

She threw herself onto the couch.

Now what the hell was he supposed to do? What were they supposed to do? They worked together now and he'd made a mess of things, all in an effort to preserve his stupid sanity. Which was a worthless endeavor. He'd lost it long ago.

33

D iana opened her eyes in the forest in central England. Esha had created a portal for her that morning, and though stepping into it alone had been like stepping off a bridge, she'd done it. She'd learned that Esha was friends with Andrasta, but that she didn't have the power to summon the goddess.

It was fine, though. Diana had a good feeling that this would work. Her memory had restored the location of the place where she'd originally called upon Andrasta for help. It was also the place where she'd died, but Diana pushed the nerves away and looked around at the forest. She was only a few miles from the Roman fort she'd visited with Cadan. She had to come alone to ensure that Andrasta would show, and she was probably safe, but she gripped her sword tighter just in case.

The smell of the trees hit her first. It had smelled like this when she'd died. A light sweat broke out on her skin. Everything else was different, but as she walked through the forest, she swore she could smell the mud and the blood of war that lingered in the earth. Though they hadn't fought on this ground, the battle had been waged only a hundred yards away.

No, this ground was soaked with her own blood. She stopped in a particularly thick copse of trees and began to dig at the soil with her foot, nudging aside fallen branches and piles of dead autumn leaves. It wasn't long before she found the tumbled ring of stones that had once formed the walls of the house where she'd died. Dappled sunlight shone through the oaks above and danced in patterns on the stone.

As she revealed the rest of the ring, now rising only a couple of inches above the ground, she fought the nausea rising in her stomach. Instinct had led her here, as it had told her to clear the stones.

A raven called as she brushed the leaves off the last stone. Diana shivered. Once every stone was revealed, she stood in the spot where she had died. Where she'd been trussed up by Cadan on the night of the battle.

She had to assume he'd be able to resist his instincts this time around and let her fight her battles. He'd managed to in their first attempt against Paulinus, but there had been little risk then. With everything she'd learned, this was only getting more dangerous. Honestly, though Boudica had wanted to go it alone, she, Diana, would rather work with Cadan. She just hoped he would agree to do it on her terms. She shook the thought away and knelt on the ground.

With a steady hand, she opened the basket that she'd brought with her and released the hare, Andrasta's sacred animal, who ran to the center of the circle. Would this even work? But as she recited the ancient words to call the goddess of victory, the words her soul still remembered, a tingle of knowledge and recognition ran over her skin.

It felt like an age, but finally the mist swirled and a woman appeared in place of the hare. Diana stared her straight in the eyes, knowing that this goddess needed no obsequious bowing or scraping. After the day she'd had, she wasn't going to get it anyway.

Andrasta was smaller than Diana recalled, and much more delicate than one would expect of a warrior goddess. Her pale hair was pulled away from her face to reveal wise, even features. She looked so...young. She wore a leather breastplate and brown leather pants. A bow hung casually from her right hand and a quiver of arrows peeked out above one shoulder.

How did one greet a warrior goddess? Apparently her knowledge of divine protocol hadn't transferred with Boudica's memories.

"Boudica. Wow. It has been a long time." Andrasta's voice was nothing like she'd expected. Perky, and with an entirely modern cadence and word choice.

"Um, it's Diana, now."

The goddess nodded and swung the bow at her side. "Diana, then. I haven't been called out of Otherworld in centuries."

"Where are my daughters?" Diana started—she hadn't expected that to come out of her mouth. But after seeing Paulinus's son, the knowledge that they technically still existed, even if it was in another form, had been creeping in her mind.

"In Otherworld. They're happy, though." Diana could almost hear the pity in Andrasta's voice.

"So, I can't..."

"No, they're unreachable. If they're meant to be reborn, they will be." Andrasta seemed to be able to guess her thoughts before they left her mouth. Diana was grateful. The questions were almost too painful to complete.

"There's no other way to get them out?"

"I'm sorry, but no. That is the nature of our world, our beliefs."

Diana felt sick. "Then what if I don't believe it?"

"It wouldn't matter. It's what they believe that counts. And even if it were your choice, this is a matter of belief, not desire. Controlling belief is a difficult thing. You may think you are convincing yourself, but your subconscious knows. You've believed in this fate for thousands of years."

The words hit her like a brick. Memories flared in her mind. She remembered exactly what Andrasta had told her before, two thousand years ago. Her stomach roiled. "You told me my fate, the last time we met here. Told me that I would die, but that it would be so that I could complete what I had started. Did you know that this was how it would go? That as Boudica, I would kill myself so that I could keep Paulinus in hell?" *And possibly atone for the boy?*

"I didn't know exactly how it would happen, but I didn't want you to have to kill yourself. You were my favorite mortal." A small smile kicked up the corner of her mouth.

So that was the reason she'd been so quick to leave Cadan. Not just to save her people, and not just to avoid capture. So that she could do what had to be done. She'd been meant to do this for thousands of years.

"Is it true, then?" Diana asked. "The myth about you and Camulos?"

Andrasta grimaced and nodded. "There's more to it than what's recorded, but the gist of it is accurate. It sucked."

"Is that how I'm supposed to get to Erebus?"

"It would work," Andrasta said. "Paulinus will continue to send harpies after you until he has you. Going on your terms will give you an advantage. And sooner is better than later. The magic he's been working has strengthened the portal. It will become easier for beings to escape."

"And everyone will get out?" Diana's voice was weak. "Erebus is where dead Roman warriors go. There will be thousands of pissed-off warriors loose in Edinburgh?"

Andrasta shrugged. "Maybe. But probably not, since they're

only souls without bodies. That's what Paulinus needs you for—to give his soul a form and path back to this world. No, it would be the harpies and other demons who'd be able to use the portal, as they have both their bodies and their souls. As Mytheans, they can cross the barriers without the death it usually takes to grant a mortal passage."

"How do I kill Paulinus? How do I destroy him so that he never comes back?"

"The same way that you would kill him on earth. He doesn't have an earthly body, but he's no ghost either. As the person who killed him the first time, only you can kill him again. And you're the only one who can dispatch his afterworld form."

"Wait...what? What about his soul? Is that different from his afterworld form?"

"Ah, good catch. We don't know if it would be destroyed. Perhaps it would, or perhaps it would go elsewhere. Souls are pretty tough."

"But what about the myth? The story of you and Camulos? You destroyed his soul in Otherworld."

"Thought I did. And for a long time, we thought that he was gone forever. I've very recently discovered that might not actually be the case. He's probably still alive."

Were her eyes a little brighter?

"So, that's why you don't think I can destroy Paulinus's soul?"

"Yes."

Diana's chest constricted. If Camulos could come back after Andrasta had killed him...

"So, is there no way to destroy Paulinus so that he can never hurt us again?" Diana asked.

"Well, there's no way for *you* to destroy him forever." She hesitated before continuing, searching Diana's face as if she were debating her next words. "But if he were to kill *himself*, then yes, possibly. The universe allows us choice, and if he were to make the choice, particularly if it were in sacrifice, then his soul would probably disappear."

"Wait—why sacrifice?"

"It's one of the most powerful forces there is. Just killing yourself in the afterworld could destroy your soul, but it's not a sure thing. What would hell be if you could escape it? However, a sacrifice can give it that extra push."

So, like her survival, truly defeating Paulinus was possible but not probable. "And what about me? Could I survive this?"

"In some form or another, yes. You'll always survive."

"You were made a god."

"Those were very different circumstances." Andrasta frowned sympathetically.

Diana's shoulders drooped. "I didn't really want to be made a god. But I didn't want to die either."

"I know. You'll probably be reincarnated as you were before."

"That's it? That's my best bet?" Wait another two thousand years to be reborn? Where would Cadan be by then?

"Yeah, I'm really sorry I can't give you more. But you are the key to this, and it won't necessarily end in tragedy. But I've run out of earth time and the other gods will notice my absence. I've got to go."

"Thanks, Andrasta." And she was grateful. She really was. But with everything looming on the horizon, it was hard to remember.

"Of course. It's not often that I get out of Otherworld. Earth rocks." The goddess looked away from her then and around the clearing. "It's beautiful, isn't it?"

It looked pretty bleak to Diana, but maybe that was because she'd died here before. "The clearing?"

"Earth." Andrasta reached down to pick up a handful of fallen leaves. She inhaled deeply of their fragrance, then let them flutter to the ground. Diana caught sight of a hint of green in the leaves, as if the life had returned to them after Andrasta's touch.

"I suppose. But you're from the land of the gods. Isn't it beautiful there?"

Andrasta sighed. "It's not home."

The comment squeezed Diana's heart. Andrasta had been mortal, after all. "Would you return here if you could?"

"I'd give anything."

So would I. But how was she going to make that happen?

34

Diana opened her eyes in Esha's flat. Esha lay sprawled on the couch throwing cat treats to the Chairman, who didn't seem to be moving much but managed to catch them in his mouth all the same. Warren was pacing behind the kitchen island.

"Hey, warrior lady, how'd it go?" Esha looked up from the magazine she was skimming with the hand that wasn't throwing treats.

"Neither as well nor as poorly as it could have." Which was just another way of saying that she was in the same situation as before she'd left.

Screwed.

"You just can't get a break with this." Esha lobbed a high-flying treat at the cat, who snagged it out of the air.

"Too true. Where's Cadan?" Diana asked.

"On an errand. He'll be back soon." Esha set down the magazine and looked at Diana. For all her joking and treat throwing, her eyes reflected the direness of the situation. "Are you going in? To get Paulinus?"

"Yes."

Esha grimaced. "No other way, huh?"

Diana shook her head.

"Then you think you can do this? Kill him and all?"

"I don't know. But I know that if I don't try, then they'll eventually find me and kill me. And if the portal opens to more harpies, then a lot of other people will die as well." Her dreams of a tenure-track teaching position seemed silly in comparison.

There was a pounding at the door and Esha leapt up to answer it. Diana wasn't surprised to see that it was Cadan. She was in his arms before she could blink. He lifted her face to his and kissed her hard on the mouth.

"What did you find?" he asked as he drew away.

He looked so good. Alive and healthy and permanent in a way that she wanted to be. Diana relayed everything that Andrasta had told her.

"*That's* not great," Esha said.

Diana agreed. Definitely not great.

"She knows nothing, is what you're saying." The muscles of Cadan's arms were tense beneath her hands.

"No, just not much that can really help me, except for the fact that I really am the only person who can do this." While part of her soul soared at the thought, most of her felt sick over it.

Cadan yanked her to him once again and held her tightly.

"Let's discuss logistics." Diana pulled out of his arms. She'd barely accepted her fate and if she was going to go through with this, it was going to have to be soon, before she backed out and threatened the whole world, not just herself. "How do I get my entire soul into Erebus, since only sending part of it didn't work the first time around?"

"That's fairly simple." Warren's voice was calm as he turned from Esha to look at her, but there was something sad in his eyes. "You have to walk through the portal. Your body may die at the entry and collapse, but your soul would continue through."

"But I can't see the portal."

"I can guide you," Esha said.

"So then I would be in Erebus? Not Tartarus or the Fields of Asphodel or any of the other Roman afterworld realms?"

"Aye, since that is where he opened it," Warren said.

"It would be best if you could sneak up on Paulinus, since he will be expecting you. I think I can help with that," Esha said.

"Thank you."

"When will you go?" Warren asked.

"Tomorrow morning. It has to be soon." *Before I back out.*

Diana winced as Cadan squeezed her hand. She would go and kill the father, but then what would happen to the son?

35

They barely made it through the front door of his flat when they returned from Esha's. Cadan was on her in an instant. He'd meant to be gentle. Their last night should be tender, but fear for her rode his back like a demon.

He slammed the door behind him and whirled her around until she was pressed against it.

"Cadan." Her voice was breathless as he crowded her up against the door.

"Diana. I need you."

"Yes," she whispered. "Now. Please now."

He groaned as he bent his head to capture her lips. His hands gripped her hips and yanked her toward him.

Diana fumbled with his fly. *Faster.* The silk of her shirt tore beneath his hands, her pale breasts beautiful in the light. He tore off her panties, desperately grateful to find her wet and ready. His fingers lingered only briefly before desire overwhelmed him. He thrust inside her, groaning as her wet heat closed around him.

She moaned his name. Desperate longing drove him as he pounded into her. *Take me. Take all of me.* He wanted to bury his pain and his fear in this one perfect act. For just a second he wanted to forget everything the future held in store for him without her.

When her pussy began to contract around him and her cries echoed in his ears, his wish was made reality.

An hour later they lay in bed together, wrapped in one another as if they'd never have to part.

"Cadan," Diana said. Her small hand came up to rest on his cheek and he turned into it. "I'm sorry that I'm leaving you again."

Nay, you're not leaving me again. I won't be letting you. He crushed those thoughts, and waited before speaking, desperately hoping that she would ask for his help. It was *fucking hard* to resist the instinct to keep her safe by fighting her battles for her.

"If there was any other way for me to stay, to not go through with this, I would do it. But I have to save Vivienne. To close the portal."

Ask me. Ask me to help. Ask me. It was torture not to tell her his plans, but he wanted her to ask for his help rather than force it on her.

DIANA LOOKED at the man holding her as if he were afraid to ever let go. How could she not love this tortured, complex man?

"Cadan," she said, hoping to prove to both of them that she trusted his word, "would you escort me to the portal tomorrow? I want you to be there when I go."

And in truth, she needed him to be there. Even worse, she might need him to carry her there because she wasn't sure if she could walk to her death on two steady feet.

"Aye, Diana."

Thank God.

"But I'll be going through with you." His voice brooked no argument.

Shocked, she broke out of his arms and looked up at him. His jaw was set and his eyes fierce.

"But you can't. You'll die. Your soul could be stuck there."

"Aye, possibly. You think that would stop me?"

A hard lump formed in her throat, painful in its intensity, and her eyes prickled. She didn't want to be alone in this, but she didn't want him to die, either.

"I was at the university today," he said. "Trying to figure out if I could survive going through the portal. There's a chance I can."

"Really? How?"

"Some species, like the demons, can pass through safely. Because Erebus is the region of the Roman underworld that is reserved for warriors, it's possible that Mythean Guardians, who are warriors and immortal, can pass over the boundary without losing our earthly bodies and becoming trapped."

"You're sure?" Her heart raced.

"Nay."

"But what if I'm trapped there? Is that how I'm supposed to die? By becoming trapped? What if I succeed in killing him, but I can't get back out because I'm mortal and can't get back to my body?"

His arms squeezed the breath from her lungs. "Then I'll stay. I'll find a way to get you out—or I'll stay."

"In hell?" Her heart constricted at the thought of the man she loved trapped in hell with her soul.

"Do you think it hasn't been hell here on earth without you? Hell is wherever *you* are no'."

She gripped him fiercely in return. Could he possibly love her? "And if he kills me?"

"Won't let him." Determination flashed behind his eyes.

"But if he does, and I'm reincarnated as another person… you'll wait for me, right? You'll *know* me? You'll make me remember us?"

Her throat tightened, a jagged rock lodged within. Once again, she didn't speak of love, and neither did he. Everything was too fraught with emotion and tension to add it, but she couldn't help but ask.

"Aye, I'll always know you." He crushed her mouth to his. She returned the desperation of his kiss, tangling her hands in his hair and welcoming the invasion of his tongue. He clutched her close and she poured her heart into him.

When they drew apart, she caught her breath. "You'll let *me* do this, though? You won't try to interfere as you did with Boudica?" *If I'm destined to die, I might as well get a chance to save my friend and the world.*

"You are the only one who can accomplish this task. But I'll be there, should you need me." She felt his muscles tighten beneath her.

"Then we need a plan. I'm a good fighter, thanks to my soul's memories, but it's no guarantee that I'll win. So I need something clever to ensure my victory."

And so she told him her plan, hoping he would agree.

36

H er last morning on earth was clear and bright. The crisp autumn air was cold on her throat. God, it was good to be alive.

Diana turned to look at the man she loved. They'd risen early, before dawn. The sun was beginning to peek over the tops of the buildings as they walked down one of the sets of narrow stone stairs that wound through the city, a few errant leaves scraped along the ground in front of them. Autumn was nearly past now, and winter was on its way. She tried not to think of what that meant for her. But all of these unknown people she was trying to save had better appreciate it.

They hadn't far to go, only to the base of the small cliff upon which both Edinburgh Castle and Cadan's flat sat. As they stepped off the last stair and into the Grassmarket, a small district at the bottom of the stairs, the sun crept over the buildings and cast its warm glow on their intricate, soot-stained facades.

Diana wished that it would warm her the way that it warmed the buildings, but she didn't think it would be that simple.

She reached for Cadan's hand as they walked along the

street at the base of the cliff. They were to meet Esha and Warren at the entrance to the underground and these would be her last few moments alone with Cadan when they wouldn't be fighting for their lives. Maybe they should just turn and run for it and hope for the best.

Instead, she took a bracing breath.

Too soon, they came upon Esha and Warren, who stood a few feet apart near a crevice in the cliff's side. She squeezed Cadan's hand, then let go.

I can do this.

"So, you're ready?" Esha asked. Her long, graceful form was slouched casually against the rock wall, but her face and eyes were serious.

"I am." Diana was grateful that her voice was stronger than her stomach, but it was little consolation. She hadn't been able to keep down her coffee this morning; was, in fact, barely able to comprehend that it might have been her last cup.

She felt Cadan's hand squeeze her shoulder as if to keep her from trembling.

"Good. Here—" Esha stepped forward with her hand outstretched. "These are invisibility charms." She dropped a necklace into her hand and another into Cadan's. Diana closed her fingers around it tightly. "As long as it's around your neck, you'll be invisible. The charm will wear off in a few hours, though. I've added a little extra something so that you'll be able to see each other, as long as each of you is wearing yours. If only one is wearing it, you're screwed."

"Thanks. You made them?"

Esha nodded. "Took a couple tries, but since I can't go with you I figured I'd try to use my magic this way. Send a little bit with you."

"I appreciate it. I can use every bit of help I can get."

"Then you'll like this." Esha pulled a pack off her back,

unzipped it, and withdrew a large piece of stiff leather. "It's an enchanted breastplate. It will help protect you from weapons and some magic."

Diana's throat tightened at the effort Esha was putting into keeping her alive. "You charmed this too?"

A rough chuckle escaped Esha. "No. The spell is better than anything I could manage. It's Andrasta's. She wanted you to have it for this, so she dropped it at my place last night. She said she hopes it helps."

"It will." Diana unfastened the buckles and shrugged into the ancient armor, turning around so that Esha could fasten it. "Thanks."

"Not a problem," Esha said.

"Is this the only entrance?" Diana nodded toward the crevice.

"No, but it's the one closest to the portal that doesn't go through any heavily trafficked sections of the underground. We don't want to run into anyone, and since I can't transport everyone at once, we'll just walk." Esha turned, and after shooting Warren a quick glance, headed toward the crevice.

Diana wanted to look up at Cadan, but couldn't. She teetered on the edge of a breakdown, and even a little bit of sympathy would push her over. She couldn't afford that. She had a plan. What she didn't have was another option. Fate might say she was supposed to die, but she wouldn't go down without a fight.

Esha led them through the crevice in the wall. It expanded to let them enter and the air immediately took on the old, stale scent of abandonment. Esha handed out flashlights that she pulled from the bag thrown over her shoulder.

Diana flicked hers on to provide light for Cadan to hand out their weapons now that they were hidden within the underground. He unzipped the case he'd brought and handed her Boudica's sword, then strapped a quiver of arrows and a small bow to his back. His sword came out last, though she knew he had a dagger in his boot as well.

"Ready?" Cadan asked.

She nodded and the four of them set off down the tunnel, crunching over rubble and animal bones.

They arrived at the chamber with the portal and Diana immediately started to breathe more shallowly from the stench. Stale air became dead air and her stomach dropped when Esha gestured toward the far side of the room to where the portal had opened. She still couldn't see it, but within moments she would be walking through and leaving her body behind.

When her soul tore away from her body, would it hurt? She assumed it had to, and it became harder to drag air into her struggling lungs. The desire to run back out into the sun was nearly overwhelming. She reached blindly behind her for Cadan's hand. She wasn't sure if she could do this.

He came up behind her and gripped her hand, laid one upon her shoulder and squeezed. "You doona have to do this," Cadan whispered into her ear.

"Yes—yes, I do." Her stomach jumped and her extremities trembled, but she had to do this. For all her bravado, she really didn't have another choice. "I can—"

Her words were cut off as chaos rocked the chamber. Two tall figures hurtled through the portal. Cadan pushed her behind him, but not before her flashlight highlighted a harpy. It shrieked when the light blinded it, and charged.

"Watch out!" Esha screamed, blasting a fireball from her palm at the harpy that charged toward Diana.

No! If they caught her and took her to Paulinus, she would lose the advantage. Her plan would be dead.

"Go!" Warren yelled as he clashed with the second demon. "We'll hold them off."

Diana and Cadan took off for the portal, dodging around the

harpy that had lost an arm to Esha's fireball. She grabbed Cadan's hand, and with one last breath, stepped into the area that she thought held the portal.

She gasped when the world suddenly quieted and darkened. Wait. She could breathe?

"Diana." Cadan's voice was awed. "You have your body."

She looked down at her arm. He was right. She was flesh and blood, as he was. He, she had expected. But she stared at her own arm in joy. It didn't have the pale translucence of the souls she'd seen here before. Those souls maintained the same form they'd had on earth, but were a pale imitation of themselves.

She was just...Diana. But somehow more, as if taking this last step toward courage had allowed the two aspects of her soul to knit properly together. She felt the strength and knowledge of Boudica running through her veins all the more strongly. Even if her plan failed, she would have Boudica's strength and skill to fall back on.

"You're a warrior, Diana. The portal was no barrier to you."

She hadn't died? If she still had her body, did that mean that Paulinus was meant to kill her here?

"We can do this," she told Cadan. And herself.

"Aye, always knew you could."

She nodded gratefully, then slipped the charm over her head as he did the same. His confidence acted as a buoy for her own.

She spun to look at their surroundings. It was the same place she'd visited before. Still gloomy and dark, with a foul yellowish mist creeping along the ground, but *she* was actually here this time instead of just her consciousness.

The river flowed sluggishly nearby, winding through marsh that grew on either side. A vast field of wheat stretched before them that led to the forest where Paulinus had created his altar.

She swallowed.

"Which way?" Cadan lowered his hand to the sword sheathed at his side. They hadn't seen anyone else yet, but she gripped her sword tighter as well.

"Toward the forest."

They set off in that direction, stepping cautiously on the boggy ground. It soon hardened beneath their feet as the marsh transitioned to the field. Gray wheat rose up to their thighs, waving lightly in the foul breeze.

"Go first to the boy, and stay with him."

"Aye, but I'll be keeping an eye on you as well."

She tried to smile, but she was filled with nothing but dark purpose now. She hadn't been able to stop thinking about the boy. About her daughters. Boudica had sent him here, and though she understood the rage and pain that had caused her to do so, as Diana she couldn't bear the thought.

The boy hadn't killed her daughters; he was just a child. She'd do what she could to make amends. As she couldn't for her daughters.

They reached the forest and began to pick their way around fallen limbs and branches. Black, leafless oaks twisted and reached toward a gray, starless sky of perpetual night.

Diana froze when she heard the crack of a tree limb that neither she nor Cadan had stepped on. Cadan whirled to face the noise, placing himself between her and danger.

"Hey!" she whispered.

"Just protecting you 'til you get to your final task."

That was understandable, but either way, she stepped up beside him.

Another twig snapped, this time about twenty feet to the left of the first. Cadan slipped a knife out of a sheath strapped to his forearm and whipped it into the distance. There was a soft thud, and then silence.

"Demon." His voice was short. "I could see it through the trees. I doona know if it could see us, but..."

His vision was much better than hers, so she nodded. They crept onward, stopping long enough to retrieve the knife from the demon's corpse. They passed within sight of several wandering souls, but none of them displayed interest in their presence. The charm must be working. *Thank God.*

Diana clenched her fist around the sword in her hand when she felt the energy in the air change. Maybe it was the thinning trees, but she swore she could feel it.

"We're nearly there," she whispered.

"Aye, I can hear them."

Damn. His senses were excellent.

They reached the clearing, which still held the terrible altar with Paulinus standing behind it. Out of the corner of her eye, she saw Cadan's head swivel to the left. "There's a demon, over there in the trees, who'll do fine for your purposes. It's guarding the clearing like the others."

"They're harpies. Watch out for the wings. They hide them on earth, but they've got them here." She pointed to the far edge of the clearing, behind Paulinus. "There's Vivienne and the boy."

They leaned against two trees, Vivienne bound but not the boy. He stared up at the claw-like branches.

"I'm off now. Good luck. I'll have you in my sights." He leaned down and swept her toward him. He pressed a kiss to her lips, gave her a fierce look, and then disappeared into the forest after his prey.

Diana watched him go. She was glad he was here. For her plan to work, she'd need him for backup. She turned toward the clearing and crept forward to get a better look, careful to stay behind trees or bushes. Branches that clawed at her clothes and brambles that dragged at her feet went ignored as she slipped silently through the forest. Finally, she caught sight of Paulinus again.

She began to feel Boudica's rage rise to the surface.

Control it. That was not the tool she would use here. She wanted so much more than to merely kill this man. She wanted to destroy his soul, to outsmart him, to save herself and Vi and the boy.

So she continued to squint through the gloom, attempting to assess his mood and glean anything she could about his intentions. His attention was rapt, his gaze rabid as he scanned the pages of the book.

He wasn't actually insane, despite his demeanor, but he was immensely obsessed. He was manic with energy as he flipped through the pages and muttered to himself, occasionally shooting glances back at the boy who sat slumped against a tree. The boy hummed to himself and never looked at his father.

She could empathize with Paulinus. Wouldn't she be obsessed with the same thing if she had to see her daughters in hell every day for two thousand years? At least she had the comfort of knowing her daughters were in Otherworld, a far nicer place than this.

But she was beyond forgiveness. After what he'd done, she didn't have it in her. And she wasn't going to allow herself to be led to slaughter like a goat in sacrifice, which is what he intended for her.

Diana took a deep breath and stepped toward the harpy.

37

Cadan crept through the forest, silent as he kept to the perimeter of the clearing. The air smelled vaguely of dust and mold, with an underlying scent of decay. Erebus was one of the most fucked-up places he'd ever been. Dark, dank, and depressing; who the hell envisioned this place as an afterworld for warriors? The Vikings had it right with Valhalla—partying, fighting, women. This hole, with its endless gloom and misery, seemed like pretty poor recompense for a life of war.

Leaving Diana on the other side had been one of the hardest things he'd ever had to do. His bones had ached with the need to grab her and take her back to the portal. But he'd sworn an oath. An oath that—intellectually, at least—he understood the need for.

She had a point—she didn't want him making her decisions for her—but damn, he wanted to. Stepping back was something that he never would have been able to do the first time around, and even now he fought his instinct to return to her.

But he had to have faith in her plan. This was her fight. And she truly was the only one who could kill Paulinus. As much as he wanted to, he couldn't fix this for her.

He paused, stopping to watch her as she crept toward the harpy. With her pale skin and shining hair, she was like an angel in this hell. She was dressed simply for battle, in pants and boots, with Andrasta's breastplate for protection. She moved gracefully despite it, stopping to crouch at the very edge of the clearing behind a bush.

Taking one last look, he began to move again. He'd counted four harpies when they'd neared the clearing, each positioned vaguely at the noon, three, six, and nine points to act as sentries. The first was left alive for Diana, but he would be nearing the second soon. It took him little time to find it, leaning against a boulder, dead asleep.

He didn't bother to wake the thing—just leaned down, slit its throat, and continued on. He had to reach the boy, but first, he needed to take care of the two other sentries.

The ghostly sound of an owl broke the silence of the night. He crept around the perimeter toward the third and fourth sentries, careful to stay quiet but not needing the charm to help him sneak up on them. It was nothing to slit their throats from behind. He laid them gently on the ground so that their crashing bodies wouldn't alert Paulinus.

He raced on silent feet back toward the boy and Diana's friend, both of whom sat against trees. Quickly, quietly, he slipped his hand over the boy's mouth and dragged him behind the trunk of the oak and out of sight of Vivienne, whom he didn't want to startle into screaming. His hand muffled the boy's shout and he quickly gagged him with a bit of cloth he'd brought along, suppressing a shudder at the tingling sensation he felt wherever he touched the boy's skin.

There was something not right about touching someone else's soul. He wrapped the Maoin straps around the boy's wrists to hold him steady. They hadn't been sure if regular materials could hold a soul captive, but the straps seemed to be working.

The boy couldn't see what was abducting him and fear had him struggling harder to get away from the unknown threat. But he was small for his age and Cadan had no trouble holding on to him.

"Settle down, lad," he whispered. "You're no' gettin' away."

He quickly tied the boy's ankles and placed him at the roots of the towering dead oak that rose above them. They were just behind the first line of trees and couldn't be seen by anyone inside the circle.

Paulinus hadn't noticed his son's disappearance yet, and Cadan glanced down to meet the boy's frightened eyes, which were searching blindly in his general direction. He was pale and blond, with dirt marring his translucent skin. Not a full Roman. He might even be part Celt. The thought of the union between the bastard Roman general and a Celtic woman made him grimace. But that wasn't the boy's fault.

He almost offered words of assurance, but since the boy couldn't see him and he didn't know what to say, he turned back toward the circle and peered out between the trees, searching for Diana.

There. She stepped toward the harpy he'd left alive, then reached up to remove her charm. With one last glance at the boy to make sure he was gagged and secure, he removed his invisibility charm, crept up behind Vivienne and placed a hand over her mouth.

"I'm Cadan. I've come with Diana to save you."

She jerked, then nodded against his hand.

"I'm going to undo the ropes around your wrists and ankles. Follow me and stay very close. And doona make a sound." She'd need to be near him when they made their escape.

She nodded again and he unbound her wrists and feet. He

reached out for her hand, shuddered at the feel of her, and helped her rise.

"Take this." He slipped a long dagger into her hand, hoping to hell she wouldn't have to use it.

She followed him as he stepped a few feet forward so that he would have an unobstructed shot into the clearing.

He could hear the snapping of twigs and rustling leaves as the harpy caught sight of Diana and moved toward her. His heart stuttered when the harpy grabbed hold of her, then pushed her ahead of it into the clearing. Cadan fought the urge to shoot it in the head.

He gripped the bow tighter, nearly splitting the wood before he could get himself under control. *Everything is fine.*

But it wasn't. Not inside his chest. It was a battle just to keep his instincts from rising to the fore. He could shoot the demon, shoot Paulinus, and then he could get Diana out of here safely.

Nay. Only she could kill Paulinus, and it had to be her way. She'd never forgive him otherwise.

She struggled as the harpy pushed her into the clearing, putting on a good show. Paulinus looked up as the demon came to a halt twenty feet from them.

"Well, well, Ignobel, what have you here?" His voice was excited, slightly crazed, and Cadan hated the fact that he couldn't see his expression. He could see Diana's, though, and hers had calmed considerably.

"It is I, Paulinus." Her voice was strong and sure. "Boudica."

But it wasn't Boudica. He could see Diana shining through her eyes. But Paulinus couldn't tell that she was playing on his anger, and it was likely he didn't care.

"Yes," he hissed, "I've been waiting for you. It's about time they caught you. Thought you could come to me on your own terms? Didn't work so well the last time, did it?" He snapped closed the book that he had been holding and stalked around the altar toward Diana and the harpy holding her.

Cadan's muscles tensed with the restraint it took not to throw the bow aside and charge him.

Not just to protect Boudica, but to avenge his family. It had been two thousand years since he'd looked upon the man who had ordered the destruction of his village that had resulted in their deaths. This man had changed the course of his life, both for ill and for good.

He couldn't go back and save their lives, he couldn't rationalize their deaths as being for a greater cause, but the disastrous results of the Roman incursion into Britain had led him to Boudica.

And in the end, even more important, to Diana.

38

Diana stared across the clearing at the man her subconscious recognized as the ultimate evil. She could barely feel the harpy gripping her arms behind her. She knew that Cadan was behind the line of trees waiting for her signal.

It was working. As long as she could keep her rage in check, she might get everything she'd come for. Maybe even her life.

But it was hard. Boudica's rage scrabbled for the surface. Diana focused on her breathing and her plan. She *couldn't* fail.

"I know what you're trying to do, Paulinus. And it won't work." Her voice carried clearly through the forest. Oh, she was pretty damn sure his plan would actually work, but everything depended upon her convincing him otherwise. She wanted him bragging, boasting, while he thought that she was helpless; details were the difference between success and failure. "You want to sacrifice me." She jerked her chin toward the altar.

"Indeed. Put her on the altar," he said to the harpy. "I've waited long enough."

"Why?" She struggled against the harpy that dragged her to the altar. She'd wanted to get Paulinus talking more. This was happening too fast. She jabbed an elbow at the harpy, but it only grunted. "Why did you wait so long? You've waited here nearly two thousand years."

The harpy wrestled her up the stone stairs to the altar. She dropped to her knees, hoping the harpy would let go, and winced as the stone bit into them. It didn't let go, just dragged her up. God, this was going too fast, she was almost at the top. *Don't shoot, Cadan.* She craned her neck around to watch Paulinus.

"Because of you, you stupid bitch!" His eyes flared, the light of rage glowing within them. "We needed the ultimate sacrifice —that of the one complicit in our deaths—to escape."

Bingo. "*Our* deaths?" She emphasized the plural. "I assume you mean your son? But only one can escape through the sacrifice of another. The universe wants equality that way."

"Indeed," he seethed.

"What kind of coward would leave his son behind?"

He was on her in an instant, backhanding her as the harpy dropped her arms. She flew back from the blow and collapsed against the stairs. Pain exploded in her head, rage flaring quickly on its heels. She fought it as she tasted the blood welling in her mouth. *Don't shoot, Cadan. Please, please not yet.*

He didn't, likely because Paulinus had backed up again, breathing heavily, as she struggled to quell the rage turning her insides to fire. She glared up at Paulinus through her hair as the harpy dragged her to her feet.

"You won't leave him behind." She spat blood after the words, grateful not to see any teeth fly out of her mouth.

The harpy forced her onto the altar. The stone was cold and hard beneath her back.

"He'll find a way to free me when he's on the other side." He growled the words.

She almost sagged with relief. It *was* his son he wanted to free. Her plan could work.

"You think to sacrifice me for him." She laughed. A surge of confidence drowned out her fear, despite the cold stone of the altar that bit into her back. Boudica's courage—no, her own—was rising to the surface. But she was going to try to win this with her mind, not her sword. Because she wanted to get the boy out. She *needed* to get the boy out.

"What kind of sacrifice is that?" She laughed again and watched as he trembled with rage at her ridicule. She, who was pinned to the altar, ridiculed him. "Killing your enemy is no sacrifice. It's like a shepherd sacrificing a wolf and asking the gods to keep the wolf's brothers from attacking his flock." She chuckled. "Do you think they would listen? Do you think they would give him what he wanted? It's no sacrifice."

He threw his book to the side. "*You* caused his death. When he kills you on the altar, it will be sacrifice." He swung his head around, searching the clearing. "Maximus! Come here. It is time!"

"Where is this son of yours?"

Cadan stepped from the trees. Vivienne followed close behind. The trembling boy was cradled in his arms, but Diana couldn't bear to look at his face and see the fear there. It wasn't a truly perfect plan, but it was the only compromise she could make. She craned her neck and watched Cadan lay the bound boy on the ground at his feet and raise his bow.

"Hello, Paulinus." Cadan's voice was harsh, his smile evil.

Had she not known him, she'd have wondered who the bad guy was here.

"You remember the Trinovante clan, do you no', Paulinus? My father was king, until you burned our homes and killed my family. I'd be happy to return the favor." Cadan dipped his bow toward the boy, but not enough so the boy could see.

Through her rage and fear, Diana was grateful for his foresight.

"Let him go." Paulinus' voice cracked with fear. He stepped forward; Cadan stepped back. "You can't kill his soul," he blustered.

"Are you sure?" Cadan asked.

She could see in his eyes that he wasn't.

"Now," Diana said.

Cadan raised the bow and shot the harpy who held her down. Its body thudded to the ground and Diana scrambled off the altar. She yanked the short sword from the sheath at the harpy's side and crouched behind the altar, glaring at Paulinus. Now they would fight.

"Harpies!" Paulinus roared.

The trees seemed to quiver as his voice echoed through the forest. Creatures skittered through the brush, heading away from the clearing. Diana glanced frantically at the sky. They'd killed all the harpies in the clearing, but he must be calling others to him.

An ominous flapping sound cut through the forest. Four harpies dropped from the sky, their black wings spread and their beady eyes trained on her, Cadan, and Vivienne.

"Stay with the boy," Diana yelled at Cadan.

She charged the harpy nearest her and met it with a clash of steel. The first blow sent a vibration singing up her arm. Harpies were damned strong. Fast too, and its blade swiped across Diana's side. Pain streaked through her, but not so much that she feared for her life.

Out of the corner of her eye, she caught sight of Cadan felling one harpy with an arrow and turning to sight another. Vivienne battled one with the long dagger in her hand. Her eyes were bright with a lust for vengeance.

The desire to help Vi gave Diana a burst of strength. She

used it to decapitate the harpy. She turned to help Vi and saw that her friend had somehow stabbed the harpy through the throat. Vi was bleeding from her arm and thigh, but was standing tall. The other harpies were on the ground, demon pincushions stuck with arrows.

Vi joined Cadan, who now stood between Paulinus and his son, his arrow trained on the general.

"A step closer, Paulinus, and the first arrow goes into you and the second into your son," he said.

Paulinus shot him a look of such hatred that Diana shivered. Then he turned the glare on her.

"We can fight," she told him. "And I *will* destroy you. I killed your earthly body. You know that I'm the only one who can kill you here. Who knows where you'll go then? Away from your son, that's for sure. Leaving him here, alone with us."

His face twisted, flames behind his eyes that reached out for her. She took a few steps back from his advancing form.

"Or, you can sacrifice yourself and ensure that your son lives," she said.

He stopped short but kept his sword raised. "What do you mean? I didn't kill him."

"*Didn't kill him?* Just as I didn't kill my daughters by making them joint heirs to the throne with Rome?"

"You knew that Rome was to be sole heir to your husband's land upon his death! That was the deal we gave every kingdom. Trying to slip by the rules by naming your daughters as co-heirs sealed their fates!" Spittle flew from his mouth as he shouted. But as the words left his lips, the sick light of dawning knowledge filled his eyes.

"Exactly." The decision had been her husband's, but she too was to blame. Paulinus had swung the sword over her daughters' necks, but she had handed him that sword. "Just as you are complicit in your son's death. I, Boudica, swung the blade. But would he have been on the battlefield if not for your hubris? Should you have led a child into that nightmare?"

Indecision and doubt warred on his face. "He was strong, the bravest of them all."

"Not strong enough." The words were harsh, her tone worse.

He began to advance on her, his body swift and agile despite his ghostly form. Or perhaps because of it.

"Fight me, Paulinus, and die. And lose your only hope of saving your son."

Her sword crashed with his as he reached her. She danced to the side, narrowly avoiding his blade. The now familiar unworldly skill and confidence sang through her.

"He must kill me on the altar for the spell to *possibly* work. We've killed your harpies. You have no help."

She spun on him and met his burning eyes as she sank the blade into his side. His mouth gaped and she twisted. He stumbled away from her blade, then rose again with his own clutched in his fist.

"Make the sacrifice you know is required," she said.

He was strong, but she was faster. Doubt slowed him. He couldn't kill her off the altar or his plan was lost. Her sword clashed with his as she drove him backward. She dodged his blade once more, then cursed as it swiped at her arm.

Sweat poured down her face and her wound burned. What if he settled for saving his own life and decided to kill her instead of having his son do it?

No. *Think only forward.* Only a few more steps. The forest was silent but for their sawing breaths. She thrust her blade at him, driving him toward the altar. He was faltering.

"Why?" He gasped. "Why give me the chance to save him?"

He stumbled on the first step leading to the altar.

"Because I can't do the same for my daughters."

Her heart burned with rage at this man for taking them from

her. Boudica would never have spared his son, but Diana could. Two thousand years allowed her to see clearly. The world would be well rid of this madman, but not his son.

"Do you hate me more than you love him?" She drove him up to the last step until he bent backward over the altar. His eyes met hers, rage in their depths, but also hopelessness. She had her sword at his throat, giving him just enough space to look to the side for his son.

Her heart pounded as she glanced up briefly. Cadan held the boy so that he couldn't see. With her sword at his throat and his son captive, he had only one viable option.

With a last burning look at the boy and not a second spared for her, Paulinus plunged the dagger into his own heart.

Diana gasped and lunged backward as he began to slip from the altar. It gave her chills to watch him die in the same way she had. He'd plunged his blade more truly, though, and within seconds the life slipped from his eyes. His soul was beginning to disappear; she jerked her gaze up and searched for Cadan, but he too was beginning to fade. He, Vi, and the boy were disappearing before her eyes.

No. She ran for Cadan. The boy was the key to making it back out. His restored soul would lead them out of Erebus. She crashed through the clearing, her lungs burning as she pushed harder, faster. *Please, oh please let me make it in time.*

Cadan ran to meet her, arm outstretched, but just as they neared each other, he and the boy disappeared, Vivienne in tow.

Diana stumbled to a halt. *No!* She doubled over, helpless fear overwhelming her.

Now what? With Paulinus' death, the portal was closed. She should have been able to make it in time, but he'd died so quickly.

Now she was stuck in hell.

39

Cadan fell to his knees in the chamber beneath Edinburgh, the boy still gripped in his arms. Vivienne's soul had disappeared as soon as they'd appeared in the chamber.

"Where's Diana?" Esha's voice was frantic.

He opened his eyes to see Warren jerk the silent boy out of his arms. He surged to his feet and frantically searched the room. "Nay." His voice was hoarse, desperate. "No' possible."

He sprinted toward the portal, but could see nothing more than he had earlier that morning.

"The portal is closed!" Esha's voice was unusually high-pitched. "Didn't she make it to you in time?"

Her hand hadn't touched his. When Paulinus had been destroyed and the portal had closed, *her hand hadn't been touching his. They were supposed to have had more time!*

He threw his head back and roared, "Diana!"

His hands clawed at the stone wall where the portal had been. He *had* to get to her. Diana was trapped. His heart thundered and his head pounded. Rage and despair fought for supremacy. The battle would send him into madness.

He couldn't lose her again. Not to hell. She was conscious, not dead, and she was trapped in hell. She could be killed.

He spun to face Esha, who was frantically and almost blindly looking into the space around him.

"How?" he yelled. "How do we get back?"

Her panicked gaze snapped to his. "I don't know. I don't know how to make it come back!" She clenched her fists in her hair. "Fuck!"

"Is she still alive, Cadan?" Warren was bent over the boy.

"Aye." *Please gods, let Diana still be alive.*

Warren turned toward Esha. "How much longer should your invisibility charm work, Esha?"

"I—I don't know. Minutes, maybe an hour." She ran her hands down her front and scrubbed them nervously over her hips. He'd never seen her so frantic. "Damn it!"

She couldn't stay still, and he couldn't seem to move.

DIANA DRAGGED in a breath and stood to search the clearing. There had to be a way out. She had a *body*. She wasn't just a soul. She shouldn't be here.

Panic tore at her insides with scrabbling claws as she fumbled in her pocket for her invisibility charm. *Please still work.* She didn't want to be sighted by any of the harpies who still lurked in the forest. She slipped it over her head and looked at her arm.

Shit. Still there. But she could still see herself when she'd first put it on and it had presumably worked then. Since she couldn't be sure, she ran for the cover of the forest.

Think, Diana, think! She crouched behind a bush, staring blindly at the thick yellow mist that crawled along the ground as she searched her brain for an idea. *Any* idea.

She tried to ignore the bushes that scraped at her back and the skitter of animals above her in the trees as her mind scrabbled frantically for answers. *The spell book.* Paulinus had thrown aside his spell book. Maybe it held answers.

She peered out from behind the bush and searched the clearing for any sign of danger. They'd killed the demon sentries. Would more show up? If a human soul saw her, would it matter?

She couldn't worry about that right now. She *had* to get that book. She took a bracing breath and raced from her spot. The ground flew beneath her feet as she sprinted toward the book. She jerked as a hare streaked by her but didn't stop running. She scooped the book up out of the yellow mist and sprinted back to her hiding spot.

Frantically, she skimmed through the pages of the spell book. Latin. All in damned Latin. She wasn't terrible at Latin. As an historian, it had been one of the languages she'd learned for her degree. She even used it sometimes.

But trying to read a spell book in Latin while she was in hell took more concentration than she had. The lines blurred before her face and a tear dropped to the page.

Searching the book for answers was stupid. Paulinus had been using it to escape and look where it had gotten him. A complex spell with ingredients she didn't have.

A bitter laugh escaped her. She was in the same predicament as her enemy now. She buried her head in her hands, but jumped when an owl hooted. That was weird. She'd heard it before, but she hadn't expected animals to be in human hell. And a hare had jumped through the clearing earlier.

A hare. She looked up. If there was a hare here, then maybe she could call Andrasta. It was the animal she'd used as Boudica to help call the goddess to her, and it had worked before. But how was she going to catch a hare? Chase it?

Maybe she didn't need it. If it was still here, perhaps if she just said the words, it would work.

Here goes nothing. Diana took a deep breath and began to recite the words. They echoed creepily in the clearing and she shivered. When she finished the last verse, she looked around, hoping to see Andrasta.

Nothing.

Damn. Well, she'd try again. And again.

"Diana."

She jumped. "Andrasta?"

Diana turned to see the goddess. She stood in the middle of the clearing, dressed once again in her warrior's garb, this time with a different breastplate. Her stance was confident, her mien unconcerned, if slightly paler than when she had seen her last. Apparently hell didn't bother a goddess as much as it did a mere mortal.

"Oh, thank you! You didn't have trouble coming here?"

"As a Celtic god in a Roman hell?" She asked, smiling just slightly.

"Yes. Is that allowed?" Was shock making her ask these inane questions? She should be begging to be let out of here!

"I had to get special permission," she said wryly.

Diana clutched the book in one hand, her sword in the other. Thank goodness she'd kept trying. "So, um, can I get out of here?"

Andrasta smiled. "I think so. You did well today."

Diana nodded her thanks. She'd be able to appreciate the compliment better once she was out of Erebus.

"You showed uncommon wisdom, as I did so many years ago. You also showed mercy."

Diana shook her head. "No, not mercy. The boy had nothing to do with my daughters' deaths. I shouldn't have killed him in my past life. I just wanted to undo that wrong."

Andrasta smiled. "I see. Well, be that as it may, it is because of that action that I am permitted to offer you a choice."

Diana looked at her quizzically.

"Your soul is immortal, Diana, as is everyone's. But yours is particularly strong. Possibly because of how long you waited to be reborn, or possibly because of who you are and the decisions you've made. Maybe a little of both. Because of it, you have a choice."

A chill passed over Diana as she waited for her to continue, almost lightheaded from holding her breath. Would this choice get her out of hell?

"The strongest souls cling to earth. It's the center of all of our worlds, the birthplace of the beliefs that make the heavens and the hells exist. As such, you'll live the rest of your mortal life on earth as everyone else does."

Diana nodded gratefully as her heart leapt. It sounded like she was going home. She'd died by coming here, but she had a second chance.

Andrasta wasn't finished. "Because of the strength of your soul, upon your death your soul will continue to be reborn to earth, most probably with your memories intact. Or…" She paused. "You can choose to remain with this body forever."

"You'd make me a Mythean?" Diana's heart clutched.

"We wouldn't *make* you anything," the goddess corrected her gently. "You've made yourself what you are. We would just give you the opportunity to choose this body and this consciousness to house your soul as long as it should exist."

Diana's mind reeled. To be on earth for hundreds, maybe thousands of years? Did she *want* that?

Yes. She could be with Cadan. Never to sicken and die, to stay young and strong as he had. If her soul was going to be reborn anyway, wouldn't it be better to stay intact as she was?

"Yes. I want that." The words came in a rush. "Wait. Could I ever die?"

The idea of living forever with no escape was terrifying. She assumed it would be a good life, but shouldn't she know all the details first?

"Your body would be made strong in the way of the Mythean Guardians. Only incredibly grievous injury could kill you. But you would be reborn as if you had died of old age. There's no getting around that part. It's the nature of your soul."

Diana felt as if she were about to step off a precipice. Dare she? There really was only one choice. "All right. This is what I want."

Andrasta nodded. "Wise. I'd take it if I were in your position."

"Really?" How surprising. "But you're a goddess."

"I was mortal first. I miss earth." She looked younger then, lonely in a way that a goddess shouldn't be. Diana wanted to ask, but more than anything she wanted to get out of Erebus.

She ignored her guilt, and instead asked, "How will I get home?"

"I'll see to it." Andrasta gave a small smile and reached out to touch her shoulder.

VIVIENNE WAS FLOATING in the sea. Or in the clouds. She wasn't sure. Her body felt both weightless and heavy, her mind a calm, joyful serenity. Had she died? The horror of the past few days or months or years—she had no idea how long it had been—was a distant, foggy memory.

But Diana. Where was Diana? Vivienne could only hold onto the thought for the barest second before the calm joy replaced it. She stared into the whiteness above her, wondering if it was made of clouds.

"Vivienne." A sweet voice echoed from behind her.

Weightlessly, Vivienne shifted to find the voice. A woman stood behind her, tall and dark-haired. She looked vaguely familiar. "Am I in heaven?"

"No." The figure laughed lightly.

"You're not God, then?"

"No, certainly not. I'm your mother."

Vivienne would have been shocked if she hadn't been riding this false morphine high. Instead, she felt the purest quiet joy.

"You're dead. You died giving birth to me."

"No. I'm a Sila. We're a type of Jinn, an Arabic spirit that's unusually intelligent and can shapeshift. My body can't stay on earth for extended periods of time, which is why I had to leave you when you were a baby. It was one of the hardest things I've ever had to do." Her dark eyes were heavy with sadness.

"Wait, what?"

"I would have stayed, if I could. But you had your father."

"He's dead now." The piercing sensation she'd normally get when she thought of her father was dulled by the morphine feeling of being in this white cloud.

"I know he's gone from earth. I see him, now that he's on the other side."

"He's happy?"

"Oh, yes."

Vivienne smiled, calmly packing that little tidbit away. "If I'm not in heaven, where am I?"

"The aether. It connects the here and nowhere, the earth and the afterworlds. Your soul just escaped Erebus. It returned to your body as soon it escaped. You'll wake up soon, once your body readjusts to housing your soul. As long as you are in the aether, I can visit with you."

"Will I ever see you again?"

"Probably. You're part Sila. If you were full-blood, you'd have grown up with our characteristics. As a half-blood, you adopted them in adulthood. The change was probably spurred on by your proximity to Diana when she went through her own change, and completed when you were dragged to Erebus. All that magical energy gave you a jumpstart. Because you're a half-blood, I don't know if you are immortal like other Mytheans. But when you die—if you die—your soul will probably join your father and me in our afterworld."

Vivienne smiled. This really was the loveliest place and the loveliest news.

And her mother was the loveliest woman.

40

D iana opened her eyes to the chaos of Warren's office. They'd appeared in the corner of the room, Andrasta's arm wrapped around her waist for support.

"Can you no' create another portal or something?" Warren asked Esha, who paced back and forth in front of the fireplace. Her hair was askew and her cat was striding closely behind her.

"No! Damn it, Warren, I've already told you that. If I could do something, I would have."

"Are they always like this?" Andrasta asked out of the side of her mouth as she glanced at Diana. She'd removed her arm once she'd realized Diana could support herself and they watched the room's occupants argue. It was like watching a hurricane, but the undercurrents of tension suggested there was more than just a storm brewing between Esha and Warren.

"No. Where's Cadan?" He was the first person she'd looked for and he was nowhere to be found.

"I don't know. I thought this was your headquarters of sorts so I brought you here." Andrasta had eyes only for the fight raging in front of them. "Nothing so passionate ever occurs in Otherworld. I wish—"

"Diana! Oh, thank gods, you're back." Esha rushed toward her and gripped her in a tight hug. The cat lay down in front of the fire as Warren relaxed against the desk on which he was leaning. The tension leaving the room was almost palpable. Esha spun toward the goddess. "Ana! You saved her!"

"Where is Cadan? Did Vivienne make it?" Diana asked.

Esha drew back. "Ah, well." She hesitated. "He's still in the chamber. We couldn't get him to leave. But Vivienne is fine."

Relief rushed through her at the news that Vivienne was fine, but something in Esha's expression made Diana's insides cramp. "Why? How bad is that? Why'd you leave him?"

"It's been almost a week, Diana."

"A week?" The breath whooshed out of Diana's lungs. "What do you mean? A week since we went in?"

"No, more than a month since you first went in." Esha tried to push her down into a chair, but Diana resisted. There wasn't time to be sitting if Cadan was in that chamber. "Time passes much more quickly in Erebus. It didn't affect us when we were only looking in. But when you went in fully, you became subject to it. Warren and I left the chamber once you went in, since I can feel when the energy of the portal changes. When it was about to close, Warren and I went back. But only Cadan, Vivienne, and the boy came out."

Diana's mind reeled. To lose weeks when it only felt like hours? What was Cadan doing there? She felt Andrasta rub her shoulder to comfort her, but the gesture was awkward, as if she knew why one would do such a thing, but not how.

"Diana?" Vivienne's voice sounded from the doorway. "You're back!"

Her friend ran to her and threw her arms about her.

"Vi! You're alive! I didn't know if it would work! How?" Her eyes raced over her friend, thrilled to see that she looked normal.

"I'm not totally human, apparently," Vivienne said. "You remember me talking about my mom? Apparently she was a Sila, an Arabic spirit. Like a Jinn. My parents met when my father was working in Egypt."

Diana's mouth dropped open.

"She couldn't stay in the mortal world with me. But because I'm only half Sila, I can. Though this changes everything about my life."

"Wow." Elation and confusion buzzed through Diana. "I'm so happy for you. You're going to have to tell me all about it. But now, I have to go find Cadan."

Vivienne nodded.

Esha said, "I'll take you."

Diana nodded gratefully and squeezed Vivienne's hand. She turned to Andrasta and said, "Thank you, Andrasta. For everything."

"It was a pleasure. Thank you for calling on me. I don't get requests to come out of Otherworld often." She beamed and Diana smiled back.

Diana turned back to Esha. "Okay, let's go."

WARREN WATCHED with relief as Esha and Diana disappeared. Damn, it had been a long month. The last two weeks of fighting with Esha on top of everything else hadn't done him any good.

He looked up at the woman standing in the corner. She didn't look nearly as goddess-like as Aerten. Her clothes were less ethereal and more like those of a field soldier from long ago. Her breastplate was leather rather than metal. He was relatively young compared to others in this world. This woman looked like she had been around a lot longer, despite the fact that she physically looked to be in her mid-twenties.

Since it didn't seem like she had plans to disappear anytime soon and she was looking vaguely ill, he figured he'd better offer her something.

"Can I get you a cup of tea?"

She nodded eagerly. "Absolutely. I love tea. We don't have it in Otherworld."

"Vivienne?" he asked.

"Sure," Vivienne said. She walked over to the couch and sat.

"Where is the boy?" Andrasta asked.

"Maximus? He's at the orphanage." Warren handed her a cup of tea and gave another to Vivienne.

"Not a mortal one?" Andrasta said, aghast.

"Nay, he would no' do well there." They still had no idea what the kid could do, if anything. "We have a small one here at the university that will raise the children of Mytheans who are killed." There were a couple dozen kids in all, but he never really went over to that side of campus.

"Is he doing all right?" Andrasta asked.

"Hasn't spoken. They think he may be in shock."

"Well, he's been in hell for millennia. He also just lost his father."

Warren grimaced. That had been the downside of Diana's plan, though he'd agreed that she had to kill that bastard Paulinus. And bringing the boy back had been the right thing to do.

"Do you have any idea what he might be now that he's out of hell? Mortal? Mythean?" He hadn't really had time to ask around much, but anybody he'd spoken to hadn't known. Hell, she was a goddess, so maybe she had an idea.

"No, I'm sorry," Andrasta said. "My powers are really only limited to the Celtic faith. I don't know much outside of that."

Her fingers whitened where she gripped the arm of the chair. Her pallor was more pronounced than it had been just moments ago.

"Hey, are you sure I can't get you something? You're not looking very well." He reached out.

"No, I—" She gasped. "Camulos." She swayed, then disappeared.

Well, hell. That couldn't be good.

41

Diana squinted as her eyes adjusted to the gloom of the chamber below the city. It was as dank and dark as ever, with water dripping from the ceiling in disconsolate drops. She shuddered. The chill crept not only over her skin, but inside her as well. The smear of evil left behind by the portal seemed to linger.

There. She spotted Cadan at the far end of the chamber where the portal had been. He sat on a ragged outcropping of stone, his head in his hands. She could swear there was more stone scattered around the chamber. More giant holes in the walls, as if he'd torn at them.

"He's been like this," Esha whispered. "We can't get him to leave. It's the last place he saw you and he's convinced that this is where you'll return."

"Can you keep your phone on you? If we need to get out of here quick, I'll call you. Otherwise, we'll get ourselves out."

"Soulceress taxi, at your service." Esha saluted before she disappeared.

Diana might have smiled if the situation hadn't been so miserable. She walked toward Cadan.

"Cadan? It's me, Diana. Are you all right?"

His head whipped up and her heart broke at the sight of his gaunt face. He'd clearly neither eaten nor drank anything since she'd seen him last. Being immortal might keep him alive, but it didn't necessarily keep him healthy. Her heart clutched at the sight of his bloodied hands. He *had* been clawing at the walls.

"Diana." His voice was hoarse from disuse.

He stood slowly, as if unable to believe his eyes, and she couldn't stop herself from running to him. He caught her up in his arms. His hand fisted in her hair as she clung to him.

"Are you real?" His gaze burned into her.

"Yes."

"You're no' a ghost." He shook his head as though he couldn't believe his eyes.

"No, I'm me."

He held her face and looked into her eyes. "Then I've died as well?"

"No, Cadan. I'm alive, you're alive. We're still in Edinburgh."

He shook his head, clearly still disbelieving. "Nay." His voice was hoarse. "Nay, it's been weeks since I left you in Erebus. You're just another vision."

He'd had visions of her?

"I *left* you. A mortal couldn't survive in Erebus that long." Guilt was etched into his face and his arms tightened.

"You didn't leave me. You had no choice."

"There's always a choice." He bowed his head until his forehead touched hers.

"No, sometimes there isn't. And I'm *fine*. Andrasta came to get me. I'm here now."

He shook his head.

"Cadan, you believe in nothing. If you'd died, we wouldn't be together here."

"I believe in *you*. You are my heaven." He looked at her fiercely.

That punched the breath right out of her and the words followed. "I love you." She did. Forever loved him. What had been an inkling before was now a full-fledged storm within her. "I love you."

CADAN STARED down at the vision in front of him. It was the most realistic yet. And she *loved* him. It was a dream, as the others had been.

The last days had passed in a blur as he'd searched for her in the tunnels, out of his mind with grief. To have her here, now, after he'd thought her dead for so long was too much to believe.

But even his fevered imagination couldn't conjure her love for him. And she felt warm under his hands, and real. As solid and alive as she had before they'd gone into Erebus.

"Diana," he whispered, and searched her eyes for the truth. She was everything that was strong and beautiful and good in the world, and she loved him?

He felt her hands slide up his back and around to his front. She gripped his face gently and drew it down to hers. "I'm real, Cadan, and alive. And so are you. And *I love you*." She crushed her mouth to his and he finally believed her. Even he couldn't come up with a vision this realistic.

"Diana. I love you. More than you'll ever know."

She broke away from him and reached for one of his bloodied hands. It had long since healed, but it bore the evidence of his first crazed attempts to reach the portal to Erebus again.

She kissed his hands. She looked up at him, her expression

vulnerable. "You love me, right? Not Boudica? I couldn't bear to fight for a love I can't get."

She thought she was unloved? "Diana, you are loved. I love you, more than I ever loved anyone else, more than my own soul." He pressed one hard kiss to her mouth. "She was special to me, and she brought me to you. But I didn't know what love was then. *You* taught me that."

She smiled up at him, the most beautiful thing he'd ever seen.

"You were right," he said. "What we had then was strong, but neither of us was ready to truly love. She, because of her daughters and her cause, and I, because I hadn't met you yet."

The smile she gave him was brilliant. When he looked down at her, he saw a future that he'd never known to hope for. But an errant thought sucked the breath from him. She was *mortal.* How long could she possibly live? He couldn't survive losing her again.

"Diana, doona worry, we'll find a way to make you immortal like me. And if no', when you die, so will I."

She looked at him quizzically. "When I die, you will, too?"

"I'll find a way." That, he was absolutely certain of. There would be no more penance with the Mythean Guard, and there would be no more life without her. It would be with her, or it wouldn't be at all.

"You won't have to." She reached up to stroke his cheek and he leaned into her hand. "Because of the strength of my soul, Andrasta gave me the option of the same type of immortality that you have. I want to be with you, so I took it."

Hope blossomed within him, a light that he hadn't felt in millennia. "Really?"

"Of course. It was no decision at all."

A grin spread across his face. It had been an impossible situation, yet Diana had managed it. "All right, then—let's get out of here. We've got some living to do."

Thank you for reading! Click here to get book 2 from Amazon.
Want to read an excerpt first? There's one in a few pages.

THANK YOU FOR READING!

Reviews are *so* helpful to authors. I appreciate all reviews, both positive and negative, and I really appreciate the time you take if you choose to leave one. You can click here to leave a review.

If you'd like to know when my next book is available, you can sign up for my newsletter here. You'll also get a free copy of Hidden Magic, one of my urban fantasy novellas.

If you'd like a peak at how Warren and Esha are getting along (or not getting along :-), turn the page for an excerpt of *Soulceress*.

EXCERPT OF SOULCERESS

"Can you repeat that?" Warren Campbell asked, his head buzzing.

"The witches are losing control of their prison." Cadan, his friend and colleague, looked grim. "They think the barrier will break within the week."

"A week?" Warren's stomach pitched.

"Aye. The only prisoner is too powerful to contain any longer. A soulceress called Aurora."

Aurora. The name made the blood pound so hard in his head that his eyes throbbed. He hadn't heard anyone speak of her since she'd stolen his soul more than three hundred years ago.

"You all right, mate?" Cadan asked.

Warren blinked and met his friend's dark gaze. He was spacing out—back to the past when he'd fucked up his entire life.

"Aye." He shook his head, then surged to his feet. He had to get his act together. "I'll go see them and figure out how we can help."

"I'll come too."

"Ah, doona worry about it. You've done enough by telling

me." More than that, he didn't want Cadan to know the truth about him. Closest friend or not, the fact that Warren was a monster without a soul was something he didn't want to share.

"Aye, well, you know the witches. Prideful lot. Won't seek help 'til it blows up in their faces."

Which made his job a hell of a lot harder. As the head of the Praesidium, the security division of the Immortal University, it was Warren's job to keep things like this from happening.

Intent on doing so, Warren strode out of his office and down the beautiful old hallway of his building on the university campus. Cadan kept pace with him, ignoring Warren's assertions that his help wasn't needed.

Cadan was a Mythean Guardian, as the warriors who worked for the Praesidium were called, and was tasked with protecting the individuals most important to humanity while keeping the dangerous Mytheans like Aurora in check. He was also his closest friend and nosy as hell.

Which meant he was right on Warren's arse as he strode through the great atrium that marked the entrance to the Praesidium's building and pushed out through the heavy wooden doors.

"You're acting damned strange. What the hell's the matter?" Cadan asked as they descended the stone stairs leading to the cobblestone courtyard.

Warren ignored him and focused on the stone buildings rising on all sides of the courtyard, their gray faces dour on this *dreich* day. The sun couldn't beat its way past the heavy gray clouds, and it suited his mood just fine. He strode across the courtyard toward the rolling green hills surrounding the main part of campus. The witches kept to themselves in cottages near the forest. Private, but still within the protection of the university.

"Seriously, mate, what the hell is wrong?" Cadan demanded. "You look like death."

Where would he start? With the fact that the soulceress who owned his soul and could use it to power her own evil magic was the one who would be released? Or perhaps with the deaths he'd caused that had landed him in this mess? That everything he'd worked for was about to come crashing down around his head? That he lacked any humanity at all?

No. He'd kept those secrets for years and would continue to keep them. The life he'd created here at the Immortal University wasn't perfect, but it was something good he'd worked hard to create out of the ashes of his past. Aurora might have made him into a soulless monster, but he'd tried to do good with his life in the years following the loss of his soul and his humanity.

"I'm fine. Just doona like the idea of this soulceress getting out, that's all," he said.

Out of the corner of his eye, he saw Cadan shrug. His friend didn't buy his excuses, but Warren couldn't bring himself to care.

They arrived at the lushly gardened section of the university that housed the witches' cottages and strode down the path leading to the main cottage in the middle. Roses climbed up the gray stone, pink and red and yellow, all vibrantly in bloom despite the fact that it was a dreary November day. Smoke drifted from a chimney that speared up from the side of the slate roof and the windows were aglow with golden light.

Good, they were within. He banged on the wooden door, meeting his friend's eyes as he did so. Concern tightened Cadan's brow, and Warren realized he probably looked crazed. He tried to flatten his features into calm even as his insides roiled.

"Be quiet," a voice hissed from within.

Warren turned to see one of the witches peering through a little slot in the door. Her eyes blazed green and threatening.

"I'm here to talk about the problem with your prison in the aether," he said.

It was the only prison of its type, a jail without bars or stone. It floated within the aether, that ephemeral substance connecting earth and the afterworlds—known to mortals as the heavens and hells of their religions. It was between here and nowhere, and as such was impossible for him to manipulate. Only the witches had access because they had created the prison.

"We're working on it. Right now, in fact. And you're going to screw it up. Come back tomorrow."

"Now." Warren's voice rumbled.

The witch squinted, glowering. "Tomorrow. We're in the middle of a containment spell. You're going to screw us up. We're trying to shore up the boundaries and you're messing with our concentration. *Come back tomorrow.*"

Warren frowned, but the seriousness of her voice penetrated. A flash of light bursting from the windows convinced him. If they were doing what they could, he wouldn't interfere.

For now.

"Tomorrow," he said.

She slammed the little slot in the door shut.

Warren heaved a frustrated sigh and pinched the bridge of his nose. A huge part of him wanted Aurora to be released so that he could hunt her and retrieve his soul. *No.* The risk to others was too great if she was released. She could aetherwalk away from the university as soon as she escaped, free to wreak havoc anywhere she chose. There was no telling how long it'd take him to find her, or what she could do in the interim. He'd made a vow to protect others when he'd joined the Praesidium. Serving his own selfish needs at the expense of the safety of others was not an option.

He met Cadan's worried eyes. "We're done here."

Cadan nodded. "Come on, let me buy you a pint. Work day's almost over."

"Thanks, but nay. Go back to your Diana."

"I've got time. She'll be in the library for another couple of hours."

Warren liked Cadan's woman, an American scholar who was the reincarnate of Boudica. But his friend would be happier with her this evening, no matter how much he protested. Warren was shite company right now.

"I've got some things to take care of. Give my best to Diana." He clapped Cadan on the shoulder, then spun and strode away, desperate to get some space and clear his head.

The possibility that Aurora might escape made his skin feel like it was stretched too tight over his muscles. He felt trapped in his own body, torn between duty and possibility. He spun on his heel, changing direction and heading to his house instead of back to his office. All he needed was some space.

He told himself he'd do the right thing by seeing to it that she stayed in prison.

But he couldn't say if he believed it.

CHAPTER TWO

"It's a freaking miserable night to be hunting rogues," Esha Connor whispered to Chairman Meow, her feline familiar.

They crept silently through the darkened tunnels of the Edinburgh underground, each dodging the deepest puddles in the worn dirt floor. Unrelenting rain had leaked through the porous ceiling, which was actually the street above, and Esha could feel the Chairman's foul mood. It matched her own, which was the reason she'd leapt at the job to kill the rogue demon who'd been lurking down here.

She caught sight of a cluster of remnant shadows to her left and gave them a wide berth. Shadows of old evil that lingered after the death of the evildoer were thick down in the underground—one of the reasons Edinburgh was considered the most haunted city in Europe. She could have banished the shadows, but the shadows were relatively harmless and any magical activity might alert her prey.

Anyway, she kind of liked Edinburgh's reputation.

A soft rustling noise made Esha and the Chairman freeze. Esha squinted into the darkness, knowing the Chairman did the same. She hadn't wanted to alert the demon to her presence before they managed to find him, so she carried no light.

Instead, she instinctively followed her connection with her familiar, whose night vision was far better. But the Chairman was antsy in the unusual damp of the underground, and her skin almost crawled in empathetic annoyance.

It was turning out to be a shitty night.

The rustling grew louder and the smell more rank. Like dead bodies and misery. She covered her mouth and nose with the sleeve of her shirt. The Chairman crowded up against her legs. With a tinge of dread, she held out her right hand and willed a bright fireball into existence in her palm.

"Ugh," she said at the sight of her prey.

The Chairman hissed. In less than a second, she took in the small cavern that opened up from where they stood. A tall but spindly red demon crouched along one wall, some kind of body part—she didn't want to dwell on which—gripped in its claws. Red splattered the walls and more unidentifiable pieces of gore littered the floor.

The Chairman's revulsion, combined with her own, made her gag.

Disappointed, she pumped more power into the fireball and flung it at the demon. It shrieked. She flinched.

The Chairman turned to smoke, becoming incorporeal so that the noise and other earthly threats couldn't hurt him.

Bile rose in her throat as she watched the demon burn. She made herself watch so she could be certain that she'd accomplished the job, even though she wanted to turn away to save her appetite.

When the demon was nothing but ash, she waved her hand and forced a cleansing wind through the dark space. It was the wind of time, which she used rarely, and never in the presence of another except her familiar.

Time accelerated within the wind — in this case, enough to disintegrate the gore into dust, as though a hundred years had passed.

She felt grief for the mortal families who would never know what had happened to their loved ones, but she couldn't leave the bodies down here to be discovered by mortal police. They were unlikely to find the place since they didn't know it existed, but she couldn't take the chance.

Remaining secret from mortals was a Mythean's number-one priority and one of the main goals of the Immortal University, her employer. To ignore the importance of secrecy made one a rogue. A lesser criminal than the one she had just slain, but a rogue nonetheless. If one alerted the mortals to the existence of Mytheans—creatures from myth made real by mortal belief— then one would be targeted for imprisonment or death.

In which case, Esha was sent to deal with the lawbreaker.

"Come on, let's get a drink," she said to the cat and turned to make her way out of the underground. After that, she sure as hell needed one. She'd been in a pissy mood lately, and this rogue hunt had been an opportunity to get some aggression out.

It was one reason she liked her job as a mercenary for the

university. Esha was a soulceress, the only one in Britain, and she was perfectly suited to her field, given her ability to see the shadows of evil that lingered around a person. Without a doubt, she could determine if the one she'd been sent to kill was deserving of death.

Since they were no longer worried about running into a rogue, it didn't take long for Esha and the Chairman to get out of the underground. They exited through an opening in the cliff beneath Edinburgh Castle, close to the Grassmarket and some of Edinburgh's older pubs.

A quick sprint through the rain and soon she strolled into an ancient little pub, looking for a man to take her mind off things. Stormy winds slammed the heavy wooden door behind her as she shook the raindrops off her short, honey-brown leather jacket.

"Who do you think we'll find tonight?" she whispered to the Chairman, who had turned to smoke again when they'd entered the mortal-run establishment.

He glided along next to her, invisible to all eyes but hers. He couldn't answer her, but no matter. She knew what she'd find at The White Stag. A willing man to make her forget *him*. She didn't go for one-night stands often, but since a real relationship was out of the question for her kind because soulceresses were reviled, she'd gotten used to making do.

"A pint of Tennent's," she told the bartender.

As he pulled her pint, she turned and leaned back against the worn oak bar and scanned the wooden-walled room that was crowded with little tables and small leather-backed chairs, searching for a guy who looked dangerous enough to be intriguing but shallow enough not to mind a one-night stand. And definitely mortal. He had to be mortal.

Her brows shot up when she caught sight of a table of

giggling witches in the corner of the pub. Their familiars had turned to smoke as well.

"Damn," she muttered, and turned around to lean on her elbows on the bar. What were they doing here?

Mytheans didn't normally come to mortal pubs. She hadn't expected them to be here since they generally liked to keep to their own kind, especially when drinking. It was one of the reasons she liked to hang out in mortal pubs; she didn't have to be reminded why she was alone. Like a high-schooler who didn't have a lunch table full of friends, she found it easier to go to the library when the lunch bell rang. Or a mortal bar, where she didn't expect there to be other Mytheans cringing when she walked by.

"Bunch of losers and half-rate spell chanters," she muttered to the Chairman.

When his warmth pressed up against her leg, she looked down to see that he'd gone corporeal for a moment to comfort her. Then back to smoke. A small smile pulled at her lips, but it faded as soon as she peeked over her shoulder at the other witches. Still laughing, like girls in movies always did when they were out in a group.

She spun to face the door and head out, then stopped. She didn't give a damn what they thought. The bartender finally handed over her beer, and she figured she might as well get half of what she'd come for.

Anyway, she wouldn't have to worry about steering clear of the other witches because there was no doubt that they'd steer clear of her. Smart. She'd suck the power right out of them and enjoy every second. Oh, they'd regenerate it eventually, but no immortal liked giving up their energy to a soulceress.

It wasn't like she could help how she collected power, but no one cared about the details when they felt the extra power that made them immortal slipping from their souls. They didn't actually become mortal, just weaker for a little while as they temporarily lost whatever special ability their species possessed.

She sidled down the bar toward a towering man at the end. "Hey, handsome," she said, giving him a bold once-over. Not bad, for a mortal.

He returned the gesture, apparently liking what he saw, if his grin was any indication. "Hello, lassie. American, are you? On a bit of vacation?"

She smiled when she heard his rough brogue; he was a local. And a damn fine one, at that. Not that she'd keep him around past tonight. Relationships between mortals and Mytheans always ended in disaster. The life-span differential was a bitch. But he'd do fine for her purposes.

"Sure am." The lie slipped easily off her tongue. After they'd slept together and he'd chipped away at the despicable block of loneliness sitting in her chest, it would be easier to say she had a flight to catch than to explain that she didn't date. Mortals eventually died on you. And it hurt. "What do you do?"

~~~

What the hell was *she* doing here?

Warren's eyes were glued on the entrance to the pub where Esha stood, shaking the rain from her jacket. When she unzipped the leather, she revealed a plain cotton shirt that was too tight for his peace of mind. He swallowed hard and looked away.

Within seconds, his gaze was dragged back to her. She glanced around the pub, her amber eyes bright. She didn't see him in the darkened corner, and he sat back, no longer intent on leaving.

There was nothing he could do tonight to ensure Aurora wasn't released, and the idea of twiddling his thumbs at home had been unbearable. He'd come here because he wanted a place to think that was far from the university and devoid of Mytheans.

The White Stag had been fine for all of ten minutes. Then the witches had shown up. Initially, he'd been annoyed. They should be hard at work shoring up the aetherwalls of their prison. But then he'd noticed that they were the youngest witches in the coven. Still in training and likely more of a distraction than a help with difficult spells.

Either way, they ruined the anonymity of the place. As he'd been getting up to leave, Esha had walked in.

Now, his eyes tracked her as she sauntered across the pub toward the bar. He liked the way she walked. It was very *her*, with her chipped-shoulder, couldn't-give-a-shite attitude. Her hips swayed in jeans molded to every inch of her. She was tall and lean, all strength and supple muscles that made him think she'd give as good as she got.

He shook his head. Not that it fucking mattered. He couldn't let it matter. She was hell on his celibacy and peace of mind. Iron control kept him sane. She threatened that, and he did his damnedest to avoid her because of it. He'd been pretty successful for the ten years that she'd been at the university.

Until their work had thrown them temporarily together a month ago. Once, she'd asked him why the signals he sent were so hot and cold. She could see that he wanted her as easily as she could see that he resisted it. And she wanted him back. That day, they'd come so close to kissing that he could still feel the heat of her breath.

But he'd pulled away. He'd been an arse to her when she'd asked why. He'd thrown her species in her face. Blaming his rejection on the fact that she was a soulceress was a lie, but it had come out easily, pushed by the panic over what he felt for her.

He could still remember her words. *"Always with the soulcery business. Like I have the fucking plague or something. I really thought you were different, Warren. What's your problem, anyway? You're a damned mystery monster. I don't drain your power, so what have you got against me?"*

He hadn't known how to answer, and his words had only made it worse. He'd hurt her feelings, he knew that much. She'd said that she didn't need him, that she didn't need anybody. He'd almost believed it.

Warren snapped out of his memories of the past at the sight of Esha sidling up to another man at the bar. No matter how bad an idea it was, he couldn't stop himself from becoming jealous. Which was a gods-damned worthless emotion, when everything between them was not only fucked up, it was impossible.

~~~

Though Esha lent one ear to the rumbling brogue of the man she'd approached at the bar, her attention was dedicated to scanning the room for enemies. It was a hazard of the job, but she didn't mind, because it wasn't like she left any of her assignments living. She smirked at the thought. But they sometimes had partners in crime who'd like to exact a little vengeance, so keeping a wary eye out was just good business.

She felt the smirk slip from her face when her gaze connected with that of a man sitting alone at a table in the corner of the pub.

No way.

Warren. The man she'd wanted for almost the entire ten years she'd been at the university.

Her heart shivered and goose bumps rose on her arms at the sight of him. The light from a cheery fire cast shadows over his harshly beautiful face. His fierce gaze was trained on her—probably had been since she walked in—and she kicked herself for not noticing.

The voice of the man speaking to her became nothing but a buzz. She licked her lips nervously, but managed to lean back against the bar and glare at Warren. What the hell was he doing here?

"Lassie." The sexy Scot tapped her shoulder and she jerked back to attention, blinking stupidly up at him as her brain returned to the present. She should focus on the hot man who actually liked her, not on the elusive Mythean who treated her like a bug.

Because the mortal doesn't know what you are.

But as she stared up into his handsome face, she could feel Warren's gaze burning into her. Impossible to ignore. She really should try to make him jealous, but her heart wasn't in it.

"I'm sorry. You know—" Shit, she didn't know the Scot's name. Whatever. "It was nice talking to you."

She tried to smile at him, but all she could think about was the man whose gaze continued to light her up from across the room.

She wasn't going to go over there. Avoiding him had been working out really well for her.

But she felt herself turning and her feet carrying her closer to him, her body weaving around raucous pub patrons. He was like a giant planet and she some puny little moon, helplessly drawn to him.

She'd thought there could be more between them, had wanted there to be. From what she could tell, he kept to himself and focused almost all of his energy on work. Where her isolation was forced on her by others—their loss—his was self-imposed. He was the only person she knew who was more isolated than she; it intrigued her.

And it had been a shitty night. If anything, he would distract her. True, he'd kicked her to the curb less than a month ago, and it had hurt, yet she'd slapped a bandage over that wound. She'd suffered worse.

As she made her way to him, she took in the olive sweater stretched over broad shoulders, which tensed as he watched her.

Good. He tied her up in knots; it should be mutual. His other-worldly stature and confident mien made him stand out among the other pub patrons. Golden hair glinted in the firelight, too angelic for what he was capable of.

It was such a contrast to the dark shadows that always hovered at his feet. They were the shadows of evil deeds, visible only to a soulceress. Normally, she'd only see them on rogues or other evil beings, where they clung like a black mist. But on Warren, they hovered around his ankles, like they couldn't stick to him.

Why would he have them? Was it because she couldn't see his soul? She'd heard of some Mytheans who used magic to hide theirs. Because a Mythean's power originated from his soul, it was closely guarded, even hidden at times.

The whys of his shadows intrigued her. They didn't mesh with the decent guy she knew him to be. He might be a jerk to her, but overall he was good. Too good to have the shadows.

She sank into the chair across from him, holding his green gaze and propping her feet on the chair closest to him. He was so big she could almost feel the heat of him. At nearly six and a half feet, his head would probably brush the low ceiling of the pub, hitting the decorative copper mugs that hung from it.

"So, boss, what brings you here?" she asked, her eyes racing over his face, taking in the features that had haunted her dreams. A strong jaw, full lips, and a loaded gaze. It was a face that had seen a lot of bad. The shadows that hovered around his feet were sometimes reflected in his eyes. She didn't know what he'd done to get those shadows, but she wanted to.

"No' your boss, Esha."

Right. Thanks for the reminder. She was only a consultant, not a full member of his team. She was powerful enough that no one wanted her working against them—hence the invitation to join the university staff and eventually his department, the Praesidium—but her method of collecting the magical energy that fed her power made everyone loath to include her as an actual team member. Not that she cared, of course.

"Semantics." She sipped her beer and looked at him over the rim of her glass. His expression was unreadable, nearly unwelcoming. But she hadn't made a mistake in coming over here; she didn't make mistakes.

"What's with all the Mytheans in a mortal pub?" she asked. He ranked higher than she did, so maybe he'd know.

He shrugged. "What's your reason?"

"Here? I come here all the time." She gestured to the crowd behind her. "Easy pickings."

A disgusted sigh escaped his strong throat. "To replenish your power from unwitting victims?"

She ignored the disgust. She had to, to survive. "Please. Mortals don't have enough to speak of."

It was one of the reasons she usually slept with them instead of the immortal Mytheans. Her unconscious power collection didn't cause mortals the shivery sense of powerlessness that Mytheans felt in her presence. What felt like a hit of glorious energy to her felt like a siphoning of strength for any immortal with whom she came into contact.

Except for Warren.

"So, why is it that I never feel your power? You don't have enough to speak of?" she asked.

Everyone hated her for something she couldn't control, but he was the only one who didn't like her out of spite, because he wasn't even affected by her.

He shrugged again, but she saw a flicker in his eyes.

"You know why I can't feel the power of your soul, but you won't tell me. Cat got your tongue?" She snickered and looked at the shadow that was the Chairman, lounging on a chair next to her.

"There's no' a fae's chance in hell I'm going to tell you."

She frowned as she searched his eyes for any hint, but saw nothing. "Does it have anything to do with the fact that you have shadows that don't stick to you?"

His eyes iced over, but still, she swore they beckoned. She was clearly mad, but she couldn't help herself. "I have no idea what you're talking about."

She shivered. She was pushing him, but she couldn't stop herself. He was a mystery that she'd wanted to solve since she'd met him. "You know, you're pretty much the only one at the university who has shadows. You're different."

Their place of employment was committed to maintaining balance between the heavens and the hells and to protecting earth. Someone evil wouldn't give a damn about keeping the power balance. So if Warren wasn't evil, why did he have shadows?

CHAPTER THREE

"You know nothing of my soul." Warren's fists clenched.

But she did, he realized. Not the details, but the cocky soulceress sitting across from him saw enough to know that he'd done such monstrous things that if he still had his soul, it would be as black and empty as space. All the attempts at atonement in the world weren't going to wash him clean.

"I think that no matter what you said before, you want me," she said. "You've been watching me since I walked in here."

True, his subconscious whispered, as her gaze caught and

held his. Her eyes captured him. Not merely their shape and color, but what swirled within them. Something unidentifiable, but familiar. Like a window not only into her soul, but into himself as well. Except that he had no way to decipher their contents, no context for the messages they might send. He knew little of her except that she was brave and brash—a cocky mercenary who took no prisoners and asked questions later.

"I want any hot pieces of ass that I see." His tone was harsh, the words a lie. Such a ridiculous lie, but pushing her away was the only way to keep himself sane.

Esha was the one he thought about at night.

"Maybe," she said, and leaned back in her chair.

"Why are you here?" he asked.

"I already told you that."

"No, you dinna. You changed the subject. Why are you here at my table? You were mad as hell last time we spoke." He'd been an arse then, for the same reason he was being one now.

"How insightful of you to notice."

"Just being honest."

She laughed. "Honest that you don't like what I am. Here's the thing, though, that doesn't bother me since I know that you want me. No Mythean likes my species, so why should you be any different? And it's not like I want much from you. Just a distraction."

The smile she gave him told him exactly what kind of distraction she was looking for, and gods, he was tempted. Though her tone was confident, he thought he could see a shadow of something in her eyes that belied the claim that she didn't care. He hated that she expected so little of others. So little for herself.

Gods, she was probably as fucked up as he was. It made him feel less alone.

These were dangerous thoughts. He surged to his feet and

skirted the table toward the door. "I'm leaving. Have a good night."

"Good idea." Her voice came from behind him.

She was following him outside.

The pub was small, and they were out the door in seconds. Wind and rain pelted them as he grabbed her arm and swung her into the small alley to the left of the entrance.

He pressed her up against the wall in the darkness and growled, "Why are you following me?"

~~~

Book 2, Soulceress, is available now. Click here to check it out on Amazon.

ACKNOWLEDGMENTS

This story benefited so greatly from the time and effort of many people. There aren't enough words to express my gratitude (if there were, I'd have thought of them!)

Thank you, Ben, for helping me not only with the story, but with the countless hours you put toward getting this book into publishable shape. Thank you Catherine Bowler for all your help throughout the process of creating the book. Thank you to Carol and Mark Thomas for your help and support—it has made all the difference.

Thank you, Emily Keane, for reading every story I've written, even when you were studying for the bar, and always being there for me with great ideas and support. To Doug Inglis, thank you for your enthusiasm and amazing, clever ideas. Thank you to Cathy Hall for always being there for me, and Elaine and John Thomas for being so supportive.

Thank you to Valerie Hayward, Shelley Bates, and Jena O'Connor for various forms of editing. The story is much better because of your expertise. Thank you Simone Seguin for your help with back cover copy - I don't have anywhere near your skill with that!

Thank you to my beta readers, Christy Huber, Alana Lee Rock, and Charisma Cassidy. I appreciate so much that you volunteered your time and expertise to help make this story the best it could be.

And last, but not least, thank you Kitty, Mouse, and Poa for being excellent assistants. Thank you, Chairman, for being inspiration for the best character in the book.

AUTHOR'S NOTE

Boudica is the historical figure who most captivated me from a young age. She was brave, strong, and she fought against incredible odds. Her story stuck in my mind for years. It was only natural that she become the heroine of *Braving Fate*. I wanted to create a world where Boudica could have a happy ending. The only way to do that without messing with history too much was to bring her back through reincarnation and give her the life she deserved. If you're interested in learning which history I portrayed accurately and where I outright lied to improve the story, please read on...

Boudica was one of Britain's greatest warriors. Most of what I said about her is true according to archaeology and history (take this with a grain of salt—scholars do their best to learn the truth about the past, but some of it is always shrouded in fog). One place that I fudged a bit was the fate of her daughters. According to the Roman historian Tacitus, when the Romans attacked Boudica's kingdom following the death of her husband Prasutagus, they whipped Boudica and raped her daughters. This does not happen to her daughters in *Braving Fate*. Instead, I had the Romans killed them outright. I made this decision because it suited the story better. Also, I invented the names of her daughters, as they were not recorded by history. Aela and Calea, however, are Celtic names.

Boudica waged a year-long campaign across Britain. She united several Celtic kingdoms and succeeded in destroying several Roman settlements. She nearly evicted the Romans. The fate of her campaign, and of the Romans' endeavors in Britain, relied upon the final battle mentioned in this book. Unfortunately, or fortunately, depending upon how you look at it, she failed and died shortly thereafter.

There are two theories about Boudica's death. Tacitus states that she poisoned herself, while the Roman historian Cassius Dio writes that she died of illness. Suicide suited the Boudica of *Braving Fate*. Would her fate have been as I described it had she been captured by the Romans? I wouldn't be surprised, as I borrowed that fate from France's Celtic hero Vercingetorix.

As for her enemy, Gaius Seutonius Paullinus? He actually survived the battle. However, he didn't have a son that he brought onto the battlefield with him. We can also assume that he didn't do any of the crazy stuff that I said he did in Erebus.

Cadan Trinovante is not a historic figure. However, the Celtic Trinovante kingdom was located to the south of the Iceni kingdom and was one of the kingdoms that joined Boudica in her revolt. Cadan is a Celtic name, and Cadan has carried his kingdom's name as his surname. His village, Camulodunum, was real and was destroyed by the Romans. In an interesting twist of fate that did not make it into the book, the Boudica of history attacked the newly built Roman fort at Camulodunum during her year-long attack of Roman forts.

I had the hardest time deciding on a place to spur Diana's memory about her past. I settled on Verulamium, which was a Roman fort during Boudica's time and is located near Watling Street, one place that historians believe may have been the location of her final battle. Boudica destroyed this Roman settlement while attempting to evict the Romans from Britain, though Diana doesn't yet make the connection with Boudica when she sees Verulamium because she doesn't think she could possibly be one of Britain's most famous warriors.

Finally, Andrasta and the Celtic gods of Otherworld. Andrasta was Boudica's patron goddess and the Icenic goddess of victory. She is one of hundreds of Celtic gods from dozens of kingdoms and tribes. However, the Celts weren't one people in one place at one time. Rather, they were a culture that originated in central Europe and spread out to encompass most of Europe and the British Isles during the first millennium B.C. They spoke many languages and worshiped many gods, but were linked by their material culture and advanced use of metalwork. They were known to the Romans and the Greeks as great warriors.

GLOSSARY

Aether - The invisible substance that connects the afterworlds and earth. It is both nothing and everything.

Aetherwalking - A method of traveling through the aether to access the afterworlds or different places on earth. Some Mytheans have this power and can bring another person with them.

Afterworld - A heaven or hell created by mortal belief. Mortals can access them only through death. Some Mytheans can aetherwalk to them.

Immortal University - An organization created thousands of years ago to protect Mytheans and keep them secret from mortals. It was initially founded as a true university, hence the name, but over time it morphed into an institution with greater power and responsibility. The university's primary goal is to maintain the secrecy of Mytheans and to keep the gods from warring to obtain more followers. They do this primarily through diplomacy. The university also provides services to Mytheans that they can't get elsewhere, lest mortals figure out that their clients never die. Things like education, health services, and banking.

Mortals - Humans. They are unaware of the existence of Mytheans or that all heavens and hells truly exist. They are immortal in the sense that their soul will pass on to whatever afterworld they believe in.

Mythean - Supernatural individuals created by mortal belief. They are gods and goddesses, demons and monsters, witches and other supernatural creatures. They are immortal in the sense that if they live on earth, only beheading or grievous injury from magic can kill them. If they are killed their soul will pass on to an afterworld. Secrecy from mortals is one of their highest priorities. Some Mytheans, particularly species of demons and some gods, are trapped in their afterworlds. Others have access to both earth and the afterworlds.

Mythean Guardians - Powerful mortals made immortal, or other supernatural beings who serve at the Praesidium. They protect those mortals and Mytheans who are important to the fate of humanity.

Praesidium - The protection division of the Immortal University. Mythean Guardians work here. Their job is to protect those important to humanity and maintain law and order by keeping Mytheans secret from humans and keeping the gods from warring.

Soulceresses - Mytheans who fuel their power by draining the immortal power of other Mytheans' souls. When fueled by the power of others, they can manifest their magic with a thought. They are hated by other Mytheans because of this. They also have the ability to see the evil in a person's soul.

ABOUT LINSEY

Before becoming a writer, Linsey Hall was a nautical archaeologist who studied shipwrecks from Hawaii and the Yukon to the UK and the Mediterranean. She credits fantasy and historical romances with her love of history and her career as an archaeologist. After a decade of tromping around the globe in search of old bits of stuff that people left lying about, she settled down and started penning her own romance novels. Her Dragon's Gift series draws upon her love of history and the paranormal elements that she can't help but include.

COPYRIGHT

www.ingramcontent.com/pod-product-compliance
Lightning Source LLC
Chambersburg PA
CBHW020333180626
46812CB00001B/190